Lost in the Tallgrass

To Lavae & Patience Hoskins
3 February 2015

Lost in the Tallgrass

CLYDE WITT

ISBN: 978-0-9916528-2-2

Published and printed in the United States of America by the Write Place. Cover design by Alexis Thomas and interior design by Michelle Stam, the Write Place. For more information, please contact:

the Write Place
709 Main Street, Suite 2
Pella, Iowa 50219
www.thewriteplace.biz

Susan Jones

Front and back cover paintings by Susan Jones.

Copies of this book may be ordered from the Write Place online at www.thewriteplace.biz/bookstore.

Dedication

For Susan, who believed in me when I did not believe in myself.

Clifton A. Witt (left) on leave from Ft. Sill with his brother Russell, circa 1917.

Acknowledgments

While places and people in this novel are of my own invention, it is based on real places and populated with sketches of real people, primarily my father, Russell A. Witt of Maple Heights, Ohio, and his brother, Clifton A. Witt of Hays, Kansas, seen in this family photo, circa 1917. I owe a huge debt of gratitude to many people who helped and guided me to and through those real and imagined places, as well as real and imagined people. The generous time offered by the folks at the Woodson County, Kansas, Historical Society, Yates Center, Kansas; the Kansas State Historical Society and its archivists, Topeka, Kansas; my cousin Jackie Witt Brieby of Salina, Kansas; professor and author Jim Hoy, Emporia State University, Emporia, Kansas—his volumes of work keeping the cowboy dream alive and his patience while driving me through the Flint Hills; the excellent guidance of the faculty at the University of Iowa Summer Writing Festival, Iowa City, Iowa, especially authors Sandra Scofield and Sands Hall; author Sarah Willis of the Advanced Fiction Workshop, Cleveland, Ohio; the skills of my editor, Hannah Crawford of the Write Place, Pella, Iowa; and the abundant talents of my wife, Susan Jones.

CHAPTER ONE

Summer 1916

Rusty decided to leave after supper, under the cover of darkness when cool evening air would make travel less of a hardship and more of an adventure. It was time to stop dreaming about being a cowboy in the Wild West and become one. He sat atop the metal boxcar, legs crossed in the manner he imagined Injuns would use at a powwow. The palms of his hands twisted on two warm steel rods as he tried to wipe away sweat and improve his grip.

As the train began to move the rumbling sound of its couplers rolled toward him in a straight line, like thunder of an approaching storm. Rusty shifted the gray newspaper boy's bag, worn bandoleer style, to a more comfortable position. The bag was loaded with his only possessions: one long-sleeved white shirt, one pair of black canvas work pants with a hole in the right knee, and two pairs of loose-fitting underpants stolen from his father's dresser. He leaned against the comforting pressure of the bag as it captured wind and transformed itself into a canvas pillow. The train's speed increased, creating an assault on his face by cicadas and hard-shelled June bugs. They clung to his sand-colored hair and crawled along the buttoned collar of his clean white shirt. The rush of wind and rattle of steel wheels increased, replacing the familiar summer sound of crickets. With head tilted back, he screamed at the stars, "Yeehaaa! I ain't never had this much fun."

Earlier in the day he'd passed up an opportunity to go fishing so that he could quietly explore ways of getting to Kansas—for free. Trains ran through his town in every direction, so the obvious choice, his only choice, was to hop a freight. To a fourteen-year-old boy it seemed easy enough: just find a train heading toward the setting sun. Yates Center, Kansas, had to be out there somewhere. Uncle George had written lots of letters to Ma telling her how great things were in Kansas, so how hard could it be to find the place?

Rusty's knowledge of trains was limited by what his father told him. If Pa said, "Stay away from the rail yard," that was the end of the discussion. He would say, "You never know what kind of people you might find hanging around there: hobos, gypsies, even worst."

Later that night, as the train began to move, Rusty felt the weight of Kendallville's humid air drift back to where he hoped it would remain, along with Pa's strange way of speaking, half-English, half-German. The smelly air could stay there too, with Sophia, the new stepma who screamed about kids always underfoot. Rusty's stomach began to rumble, and he felt water coming up into his mouth. To make himself feel better he tipped his head back and looked at the unmoving stars that belonged to the muggy August night.

Each time the train approached a crossroad, the four-note blast of its whistle carried stories about things he wanted, like life as a cowboy, any life away from Indiana, where noisy cars and trucks were fast replacing horses. Living in the west would mean he could be with his brother, whom he'd not seen in a year. Cliff was six years older and already a cowboy.

Occasionally, when rounding a curve, the train's speed decreased, easing the pressure of the wind. Rusty could relax his grip on the metal bars and expel a deep breath he didn't realize he'd been holding. The rhythmic invocation broadcast by the boxcar's wheels rose through the dark as the train traveled over uneven joints in the rails: do something, be something, do something, be something.

Rusty twisted from side to side searching for some way to ease the swaying of the railcar. He lifted his nose and sniffed, trying to identify insects, sparks, and ashes mixed in the aroma that pelted his face. He shuddered when cinders brushed his cheeks, reminding him of how Ma's chapped hand used to feel when she tucked him in at night. Occasionally, invisible particles burned and he wondered if hitching a ride atop a steel boxcar was a good idea. Running away from home—or what he had called home after Sophia tossed him out of his real house, Ma's house—had seemed like a perfect plan.

When the car swayed and rocked while rounding a turn, Rusty reacted like a bird flapping its wings to stay balanced on a wire. He rubbed his butt. His flat wool cap, first used as a seat cushion, no longer helped. His eyes became accustomed to the dark, and he studied the array of rods crossing the roof. The fat, central piece that extended the length of the car divided it into equal segments. At ninety-degree angles from the main rod, equally spaced shorter rods extended toward the darkness of the roof's edges. This jigsaw puzzle of symmetrical metal pieces reminded him of sides of beef he'd seen hanging in Mr. Kinkauff's butcher shop back home.

The railcar shook and he flattened his hands against the still-warm roof in hopes of reducing the swaying motion of the car. He leaned forward against the pressure of the wind. To keep himself awake, he searched for familiar bright stars in the night sky and imagined Cliff doing the same while rounding up stray cows or sitting near the campfire drinking coffee.

Deep in the tunnel of darkness he saw red and yellow fireflies exit the engine's smoke stack, then disappear into the night. Each time his body slipped he knew he was losing his battle to stay atop the railcar. He rubbed his tongue on the grit stuck to his lips and turned toward the back of the railcar in hopes of finding some safe way to get out of the wind.

As the direction of the train shifted his hair flowed with it, unblocking his vision and allowing the slightly bowed outline of the railcar's back edge to come into view. Even though that edge seemed hardly more than three arms' lengths away, Rusty knew the wind pressure would prevent him from standing. He could forget about trying to walk to the ladder at the back of the car.

He rubbed the tops of his thighs to relieve the numbness and feeling of pins and needles being stuck into his feet. He twisted and turned to get his legs unwrapped and under his stomach so he could balance on all fours and find a better position to fight the ceaseless rocking motion of the car. The swaying subsided long enough for him to slip his hands along the horizontal rods away from his body and seek a more secure, flattened position. Being stretched flat as possible might help reduce the wind but made it impossible to move toward the ladder. The car lurched. Rusty reached for any anchor and grabbed the metal rod that ran down the centerline. To keep himself from rolling across the top of the car, he spread his legs like a bird's tail feathers. His jaw slammed against the roof and he unleashed a string of unpracticed profanity.

Rhythmic battering of his body against the roof sent spurts of pain through his chest. To soften the blows, he pulled and pushed at his canvas bag until it wedged between his chest and the central rod on the roof. The rod gripped with his left hand felt slippery with sweat as he used his right to unbuckle the scarred leather belt he'd stolen from his father. When the tongue of the belt slipped free, he pushed the metal buckle under the central rod, rejoined the two ends, and pulled hard to cinch himself to the boxcar roof. Except for the pain in his stomach caused by the too-tight belt, he felt secure when lashed in place.

The train moved faster than he'd ever imagined—faster than any horse he'd seen at the county fair. He lifted his head to see where he was going and a sharp pain in his neck made him tuck in his chin and rest his head on his forearm. Up ahead he knew was only darkness. With each attempt to see where he was going, his eyes stung from sweat mixed with insects and soot. He knew he was going to cry. He shivered. His right hand worked the bag closer to his face to serve as a pillow against the rhythmic pounding. He felt nauseous again. Maybe, if he could splay his arms and legs a bit more, as if he was giving this railcar a hug, it would reduce the endless swaying. He closed his eyes and was soon riding on top of a sparkling white stagecoach, seated next to Buffalo Bill himself. *They were caroming between the new lamp poles of Kendallville's Center Street, the sparking hooves of eight white horses thundering so loud he couldn't hear the screams of children huddled against store windows in fear of being trampled. Buffalo Bill handed him the single-action .45 revolver, a huge Colt Peacemaker, to fire at the clouds overhead.*

Sleep lifted from Rusty. The train was no longer moving. He forced his encrusted eyelids open on a scene of railcars the color of cooked beets stretching before him in the wide sweep of a train yard. A greenish hint of land separated the tops of railcars from the gray-blue sky. The sun poked above the line, its orb reminding him of the yolk of a fresh egg dropped in a skillet. Below the green line, railcars interrupted his view of the yard as they swayed along the tracks. Bells and whistles joined unfamiliar ticking sounds as the metal roof of the boxcar warmed in the sun. Smoke made the air feel thick as wool. Despite the clamor, there was a softness to morning in this place, something he'd not felt back in Kendallville for a long time.

Rusty sensed vibrations in his stomach. It was a soft, slow padding feeling, like a cat sneaking up on a mouse, making the hair on the back of his neck stand up. He clinched his teeth as the tremors drew closer, then stopped. He lifted his head at the sound of a sharp squeak. A hissing noise followed by the unmistakable sound of the impact of a bat against the skin of a ball arrived at the same moment as searing pain in his left foot. His body jolted forward, causing his head to slam against one of the roof's cross members. Flames flared through his spine, into his neck, and exited as dry heaves from his mouth. Another sharp cracking sound, an unexpected wash of cold air, then intense pain made his body shake and his breath disappear. The smooth skin of his cheek scraped against the canvas bag. Rusty twisted in an effort to see his assailant; however, something held him captive.

CHAPTER TWO

Chicago

Rusty realized the belt, provider of safety through the night, was now an accomplice of his attacker. He swallowed, trying to hold back the rush of fire coming from his stomach. Vomit spewed across the clean red lettering on his newspaper boy's bag. He clung to the bag as he pushed against the boxcar roof. His hands slipped on what felt like wet leaves. His face slammed into the yellow-colored wet mess on the roof. The acrid smell in the liquid that came from his stomach forced him to turn his head.

He squinted against the brilliant glare of the sun, yet all around him seemed cloaked in shadow. Through a red haze of pain he strained to look back over his left shoulder at what appeared to be a tree. His eyelids fluttered, and as his vision cleared he realized he was looking at the silhouette of a giant—a huge man holding a baseball bat in his left hand.

The weapon was short, like the busted bat he remembered seeing at that game Pa took him to in Indianapolis. It was the time Benny Kauff hit the ball over the fence and half his bat sailed into center field. It looked like a bat on one end and a spear on the other.

"So, yer awake, kid. Been enjoyin' the night air and yer free ride, have ya?"

The voice of the giant was squeaky, belying his size. Rusty fumbled in search of the belt buckle. His arms refused to move when he felt the man begin to lightly tap the head of the bat against the thin sole of his right shoe.

"Hurry up and get yerself untied," came the strange, high-pitched growl, followed by a gurgling laugh. "'Cause then I'm gonna whip yer skinny little ass 'til you fall offa my train and break yer skinny little neck!"

Rusty could not move. The giant's boot slammed into the bottom of his right foot, causing his body to jerk forward. His face slipped over the vomit on the canvas bag and his body scraped along the top of the car, coming to a stop when his head collided with the steel cross rod.

From below, a voice cut through Rusty's pain. "Whatcha got, Bull? Looks like a punk kid. Get yer sorry ass down to 87. There's a dozen or so guys there that needs a lesson more than that kid. He'll learn soon enough."

"Right, boss."

Rusty looked back. His eyes alternated between the bat and the tree-trunk arms of the man called Bull. He was afraid if he looked any higher he might see the man's face.

Amid fits of coughing and laughter, Bull said, "Seems to be yer lucky day, kid."

Rusty heard the familiar whooshing sound of a baseball bat, and he squeezed his eyes and butt muscles as tight as he could. He felt a pleasant coolness in the breeze as the bat brushed past his left ear.

"Fooled ya, kid!"

Bull's next few words were swallowed by the metallic clumping sound of the big man's boots. Rusty waited until his stomach could no longer feel the reverberations of footsteps on the car's metal roof before he began to cry.

The hot metal surface of the boxcar warmed one side of his face; the sun directly overhead warmed the other. A coppery taste, like new pennies, filled his mouth, and he could smell cows. The echo of what sounded like a gunshot forced his eyes opened. Dried vomit, sweat, and tears cemented his right cheek to the boxcar's roof.

In the distance he heard men shouting words as incomprehensible as faraway thunder. Rusty's line of vision was cut off from the source of noise below by the roof's ragged edge. The frying-pan surface of the roof seared his hands as he pushed against it in an effort to raise his head. His body seemed too heavy to move. Although tears distorted his vision, he could see the belt used to lash him to the spine of the railcar the night before remained in place.

He wiped his nose and abraded cheek on his shirtsleeve. With his right hand he began to pick at the buckle. He heard men's voices below and tried to stop taking shallow gulps of air. The shouting was getting closer. Blinking his eyes did not relieve the stinging sensation caused by sweat. Using the canvas bag to protect his hands, he pushed his body up to see over the edge. There was Bull, baseball bat dangling from his left hand, a cattle whip in his right, kicking at a pile of rags on the ground.

The sharp crack of a whip pierced the noontime stillness. Rusty flinched. His face slammed into the roof of the boxcar, making a sound like a rock thrown against a hollow tree trunk. He opened his eyes and lifted his head enough to see another man, dressed in the neat black uniform and pillbox hat of a stationmaster, approach the giant. The well-dressed man grabbed the larger man's grease-stained shirt and pointed down the tracks. Bull pushed the stationmaster aside with his elbow, gave one more kick to the inanimate pile of rags on the ground, and trotted away.

Rusty tried to keep his head from touching the blistering roof as he searched the train yard below. To his front and rear stretched endless lines of railcars—he was at the apex of a metallic rainbow arching from where he'd been toward some unknown destination. Using the canvas bag to protect his hands and hunkering close to the top of the boxcar, he began his crab-like journey toward the ladder he'd climbed less than twenty-four hours before.

Just before his feet touched the ground, Rusty heard the hollow tick, tick, tick sound of water dripping. His dry tongue scraped across drier lips as he lowered himself into the gravel between the rail ties. He wiped his soot-and-grease-covered hands on his trousers as he searched for the source of dripping water. Beneath the car thirty feet across from him, he could see water leaking from the floor. And, in the glare of the sun, a pile of rags.

He worked his tongue against his upper lip and narrowed his eyes. The longer he stared at the heap of rags, the more certain he was that it had a pink foot. He blinked to clear his vision. The rags moved just slightly. It had to be a person.

Should he help? Pa's words came back to him: "Lord helps 'em what helps 'emselves. Ya stay outta trouble's way if ya walk down the other side of the street."

Razor-edged pieces of gravel pressed into his hands and knees as he crawled beneath the railcar. Mewing sounds escaped from his throat each time he took a breath. He paused when he reached the other side of the tracks. Before crawling into the heat of the rail yard, he leaned back against an iron wheel and let its coolness penetrate his sweat-soaked shirt.

He jerked awake, squinting against the glare of the rail yard's gravel. He felt the ground beneath him began to tremble and the sound of church bells rang in his ears. The iron wheel he rested against grabbed and twisted the back of his shirt. He looked at his right ankle resting on the cool steel of the rail and realized the boxcar's massive wheel was creeping along a line that would cut off his foot. He squirmed to get out of the way, but his hand found only emptiness. The downward slope of gravel offered nothing to push against, and he tumbled into the furnace of sunlight. He fought for breath that came only in fast gulps. His body stopped when his head hit what felt like a tree stump.

"Well, well, well," came a voice from above.

Rusty's body began to shake and he felt tears in his eyes. He recognized the squeaky voice of Bull. With no effort on his part, his body began to lift from the ground. He felt a crushing grip on the back of his neck. "Look at this little angel that's come to Earth. I got a special treat for you, young lad," said Bull.

Rusty felt relief from the pain in his feet since they were no longer on the ground. He could feel heat where the giant's body pressed against his and knew he'd die if he opened his eyes. He had to turn his head away from the stench of Bull's breath, which reminded him of dead animals back home.

"Please Mr. Bull, I just wanna go home. Please."

Before Bull could answer, another voice came from behind the monster that held him in its grip. "God damn, Bull, leave that kid alone and get over to 23. They's a fight there you'd enjoy more."

Bull's grip loosened and Rusty slid to the ground, fighting to hold on to the shaggy bark of the railroad guard's dirty coveralls. Rusty's knees hit first, creating enough pain to block Bull's laughter and parting words.

Except for the rhythmic sound of Rusty's crying, the yard was quiet. He rolled his head left and right and could see only the sides of rusted boxcars. The music of dripping water returned. Rusty shook his head and raised himself to a seated position. The sun burned through his sweat-soaked shirt as he crawled into the shade with only one thing on his mind. He started to get up and pitched forward as pain shot through his feet. His knees buckled. Flashes of red lightning accompanied a scorching sensation that traveled from his feet to his chest. Gravel and cinders scattered where his face plowed into the ground.

A distant keening alerted Rusty. He opened his eyes and tried to spit away the copper-flavored cotton that filled his mouth. An arm's length away was the shape that had earlier been the brunt of Bull's beating. A high-pitched whine came from the pile of rags. The longer he stared at the shape, the better its individual pieces came into focus—a man dressed in a faded homespun cotton shirt and coveralls. His clothes were varying shades of dirt, disguising the garments' original colors. No shoes, only dirty calluses that looked like raindrop splatters on a muddy street, adorned the pink soles of his feet.

Rusty looked at the sky now fading from yellow to gray-blue as the day's heat escaped through cracks in the clouds of late afternoon. He licked his lips with his dry tongue, trying to get rid of the metallic taste in his mouth. He watched the man lying in front of him breathe, his chest rising and falling with a steady rhythm just like his baby sister Pauline's. *So, this guy's not dead. Maybe I should just get out of here while I can.* He looked around, unsure of which direction might lead to safety.

He was also unsure if the man could hear, but he spoke anyway: "Mister, first I gotta get something to drink. Then, well, then I don't know what."

Placing his hands between chunks of gravel, Rusty was able to raise his body and scoot over the rough surface of the train yard in the direction of the boxcar where water dripped from the floor. Between its wooden side slats he could see pale-green heads of lettuce packed in ice. *This must be the big city, probably Chicago, otherwise people would grow their own lettuce in the backyard like Ma does at home.*

Rusty snaked his body between the rusted iron wheels to get beneath the car. He pushed gravel aside and laid his head back against a rail tie. Using his meager bag of clothes, he made a pillow behind his neck to soften the edge of the oil-soaked tie. He closed his eyes, opened his mouth, and welcomed water so cold it hurt his teeth. It dripped onto his face and he laughed as it trickled back into his ears. He reached up to let the water slide down his arms and spread his legs to find drips of water that would bring some comfort to his bruised feet.

A rumble of thunder startled him. He realized railcars were colliding; he heard the anxious sound of couplers urging the cars behind them to follow. He bolted upright and smashed his forehead against the axle brace of the moving car. His head rebounded back against his makeshift pillow and the rail tie. He fumbled through his wet canvas bag for his spare shirt and rolled it into a ball to soak up as much moisture as he could. He remained flat on his back, trying to keep his head from being sliced off by the undercarriages of the cars moving inches above his face. As the last car passed, stars in a clear night sky greeted him. *When had it turned dark outside?*

Rusty looked to his right searching for the pile of rags. A hazy half-moon provided enough light for him to see the man, now poorly concealed behind a collection of broken crates stacked alongside a boxcar. The pink-white feet against the background of dark clothes stood out as brilliant as stars. As he'd done before, Rusty alternately rolled and crawled over coarse gravel, the dripping shirt wrapped around his neck so both hands would be free.

The stranger's moans where just like the sounds Ma made when one of her headaches was coming on. He reached the man's side and unwrapped the dripping shirt. He thought the swelling lump in his throat might prevent him from breathing. Cold chills caused the hair on the back of his neck to rise. He was not prepared for the sight of the stranger's face. A burning feeling replaced the swelling in his throat and he felt tightness at the center of his chest. His mouth began to fill with water coming from his stomach and he feared he might puke again.

The stranger's left eye snapped open. On the other side of the man's flattened nose, where most people had another eye, a pink slot twitched. A red, dirt-encrusted gap replaced the spot where lips should be. Most of the man's teeth were missing. Thin cuts wriggled across his face. And he was black.

Rusty leaned forward, unsure of what he'd discovered. He looked at the filthy clothes and dirt caked in patches on the skin. In disbelief, he leaned back and took another look at the man's feet. The bottoms still showed shades of pink. Rusty looked down at the man's left hand lying open on the ground, its palm as white as his own, yet the back and wrist seemed darker than black.

"Wow, a real nigger. And who'd think they bleed red, not black, like Pa said they would."

As he looked around to see if anyone had heard him, the man's crooked mouth began to move. Rusty worked his arm under and behind the man's back to raise him up. A stench arose. Rusty turned his head and gasped for air. He felt only hardness inside the shirt where flesh should be. As he tried to prop the man into a sitting position, the stranger's body slumped against him. Rusty's breath quickened and he lowered the man's head to the ground, shoving his soaked canvas bag under the ball of curly gray hair.

"There you are, old man," he said.

The man's single eye popped open and Rusty watched as it traced an erratic pattern over his face. Without a word, the man's arm began to move. Rusty saw the hand rise and extend in his direction, the pale-pink palm unfurled in the moonlight reminding him of the night lilies opening in Ma's garden.

Rusty offered the man the dripping shirt, and when their hands touched, the boy jerked back.

"Don't worry, son. It don't come off," came a raspy croak.

Rusty leaned forward, unsure of what he'd heard.

"Huh?"

"The color. Don't worry, it won't get on you."

"Oh. It's just that I never seen a nigger up close. Like this, I mean."

"Humph. I seened too many white men up close. For sure. Thanks. Water feels good," said the man as he raised his body onto his elbow.

"That eye of yours looks pretty bad," Rusty said.

"Yeah. I think it's still in there, though. Can't really tell. That fuckin' bull was one mean individual. And being a nigger sure didn't help my cause. For sure. Ya gotta name, kid? I'm called Jupiter. It's what my master called me, anyways, 'bout fifty, sixty years ago."

"Wow! You mean you're a slave? A real slave?"

Rusty watched Jupiter's one good eye scan his face again.

"Sure ain't nothing to get all excited about. For sure."

"Well, I mean, I never met a slave 'cause that's all over."

"Slavin's far from being over, boy. Far from it."

"See, this town I come from has a sign by the city limits that says, 'Nigger don't let the sun set on you here,' so I don't see many, ah, colored folks. None really."

"Where you from, boy?"

"Kendallville."

"And where in hell's that?"

"It's in Indiana."

"Might as well be fuckin' Georgia," Jupiter said, as he lowered himself back to the ground. "So ya got a name or not, kid?"

"Oh, sorry. Sure, it's Rusty. Well, Russell, really, but my ma calls me Rusty so everybody else does, too."

"Rusty, huh? Rusty, does yer ma know you're hoppin' freights and gettin' beat up by railroad bulls?"

"Ma's dead."

"Sorry. Least you knowed your ma. For sure. Good job on finding a bit of water. You can go a long time without food, but water, that's a different story, for sure."

"Mr. Jupiter, I think we're in a bad spot here," Rusty said, looking at the undersides of railcars and iron wheels that surrounded them.

"It's just Jupiter, and I think I'm blessed to be in the company of such a perceptive young man."

"What's a 'perceptive'?"

Rusty watched Jupiter's eye lock on his face and felt he was being judged. Jupiter lowered his head. "Means you know what the fuck is goin' on. We don't have one good body among us, boy, but somehow we gotta get out this spot before that bull comes back and finishes the job."

The crunch of gravel, soft footsteps slowly moving in their direction, made Rusty and Jupiter look to the right.

In a voice that sounded to Rusty like a cricket rubbing its legs together, Jupiter said, "Quick, under here."

Rusty felt an unexpected tug on his sleeve as Jupiter pulled him into the confining space of a crate lying on its side. Jupiter lowered the lid so gently that Rusty did not hear it touch the ground.

A sharp, sour smell made Rusty turn his head and press his eyes closed. He could not tell if the smell was from him, Jupiter, or some dead animal that shared their hiding place. He'd never been this close to a colored man—never even had a good look at one—and Pa always talked about the way they smelled. Now what was he supposed to do?

Rusty locked his hands behind his neck and pushed his chin against his chest. Through a busted slat of the crate he could see two dark boots approach and stop next to the crate. He began to shake when he felt warm water run down the inside of his pant leg.

"Don't worry, friend," came a soft voice. "I can smell ya in there. I'm just makin' sure the bulls didn't follow me."

Jupiter and Rusty held their breath.

"Oh, Christ," came the voice again. "Did you pee your pants?"

Rusty closed his eyes as tight as he could and clamped his hand over his mouth, but could not stop the convulsions of his body.

"Roman? That you?" came a raspy whisper in Rusty's ear.

"Jupiter? You peed your pants?"

"Naaa. I got a kid here—"

He never finished the sentence. The crate swung up and Rusty stared at a man who could have been Mrs. Olsen's scarecrow back home. The sleeves of the man's coat hid his hands and ragged hair hid his ears. Rusty could see the man examining his feet.

"You gonna steal my shoes, mister?" Rusty said.

"Ha. I can tell which bull got ya by his signature on yer feet, kid," Roman said.

Rusty thought he heard a bit of laughter in the voice. He wanted to respond; however, sudden sobs blocked his words. The best he could do was nod his head.

"Damn, looks like he got you good, Jupiter," Roman said.

"Yeah, one mean sumanabitch. It's that guy with the whip we saw down in Louisville a week or so past, I think."

Rusty watched the scarecrow straighten, dirt falling from his coat as he rubbed his chin. "Well, let's see what we can do about getting us some grub and liquid refreshment. First, we gotta get outta this place. Too damn many bulls working this yard for us honest folk."

The three crawled beneath cars, over tracks, and around piles of busted crates. After each pause, Rusty thought he would never be able to start moving again. Gravel bit at his knees, and on his trousers he could see dark stains blossoming around the largest tears. They worked their way toward a place in the yard where he could no longer see lights, only silhouettes ahead that changed from angular outlines of railcars to softer shapes of trees and bushes.

"Where are we?" Rusty whispered.

Roman stopped, held up a hand, and stood. "Y'all wait here," he said. "I think it's okay, but ya never know."

Rusty fell on his side into a mix of coarse gravel, small chunks of coal, and the refreshing scent of grass. He found that keeping his eyes open was nearly as tough as crawling on the sharp gravel. He could not take it all in; everything had happened in just a couple days. Was that possible? The days were all jumbled in his head and made no sense. How did he get here in some far-from-home train yard with a beat up colored man, both so hurt they couldn't stand up? He'd left Indiana to become a cowboy, a simple cowboy in Kansas with his brother. He fought back the desire to cry.

Rusty awoke. He was lying on his side with his numb left arm pinned beneath him. He swatted at a bug trying to crawl into his ear. His view of the world was filtered through blades of grass.

Roman's head was turned in his direction. At the upturned corners of the man's mouth two brown teeth, like broken pencils, protruded through yellow-stained gray beard hair. In the daylight, the hobo's ragged clothes appeared like those in drawings of Jim Bridger, the fearsome mountain man, who Rusty'd seen in magazine stories. Were these the kinds of men he was going to Kansas to see and meet when he became a cowboy?

"What? How long have I been sleeping?" Rusty said.

"All night and most of the next day, or today, I guess," Roman said. "And old Jupiter over there, he's only beat ya up by a few minutes."

"Sir, I feel like something the cat puked up," Rusty said.

"Speaking of cats, let's get you two boys something to eat. Grub'll make you feel better, but I don't have much hopes for your looks. Neither of you."

Roman poked at a fire in a small depression scooped out of the gravel. The aroma of something cooking on three sticks above the flames made Rusty's stomach growl.

"What's that cookin', Roman? Sure smells good," Rusty said.

"Well, let's just call 'em rabbits, small rabbits," Roman said as he examined the meat and gave the sticks a quarter turn.

The hobo removed the creatures from the sticks, examined them again, and handed one to each of his fellow travelers. When Roman's ragged coat sleeve fell away, Rusty saw that he was white, though it was hard to tell through the dirt and grime. A cap that appeared to be some kind of animal's skin covered his head.

Rusty looked around at where they had camped for the night. Towering piles of broken rail ties, crates, and empty barrels surrounded them. In the distance he could hear clanging and banging, punctuated by the occasional shouts of men, but any activity was hidden from view.

"Where are we, Roman?"

He watched the bear-like man look up from the dying fire and make a slow scan of the landscape. "Well, the easy answer is that we're on the edge of civilization as we know it. Kinda looks like a monument to some sorta ancient lost city, don't it?"

"But we're still in the train yard, ain't we?" Rusty asked.

Roman stood, stretched his arms skyward, and looked toward where the sun hesitated above the last row of railcars. As he straightened, a cloud of dust fell from his clothes and an odor more sour than the creosote in the rail ties made Rusty's eyes water. Roman pushed his hands into his pockets, tipped his head back, and released a deep sigh.

"Well, this has been a grand party, gents, but I got a gal back there in Cleveland that is probably missing me. I don't want to keep the little lady waiting—if you get my drift."

Rusty saw Jupiter's busted lips form a small smile. The pink tip of the black man's tongue poked through a crust of dried blood and dirt to moisten his lips. Jupiter looked at the hobo with his single eye. "Tell me, Roman, you know these trains. Which ones is going to Kansas?"

At the mention of Kansas Rusty straightened.

"You going to Kansas, Jupiter?" Rusty asked.

"Yep. Plan to join my people out there. Place called Nicodemus."

"Humph. Never heard of it. North or south Kansas?" Roman said.

"North. Sorta west of central, I been told. Supposed to be the Promised Land. Like us slaves never heard that story before."

"Well, you'll have to head southwest, probably one of them trains over yonder on track eleven or twelve. Best follow the smell of shit and dead animals if you want a free ride. Nobody wants to ride in those cattle cars, so the bulls usually leaves them alone."

"Hey, I'm going to Kansas, too," Rusty said. "I'm going to be a real cowboy."

"Ya don't say," Jupiter said. "What does a kid from Indiana know about being a cowboy?"

"Everything! I read all about them in a book that cost me a dime called *Wild West*. And, I saw Buffalo Bill's show when it came to our town once, a couple years ago."

He waited for Jupiter to respond, but the colored man was too busy watching several ants work their way through the gravel.

Without looking at Rusty, Jupiter said, "Yeah, and I'm going to the Promised Land."

"Roman, do you know where the train to Yates Center is?" Rusty asked.

Roman scratched at a bug Rusty could see crawling in his beard, and said, "I been living on dreams and train smoke a long time, son. I know just about every place they is. Heard of it, maybe, but I ain't sure which trains run there. For sure they run between KC and Bazaar—that's a little place nearby Yates, I think. Big cattle shipping town, or least it was."

"That's just great!" Rusty said. "I'm going to join up with my brother out there so we can be cowboys together."

"So you says," Roman said and thrust his hands into his pants pockets.

Rusty watched the two men exchange a look he could not understand.

Roman snorted. "Ya better get a move on then, young fella. Not as many calls for cowboys as they oncest was."

After saying good-bye to Roman, Rusty and Jupiter spent a week in the wreck of a boxcar recovering from their injuries before jumping their first train going west. Together they hopped one freight after another for short rides heading south and west. Near Peoria Jupiter decided he would head toward Iowa instead of Kansas.

"I'm not sure what I should say," Rusty said.

The two stood in the dark of a rail yard, one looking to begin his journey, one looking to end his, listening to crickets and the ticking of metal railcars cooling from the day's heat. Jupiter looked to where the sun had disappeared, not at Rusty. He scratched at the back of his neck and spoke so softly Rusty had to lean forward to hear the old man's words.

"Nothin' much to say, lad. Thanks about gets it. You help me, I help you, we both promise to reach down and help somebody else the next time. That's all they is to it."

Rusty looked up at the dark slit of Jupiter's toothless smile. "Well, shouldn't we shake hands or something?" he asked.

"Yep, we sure can, unless you're afraid of some of this color getting off on you."

"I guess there's not much chance of that, sir."

Rusty released Jupiter's firm grip and turned toward the looming shape and distinct aroma of the cattle car, one in a long string of about fifty. He took only a few steps before looked back over his shoulder. The rising moon was full now and he could make out Jupiter's bent silhouette shuffling between two lines of cars. He shoved his hands deeper into his pockets, let his breath out in a low whistle, and said, "Okay, now what?"

CHAPTER THREE

Kansas

Rusty spent three more days drifting from one car to another before he crossed a big river and saw Kansas City squatting like a fat chicken on the edge of the prairie, just as Jupiter said he would. He passed those few days sitting in the open doors of boxcars that reeked of death. He slept on piles of soiled straw he'd swept together and crushed into a bed in the corner, trying to avoid dark stains in the wooden floors. The stains were dry, but what were they from? At night, he kept his nose between the wooden slats of the cattle car's wall and tried not to breathe air thick with the oppressive stench of dead animals.

Sharp edges of sunlight poked through cracks in the cattle car's sideboards, warming his face. The car's slowing pace didn't register with him until the clanging echoes of the couplers signaled a stop. The boxcars thumped into one another, and the impact caused him to bite the heel of his hand while he was trying to remove a splinter with his teeth. His thoughts had been centered on riding bucking broncos, their black coats all glistening with sweat—horses with flames shooting from their nostrils. He scanned the yard for bulls that might be working the tracks, a trick learned from Jupiter: Always check before you do anything, then exit out the blind side of the car, usually toward the center of the yard, since bulls patrol the outside edges.

He sniffed his shirt and turned away from his own body odor that seemed to have absorbed the lingering smell of dead cattle.

"Maybe I can get rid of this smell if I put on my other shirt," he said to his newspaper boy's bag.

"And maybe you cain't," came a ragged voice out of the shadows.

"Wha— Who's there? Huh?"

"Sorry to make you jumpy, kid. I hitched on last night outside a Holt. Didn't know this side-door Pullman was taken 'til this mornin'."

Rusty felt his heart pounding in his ears. He licked his lips, wiped his hands on his trousers, and strained to get a look at the man in the dark of the opposite corner.

"Aaa, it's okay. I mean, it's not like I own it or anything. You just sorta surprised me."

"Humph." The stranger turned to look through the slats of the car. "Well, forget your shirt. When they's a lotta death about, it sticks in the ground, or in these boards here. Some things ya just cain't get rid a."

"I seen lottsa dead animals at my house in Indiana. My pa kills lottsa things, but they never smelt like this."

Rusty's eyes began to focus on the man slumped against the back of the cavernous cattle car. He looked like other hobos he'd seen along the tracks in the train yards—white and ageless, wearing clothes not suitable for rags. There was no telling when the man had last shaved or had a haircut. Tobacco juice at the corners of his mouth stained his graying beard. Even the whites of the man's eyes looked dirty. Cigarettes had left their marks on the fingers of his left hand.

The stranger, now on his hands and knees, began to crawl indirectly toward Rusty, as if circling to get behind him. Their eyes locked. Rusty tried not to stare at the stranger's tongue as it worked left and right between his smiling lips.

A hand snaked along the floor in Rusty's direction, hesitated, and stopped. The man's eyes narrowed as he rested back on his haunches and worked grimy fingers through his wiry hair. He seemed in no hurry to close the gap.

Rusty hoped the ringing sound in his ears was voices. He rapidly alternated looks through the slats of the boxcar into the empty rail yard and back toward the old man.

"Say, kid. Ya don't happen to have any smokes or money on ya, do ya?"

Rusty turned his face away. The man's breath reminded him of open garbage cans. "Ah, no sir. I'm broke, too."

The stranger's hand began to move again. It rose and reached out toward Rusty's thigh. The boy jerked back as heat from the crooked fingertips penetrated his trousers. The rough wood of the car's side slats slammed into his back.

"Now there, don't go getting all jumpy on me, young man."

The clanging sound in Rusty's ears grew so loud he could hardly hear what the man was saying. His eyes could not let go of the man's swaying tongue. In a single motion he scooped up his canvas bag, leaped to his feet, catapulted over the man, and escaped through the partially opened door. Pain in his still-injured feet shot up his legs and into his groin when he landed in the gravel of the yard. He knew only that he had to run.

Rusty was not sure how far he'd run, nor if the vagrant had given chase. He stopped at the edge of a corral filled with bawling cattle and shouting men—real cowboys. Rusty glanced back toward the rail yard before walking around to the side of the corral. He didn't want any bull sneaking up on him while he watched the cowboys work. He grabbed the middle fence rail, started to pull himself up, but decided against trying to climb to the top—not a good place to be if he needed to make a quick getaway. Before him a roiling mass of humans and four-legged beasts moved in no discernable pattern. The scare of a few moments ago forgotten, he tipped his head back and drew in a deep breath of fresh western air, laden with the smell of cattle feces and urine. High-crowned, broad-brimmed hats floated past through the dust clouds. His arms pressed against rough-hewn logs that separated him from this new world. A kaleidoscope of color swirled before him. He stuck his head between the fence rails to get a better look. He could hear the faint jingle of rowels on the cowboys' spurs each time a rider passed. Horses' hooves tossed small flecks of mud in all directions. He feared his face might split from smiling.

He'd never witnessed such skill. Horses did most of the work while cowboys slapped cows on the butts with coiled ropes to maneuver them toward the railcars. Eventually the cowboy would select out some animal that a man sitting on the fence near the railcar pointed to. Even when the cow seemed to want to get back with its friends, the cowboy and his horse kept blocking the way. Finally, the cow just lowered its head and ran up the ramp into the railcar, or into a smaller corral.

"Hey mister, do you know which one of those trains over there runs over towards Yates Center?" he shouted to a cowboy who had stopped near him.

"Well, I don't think any of these trains goes to Yates. Best you can do, I think, is that un over yonder." He pointed with his nose and the brim of his hat. "She goes back to Bazaar or Matfield Green. Not sure which. Depends."

"Mister, can I ask you a question?"

"Sure."

"What's it like? I mean, do you like being a cowboy?"

"I think that's two questions, son. First off, I wouldn't do anything else. Second, it's not the kind of life I'd wish on my worst enemy."

Rusty looked out at the steers, unsure if his question had been answered. Before he could ask anything else, another cowboy rode over and stopped next to the fence. "Harper," the first man said, "this young fella's looking for the train what runs over to Yates. Got any idea?"

The man called Harper looked down at Rusty, then west.

"Nope. None does, I think, Mr. Carson."

Carson leaned forward in his saddle as if he were seeking a more comfortable position, and trying to get a better look at Rusty. The tooled leather of his saddle and stirrups groaned with each movement. His hands pushed against the thighs of his sweat and dirt-stained black trousers. He straightened. Rusty looked at the man's huge gloved hands resting on the horn of the saddle.

A shout from somewhere in the corral distracted the cowboy, and he hesitated as he pulled at the gloved fingers of his left hand. As the glove slipped away, Rusty could see the beginning of a thick, worm-like scar on the tip of the man's index finger. The pink line crawled over the back of the man's wrist and disappeared beneath the snap-buttoned cuff of his shirt.

"Yer not from around here, are ya?" Carson said.

"No sir. I'm from Indiana."

The cowboy pushed his hat back with the gloved thumb of his right hand and asked, "You mean you hopped freights all the way out here from Indiana?"

"Yes sir. I wasn't gonna walk, was I? So, is it far to Yates Center?"

"Too far to walk, pal. Harper, go check to see if that supply truck has left for Nehosho Falls. Maybe the kid can hitch a ride that far. Then Yates is just a hop, skip, and a jump."

Rusty turned to Carson, stood as tall as he could, and said, "Say, Mr. Carson, you hiring any cowboys? I could use a job."

"No kid, not now. Maybe later in the fall. Besides, ain't you kinda green, even to be a cowboy? I bet you got a ma back some place that's going to be putting you in school about the time we start the heavy shipping season."

"It's Kendallville, sir. And no sir ... I mean, I do have a ma, but Ma's dead now and I don't need schoolin' to be a cowboy."

Carson coughed, spit a long brown stream of chewing tobacco juice in the direction of the nearest steer, and said, "That's what we all said, least oncest or twicest."

It was early evening when the supply truck driver stopped at the base of a rise in the land that hid whatever lay ahead. Rusty could see they were stopped at a fork in the road that disappeared in either a northwest or southwest direction. There were no signs indicating where Yates Center or anyplace else might be. Using his nose and chin, the driver pointed to the road on the left, the one heading southwest and going up the steepest part of the hill.

"I'm going over to Yates Center to join up with my brother. He's a cowboy, there."

"She'll carry ya right on into Yates then, 'bout twelve or fifteen miles," the driver said between fits of coughing. "Don't wander off into the tallgrass this time a year. Plenty of snakes here, if you know what I mean. I can smell 'em."

Rusty looked at the man who'd not said a dozen words in the ten-hour truck drive from the stockyards in Kansas City on roads so rough he could not have slept if he had wanted.

"You can smell snakes?"

"Yup. Smell like those mothballs the wife puts in the box with our winter clothes to keep the bugs out. Smell probably scares the bugs more than anything, just like the snakes scare me."

Rusty looked at the driver, then at the empty road. The sky ahead of him had changed from deep blue to the color of fresh peaches.

He sucked in as much air as he could and said, "Thanks for the lift, mister."

"Humph. Better get a goin', then."

By the time Rusty reached the top of the rise, sweat burned his eyes and his feet ached. The top of the hill hadn't seemed so far away when he started walking an hour earlier. He lifted his nose and sniffed the air, checking for snakes. He pulled off his cap, stuffed it into his canvas bag, and used the left sleeve of his shirt to wipe his face. He was hungry and Jupiter's words about going without water rang in his head.

He blinked several times, trying to absorb the immense length of the Nehosho Valley that fell toward the orange and red band of light in the west, then climbed in low rolling hills to the north and flatness beyond. Through the graying of the evening he could see how the land fanned out and surrounded him with tallgrass. And it was alive. No matter which direction he turned the land seemed to be in motion like a huge dark green lake that would take forever to cross in a rowboat.

Alongside the road to his right he saw what appeared to be a stone fire ring and the remains of charred fence posts. He probed the ashes with a stick and turned over what had once been two soup cans riddled with bullet holes, a water bucket with no bottom, and a mud-coated brown medicine bottle. The flat rocks near the dead fire's edge, still warm from the day's sun, offered a place to rest. Rusty looked at the fence's sagging bottom strands of rusted barbed wire, then at the scar of gray clouds on the far edge of the horizon that divided the world between green and blue. *If this isn't the top of the world, it's damned close.*

Maybe a short nap would be a good idea. To his left he saw a pile of rocks that would keep him off the ground and away from rattlesnakes.

Night sounds replaced daylight as uncertainty replaced his bravado. He pulled his knees closer to his chin and fell asleep, riding a great black horse. *His spurs jangled louder than all the other riders as he chased after splotchy long-horned cattle—and rattlesnakes.*

Silence woke him. The sky to the east, where the morning sun was trying to make its appearance, was gray, dull, unpromising. His whole body protested as he uncurled from the pile of flat stones that had been his bed. These rocks were at the corner of a rectangle drawn by other piles of rocks. This must have been some sort of building, he thought. Maybe a large house. Rotted timbers lay on the ground along with scraps of wire. There was a wide break between what must have been two walls. In the break, or path, he could see two faint grooves in the ground. Wagon tracks?

He turned and asked the reluctant sun, "Was this some kind of stagecoach stop or something?"

The only answer came from the wind. A short distance from the building structure he scampered atop the tallest rock he could find. His throat was so dry it was painful to swallow. In the fresh greenness of the prairie he could see dark spots he thought must be cattle, along with smaller animals he figured were whitetail deer or maybe antelopes Cliff had written to him about. A gentle wind carried the fresh smell of grass—and mothballs. No humans, or shapes of things created by humans, in any direction.

He turned and faced southwest to where Yates Center was supposed to be. Rummaging through the emptiness of his canvas bag he found only his shirt, pants, and cap. No socks, no underwear, no food, no water.

He looked over his shoulder and watched the morning sun ride higher in the sky, then play hide-and-seek between layers of clouds. *That's the direction of Indiana. I wonder if Ralphie is tired of going fishing every day? Is Becky looking forward to school starting up in a couple weeks?*

From his vantage point atop the large rock he could see how the road to Yates curved and twisted, unconcerned about where it was headed. Cutting across all this grass in a straight line seemed like a better idea. He jumped from the rock, setting off scurrying sounds in the grass around him.

Walking a straight line through tallgrass proved more of a challenge than Rusty imagined. With no trees to walk toward he realized he had to use the constant pressure of the wind against the right side of his face, along with the moving position of the veiled sun, to keep himself headed in the general direction of town. To keep a check on his direction of travel, he frequently looked back to admire the straight path he cut through the grass.

Occasionally he came to open patches strewn with flat yellow stones that broke when he stepped on them. As he came to a rise in the land he saw the tan, sinewy line of the road that had been hidden behind the low hills and was pleased that the shortcut he took seemed to be working.

Approaching the road, he parted the bottom two strands of barbed wire fence that bordered it and stepped through. Ahead in the open space of the road lay a lifeless deer. He hunkered down to examine the animal. Carefully, he pressed his right toe against the deer's tawny front leg. The color of her body blended with the road, except for the white tail and belly fur.

He wedged the toe of his shoe farther beneath the animal and lifted. He could see a lot of hair missing down her left front leg and what appeared to be burn marks on her white belly. He grabbed the leg and lifted. The pattern of missing hair ran across her side and neck.

The constant murmur of the wind was interrupted by the metallic sound of wagon wheels and horse's hooves. Rusty looked up as a wagon approached. The driver stopped and looked at the deer, not at him.

"Lightnin', probably," the man said.

The man—most likely a farmer, Rusty thought—looked okay. His gaunt face was surrounded by a wide-brimmed straw hat. Gray hair escaped from the edges of the hat's sweatband and threatened to cover the man's ears. His denim coveralls, bleached by the sun to a quiet shade of blue, looked clean, sort of like the ones the farmers back home wore to church.

Rusty tasted salt on his dry lips, cleared his throat, and said, "Afternoon, or morning, or whatever it is, sir."

"You're not from around these parts, are ya?" the man said, staring down at him.

"No sir. I'm from over in Kendallville."

"Where's that?"

"Indiana."

"Hmmm. Big town?"

"Not as big as you'd think, unless you guessed about five hundred."

"Long ways from home then, aren't ya."

It was a statement, not a question, and Rusty was unsure if he should answer.

"Well, yes sir. I'm heading to Yates Center. I'd sure appreciate a ride, if you could, I mean ... if you're headed that direction. Please."

"Jump on up. I'm heading that way myself. Be glad for the company."

Even the hard wood of the wagon seat felt good when Rusty dropped into place next to the driver. As the man started to reach beneath the seat of the buckboard, Rusty felt the hair on the back of his neck rise. He watched the driver's every move and checked to see how far it was to the ground in case he had to jump. He released his breath when the man produced a wrinkled bag the same color as his sunburnt skin. The driver dropped the stained leather reins into his lap, dug into the bag, and offered Rusty an apple.

"Ya look scared, kid. What's the problem?"

Rusty hesitated, words stuck in his throat, and his eyes focused on the missing middle finger of the man's left hand.

"They's last fall's crop but still have some crunch to 'em. The wife kept 'em in the cellar until just the other day. I didn't even know we had 'em. She's always coming up with some kinda snacks for my trips."

"Thanks! Thanks a lot."

Rusty took a huge bite of the apple while examining dust hiding in the cracks of the man's neck.

"Name's Stockebrand, Charlie Stockebrand. Got a boy, Reggie, about the same age as you, I figure. How old are you?"

Rusty wiped his right hand on his trousers and offered it, fingers locked, thumb pointing skyward like an upside down flag caught in a stiff breeze.

"Oh, I'm nearly fifteen or so, I guess. It's my pleasure to meet you, Mr. Stockebrand. My name's Russell, but everybody calls me Rusty. Rusty Starke."

Charlie grunted, shook hands, and looked out over the undulating grass. Rusty could see thin lines forming at the corners of Charlie's eyes as the man's eyebrows moved toward each other. Charlie turned in Rusty's direction and the boy felt like he was being inspected.

"You any kin to a Cliff Starke? He stays over there on George Hardy's place—"

"Hey!" Rusty jumped to his feet and had to grab for the back of the wagon seat to keep his balance. "That's my brother! And George is my uncle. He's a big cattle rancher there, I think. I'm going to meet up with my brother and be a cowboy, too!"

Charlie continued to stare at Rusty. "Best sit down, young fella."

"What? Oh," Rusty said as he sat back on the plank seat.

"You might want to think about that cowboy life. It ain't all like what you might think you know," Charlie said.

"Well, I can ride and I can learn to rope. And if Injuns come around I can learn how to shoot 'em."

"Not at all like that. First, we don't have any Indians in this part of Kansas anymore, not hostile ones anyways. Second, nobody's gonna take time to teach you anything about punching cows this time of year. The boys will be too busy moving herds in from pasture for the next month or so."

Rusty stared at his apple, then looked over at the tallgrass, in some places as high as his head. The wagon moved along at the same speed as the breeze behind him, making it feel as if the wind had stopped. He felt the heat on his back, and sweat burned his eyes.

After a pause Charlie cleared his throat. "Maybe in the winter somebody could. Maybe. Don't know if your brother's punching cows or not. I know he and Les were riding fence a whole lot earlier this spring after that business with the crops."

Rusty turned to look at the endless lines of three-strand barbed wire running parallel to the road. "What's 'riding fence' mean?"

"Oh, it's about the worst job they is for a cowboy. See all them posts?" Charlie pointed with his chin. "Great place to scratch your back if you're a steer. Somebody's got to make sure them posts stay in place and the barbed wire stays on the post."

"Cowboying is what I came out here for. It's all I want to do. That and be with Cliff. Besides, what else can a kid do?"

He and Charlie watched three pronghorns bouncing in the distance across the open prairie. "Well," said Charlie, "I suppose, if you had a choice, you could run off and join the circus. I suppose."

The green prairie dissolved into varying shades of gold, then back to muted green as the shadows of clouds glided overhead and passed in front of them. Fields of tall corn alternated with fields of short wheat. Only when the wagon climbed to the top of a rise could Rusty view the full panorama that would be his future. The prairie seemed to have no border, just arbitrary definitions of light and shadow. The ragged mix of greens and golds reminded him of a quilt on his bed back home. When he had a home.

Endless fields gave way to occasional houses and barns. Rusty saw slab-wood houses mixed among smaller stone houses and barns, all growing out of the prairie, signaling the presence of farms and people. Near many buildings he could see stubby trees that looked like they'd been planted by fire, their limbs twisted and black.

"If you could part with it, sir, I sure could eat another of those apples," Rusty said.

"You bet, young man."

Charlie dug into the paper bag beneath his seat, smiled, and held up a bright red apple.

"Thanks," Rusty said and wondered what his next meal might be, or where it might come from.

CHAPTER FOUR

Reunion

"Afternoon Charlie. Whatcha got there?"

The woman's voice startled Rusty. He'd not realized he'd been dozing and struggled to sit upright. He ground the heels of his hands into his eyes and looked around at a scene laden with familiar farm sights and smells. He shook his head. The wagon rested in the shade of a two-story frame house. Its west side was entirely made of stone while its front appeared clad in odd-sized planks of wood the color of storm clouds. A barn more than twice the size of the house dominated the immediate view behind the house. Its vertical plank siding looked like a weathered forest. The barn leaned slightly to its right toward a smaller building as if whispering some private joke.

Like everything in Kansas, the house was planted in full sun. The downward slope of the land to the west swept away into a sea of alternating shades of green. Occasional piles of dun-colored rocks anchored the land in this sea. There seemed to be no demarcation line between land and sky, just a gradual change of color. It was a place of constant wind and cloud shadows chasing each other over tallgrass. In the distance, dark, irregular lines of brush through the fields marked the passage of a creek.

Rusty swallowed. He felt surrounded by shifting light and shadows. When he turned to face the woman, thin like Ma, his eyes met the reddest hair he'd ever seen. She must have just washed it, because it was piled in a large bird's nest on top of her head. She held a towel to the side of her face where water trickled in small rivulets toward her ear. Her eyes threatened to drill two holes into him.

"Well, I fetched you up some more kin, Belle," said Charlie. "This one was walking through Kimble's pasture up near Nehosho Falls when I found him."

Rusty saw a smile start on Charlie's lips. "Says he found a room for the night in that abandoned stagecoach stop where half the rattlesnakes in Kansas live. Says he's brother to Cliff and he's come west to be a cowboy. That about sum it up, young man?"

Rusty could feel Belle Hardy's eyes focused on his face. She reached up with her left hand and removed a pencil-sized, ivory-colored stick that had been holding her hair captive. Removing the stick gave the hair permission to surrender itself to the unseen persuasion of the wind. It collapsed on her shoulders and burst across her face, hiding everything except her deep brown, unblinking eyes.

Rusty felt trapped. He wanted to stop looking at her hair as it danced with the wind. *Maybe this is something I shouldn't see.* He licked his lips and tried to swallow. Only after she asked his name the second time was he able to respond.

"Sssssorry ma'am." The stammer in his response sounded like a stranger's voice. "Name's Russell, err, Rusty really. I mean my ma calls me Rusty, but my name's really Russell. Russell Starke. Cliff's brother. Well, and my ma's dead, so she doesn't call me anything now."

"Well, it's a pleasure meeting you, young man. You're welcome to stay, if you'd like," Belle said.

Rusty felt sweat move down his sides like tiny spiders searching for places to hide. He wondered if the flash of heat he was feeling came from this woman's red hair, her smile, or her kind words.

"Uh, thank you, ma'am." He studied a rock on the ground near her bare foot.

"I'm Carrie Hardy, but folks call me Belle. That's really my middle name. You can stay up there in the wagon all day and ride around with Charlie, or you can join us for dinner down here."

"Oh, sorry," he said, turning to Charlie. "I appreciate the ride and all you told me about the country. And thanks for those apples, too."

The older man laughed and thumped him on the shoulder. "Oh, you're welcome, young fella. You might want to mind what Belle here tells you."

"Yes sir, I will."

Without looking in Belle's direction, Rusty grabbed his canvas bag and hopped down from the wagon. He stood silent next to her as they watched Charlie turn the wagon and head down the rutted lane leading from the house to the road. Silence roared in his ears, blocking the sound of the wind.

Rusty could see Belle looking at his grease-stained canvas bag. She asked, "Is that all you have?"

"Yes ma'am. Another shirt and another pair of pants is all that's left. I lost my socks and under things someplace between here and Kendallville."

"And how is Kendallville these days? George talks a lot about that place where he was a kid, farms and trees everywhere. And Cliff says there's lakes and trees everyplace you look. Trees. It all sounds like heaven to a girl born and raised out here on a Kansas homestead and all."

Rusty watched as Belle turned toward the wind, successfully keeping hair out of her face.

"It's just fine, ma'am. At least I think so. Probably hot, but not hot like here."

"And how's your dad—Fred, isn't it?"

Rusty turned from Belle to survey the outbuildings in back of the house. He put his hands in his pockets and looked at the ground. "Oh, I guess he's okay. We didn't really talk much before I left."

Belle said, "I never met your ma, but George says she was a fine person."

"Yup."

"Cliff mentioned you live with your sister."

"Well, sort of. I mean, it was getting real crowded there since Aunt Vesta has two little ones and my sister Pauline and all," Rusty said, looking across the open land. "So that's why I decided to come here and be a cowboy, like Cliff."

Rusty jumped when he felt the light pressure of Belle's hand on his shoulder. He looked at her face as she tilted her head back and let the wind play with her hair, which now fluttered like a red flag pointing in the direction the wind raced. Wind buffeted his body and rocked him back and forth.

"Okay, young man, let's figure out what to do with you. George and Cliff are in town, playing baseball again. They'll be back soon enough. George'll have some ideas, I'm sure."

Rusty watched the endless sea of moving grass, afraid to turn his head. He felt Belle move as she leaned down until her face was even with his. She rested both hands lightly on his shoulders. He was forced to turn and look her full in the face.

"I want you to know, you, or any kin, are always welcome out here. It's our way. We never mean to bother anyone and we don't make our troubles someone else's. But I also want you to know, around here, it's only those hens over yonder that can lay around and still be thought of as productive."

Rusty's eyes narrowed a bit when he looked at Belle's smile. He noticed creamy-white flakes on her hands and apron, hands so close he could smell candle tallow mixed with fresh soap. He felt his heart beat a bit slower and looked up at her face, not sure which eye to focus on.

He decided it was best not to look into her eyes. He tried to swallow but could only lick his lips. She would not let go of his shoulders, nor turn her head—ever, he hoped. He knew he was being held captive until he could find the right thing to say.

He concentrated on her smile instead of the floating red hair.

"I'll pull my share of the load." His voice, little more than a whisper, competed with the wind. "My ma says I'm good at helping, even if I do run off to go fishing sometimes. She gets sick from time to time, so I know how to do a lot of things. Well, she used to get sick."

He knew Belle was close enough to see the tears he felt welling in his eyes. He tried to blink them away.

"And Rusty, you have to understand this: Your ma is dead. She can't help you, but you can still make her proud, understand?"

He wanted to turn away from the welcoming aroma of the candle tallow, the crispness of her apron, the nearness of her face. Then her grip on his shoulders tightened. He stopped breathing and surrendered to her.

"I guess I know. But, how will— What's gonna—"

His questions were lost in Belle's encircling arms, as she pulled the grimy, sobbing boy close to her chest. He knew he should move away from the rise and fall of her breasts and the heat that pushed against his face. He felt cool water from her hair drip onto his face, mixing with tears.

"Let's just sit here a minute. I want to tell you something my ma told me when George and I came out here," Belle said as she lowered herself to the ground and wrapped her skirt around her legs all in the same motion.

"Ma and Pa were homesteaders. There was no joy out here then, only freedom to succeed or fail. So when I was a young girl, about seventeen, back in '93, George asked my pa if he could marry me. I was scared because I didn't know anything about being married. I was the schoolteacher here in Yates Center by then. My ma said, 'Don't worry. Most of what you worry about will never happen. Worrying comes from being tired. The other part of worrying comes from things that are already past and you can't change, anyhow. Or, worrying comes from what others think they know about you—most of which is untrue and nothing you can change. And worrying about your health only makes you more sick. So, after you get rid of all those things, you'll have time to worry about what really matters.'"

"And what's that, Aunt Belle?"

"Well, I don't really know, Rusty. But let's not worry about it."

The pair sat on the warm ground for a few more minutes. They listened to the wind and watched clouds change shape and chase each other to the east.

"Well, let's get you cleaned up a bit, then maybe you can help me finish up making candles before the men folk get back."

"You mean Cliff?" Rusty was on his feet, looking toward the road.

"Yep, that's who I mean."

"Great. I bet he's already got a great lasso and a six-gun."

Belle looked at Rusty. "Are you sure you even know what a cowboy does, or looks like?"

"Sure. I saw drawings in a magazine in the barbershop back home."

"Tell me."

Rusty looked around the farm as if trying to find a cowboy to describe.

"Well, most of 'em are real tall. They have, at least the bad guys, these really big mustaches and probably lots of scars from fights with Indians. The good guys got these real pretty shirts and red bandanas and white teeth." He stopped long enough to take a deep breath. "And they have, most of 'em, two six-shooters with pearl handles."

He looked up at Belle's smile. She looked back at him and said, "Well, let's get some of that dirt off you and get you cleaned up—at least on the outside."

The pair walked around to the side of the barn and Belle pointed to the large wooden tub and a bar of gray-colored soap.

"There ya are, young man. Let's see what you look like with a little less Kansas topsoil on you."

"Thanks Aunt Belle."

Water in the large tub, warmed by the sun most of the day, felt cool against his skin. Rusty knew the large piece of Lava soap Belle gave him would scrape and burn his skin, but he welcomed scrubbing away two-weeks' worth of dirt and grime. He tipped his head back as he'd seen Belle do to let the constant wind dry his hair.

Sounds of children's laughter reached him as he slipped into his other, less-dirty shirt. He thought he was daydreaming. He stood still, mouth agape. Coming around the corner of the barn he saw a girl about the same age as his sister Pauline and two smaller children, all barefoot, being chased by a boy his own age. The boy carried the longest snake Rusty'd ever seen.

The children spotted Rusty and stopped. Rusty saw them all turn their faces to the older boy, who walked toward him. As he moved in Rusty's direction he switched the lifeless snake to his left hand and extended his right.

"My name's Lester, or Les."

Rusty looked at the boy's hand where the snake had been moments before and cautiously extended his own.

"Ah, nice to meet you. I'm Rusty. Do, uh, do you all live here?"

"Yep. And those other mutts are my sisters. You passing through?"

"No. Yes. Well, maybe. I'm here looking for my brother, Cliff."

Rusty saw Belle approaching the group, hands hidden in the pockets of her apron. "Well, I'm glad you boys had a chance to meet. Rusty here is going to be staying with us for awhile, I guess, aren't you, Rusty?"

"Yes ma'am. I mean, if it's okay, for awhile. Just until Cliff and me get jobs as cowboys."

Belle smiled and looked around, back toward the house, then at the boys. "Rusty, I guess you'll have to stay with Cliff and Les, over in the dugout."

"What's a dugout?"

"It's the place where George and I lived, as homesteaders. People called us 'nesters' then, in '93, until we proved up the land," Belle said, brushing a wayward strand of hair from her face.

"Ma, can I show Rusty the dugout?" Les asked.

"Sure. Then you two make sure those pigs have water and gather up any eggs before you come in."

The boys each grabbed a bucket from near the barn and moved toward the side of the small outbuilding. As they did, Rusty saw two riders turn into the track leading to the house. He noticed Les was looking in the same direction.

"Hey, there comes Cliff and Pa," Les said.

Rusty tried to shout. A dry, gagging sound turned into a cough and caught in his throat. The two riders coming up the lane seemed deep in conversation, both gesturing with their hands and shaking their heads. He could see they were dressed in baseball uniforms, not rumpled cowboy hats and dusty boots as he'd seen at the corral in Kansas City.

Rusty dropped the bucket and started running. A dry squeak escaped from his mouth. "Cliff!"

Cliff pulled back on his horse's reins, trying to see through the rising dust cloud where the shout came from. "What—Rusty? Rusty, is that you?"

Cliff glanced over at George and said, "Aw shit."

In a smooth motion Cliff swung his right leg over the pommel, jumped from the horse, and ran toward Rusty, arms outstretched, baseball cap abandoned to the wind. The brothers hugged and slapped each other on the back, sending up billows of dust. Rusty's eyes filled with tears as he hugged his brother.

"Well, I'll be damned," Cliff said, wiping his eyes with a dusty forearm. "How in the world did you ever get out here, little brother?"

He'd not seen the kid in more than a year, and now here he was, tall enough to look directly into his eyes. Through laughter and tears, he heard Rusty say, "I hopped a freight, lots of freights, and some folks got me on the right ones and some folks beat me up and some folks fed me and some—"

"Whoa there, catch your breath, young fella," Cliff said.

Cliff held Rusty at arm's length, looking him up and down. "I can't believe what I'm seeing. Look at the size of you."

"You better believe it, Cliff! I came out here to be a cowboy, just like you," Rusty said.

George dismounted, caught hold of Cliff's mount, and walked over to Belle as the brothers poked at each other. "Well, what have we got here?" he asked.

Belle stood, arms folded across her chest as she watched the brothers punch and slap. "It's Russell. Damn near look like two peas in a pod, don't they?" she said.

"Except the older pea's a bit taller and more serious looking. Damn if the kid don't look like his ma, though. Cliff's got Fred's mop of hair, but Russell sure has Emma's color and softer features. Is he staying?"

"I expect so. He hasn't said what drove him out here, but I can make a good guess from what Cliff's told us of their father—and about Fred's new wife."

"Might be a challenge feeding the both of them, Belle."

She looked at the ground near her feet and back to the two boys. "I'm not so sure it's food that Russell needs right now."

"Am I about to get another lesson?" George said, trying to keep the smile out of his voice.

Belle looked up at George's dust-covered face, her smile matching his. "I suppose you are. I was just thinking about how raising a child takes more attention than it does time, sort of like growing a garden."

George looked at her and said, "You know, some men might think I married you 'cause you're the prettiest woman in Kansas."

"And?"

"Well, you are that. And you're also the smartest."

With a quick shift of her hips to the right, Belle bumped against George's hand. Her arms remained across her breasts. He could see she was smiling at the patch of weeds near her feet.

"You best quit that kind of talk, George Hardy. We've enough little ones running around this farm."

Without looking down, his hand slipped around back and gently rubbed against her butt before he walked over to Rusty and Cliff.

"Hello, young man. Welcome to Woodson County," George said, hand extended.

Rusty looked at his uncle, who stood nearly a head taller than Cliff. The man's baseball cap hid most of his hair. Rusty could see from the edges that it was dark, specked with gray just like Pa's. The baseball shirt he wore, probably once white, had various food stains and large, dark half-moons beneath the arms.

"This is Uncle George, Ma's brother," said Cliff by way of introduction. "And this here's my little brother, Russell."

"Welcome, Russell. How's things back in Kendallville? In some ways I miss that place—lakes full of bluegills, trees changing in the fall. Then I turn around and look at this." George made a sweeping gesture. "God-awful windy, but beautiful. But farming tends to be farming, no matter where you live, that's why I'm trying to teach Cliff here a trade of plastering. Or maybe chimney building."

Cliff softly cleared his throat. "You have to be careful of Uncle George," he said. "He tends to make speeches anytime there's more than one person around."

Rusty toed at the ground, unable to look George in the eye. He swallowed and said, "Well, thanks for putting me up, Uncle George. I'll probably be hiring on as a cowboy someplace real soon and—"

"Well, we'll see about that," George said, cutting him off. "For now, let's get the chores done, show you the dugout, then get something to eat."

"How was the ball game, Cliff?" Belle asked.

"If Jim Weide would spend more time swinging the bat instead of running his mouth about the rest of us not hitting, we might have done better," Cliff said.

Belle chuckled. "Keep in mind, people who complain about the way the ball bounces are usually the ones that dropped it."

Though he was not sure why, Rusty joined in when Cliff and George laughed. Belle shooed Les and the other children off to their chores. As Cliff, George, and Rusty walked away, Rusty said to George, "Does Aunt Belle have those funny sayings about everything?"

"Just about, Rusty, just about. She was a schoolteacher out here for a good number of years. That does things to a woman."

George stopped as they rounded the northwest corner of the barn, and Rusty bumped into him.

"Well, there she is, Rusty. Your home away from home," George said.

Rusty looked around. On the ground in front of them he saw only the peaked section of a small roof, like something ripped from a building during a tornado that just happened to land right-side up.

"I don't get it."

"Well, you're sort of looking at the back," Cliff said. "The front's around the other side there, on the down slope of the hill."

They walked around to the front. At the sight of a lopsided door covering what looked like a huge hole in the side of the hill, Rusty lowered his voice and said, "It looks like a place for groundhogs, Cliff."

"Well, it's a bit of a dugout and a bit of a prove-up shack," said George.

Rusty stepped forward and brushed his hand against the front wall of the dugout to feel the roughness of the sod. Next to the crooked door, chopped into the sod, was a square hole. Covering the hole was a flyspecked piece of greased paper masquerading as a window. George pulled on a piece of rope that served as the handle for the door. In the gloom of the interior, Rusty could make out a colorless dark floor and a ceiling that appeared to be made of hay.

"It smells like cow shit," he said.

"True," George said, "but if you look among the grass on the roof out there, you can still see where the red, purple, and pink morning glories Belle planted in '93 are growing."

"You really don't mean we sleep in here?" Rusty said and turned toward Cliff for support.

"Beats laying in the open," George said. "These dugouts were surprisingly comfortable homes for us homesteaders: cool in summer, snug and easy to heat in winter. Solid walls cut the wind, even in a tornado. Gives you a new appreciation for the soil of this great land."

Rusty heard Cliff clear his throat with an exaggerated cough. He looked at the dugout and thought about his cramped space in the storage room where he'd been living at his sister's house back in Kendallville.

"What about snakes and spiders, Cliff?"

"Well, we have to shoo 'em out every now and again," Cliff said. "I guess it didn't bother the homesteaders much, did it Uncle George?"

"Nope, not so much."

Cliff widened the door of the dugout to let more daylight sneak in. Rusty could see the floor was made of rough-hewn planks with splinters pointing at all angles waiting for bare feet.

"This place looks kind of desperate for light and fresh air," Rusty said. Beneath the raised planks on the right side he could see a burlap bag that appeared to be moving.

"Did that bag over there just move?" he asked.

"Probably," Cliff said. "That's Ralph."

"Ralph?"

Cliff cleared his throat and said, "Ah, Ralph is a rattler we keep in here. Mornings, usually, Les opens the bag and lets Ralph have the run of the dugout to hunt mice. He usually catches him in the evening before we go to bed and puts him back in the sack."

"Usually?" Rusty asked, his eyes locked on the sack.

Rusty heard George chuckle as his uncle walked off toward the snorting pigs.

"I thought you were a cowboy, Cliff. Not some sorta animal living in a hole in the ground," Rusty said.

Cliff stepped into the dugout and lifted the toe of his boot to the edge of the lower bunk just above the bag holding the snake. He looked back through the open door at the darkening sky to the southwest. His restless hands found his pocketknife and a couple of loose coins to bother and clink together.

"Yeah," Cliff said. "Well, I guess it is sorta like shit, little brother, but it's better than the shit I had back in Kendallville. I'd have been a dirt farmer forever there. Here, with some help from an old guy in town, and Uncle Curtis, I'm beginning to learn carpentry and how to lay stone."

He watched Rusty move outside the dugout, keeping his eyes locked on the burlap bag.

"For about a month," Cliff said, "Glen and me went up to the Spring Hill Ranch—that's over near Strong City—and laid walls. You won't believe that place. It's like those castles in Germany Pa used to talk about."

The mention of their father ushered in a wave of silence.

Cliff sucked in a deep breath and said, "How's the old man doin'?"

"Oh, I guess he's okay," Rusty said. "Him getting married to Sophia so quick ... I mean, Ma was hardly ... Well, then I went and lived with Vesta so I didn't see him much. He was always too busy to visit me and Pauline. Least that's what he said. They moved over to Auburn, ya know."

"Did he talk about me? About me leavin' so quick after Ma died?"

"Nope. Not a word to me. Maybe, well, who knows?"

Through the irregular shape of the doorframe Cliff looked at his brother and tried to imagine the kid rounding up cattle.

"So, what happened to bring you out here?" Cliff asked.

Rusty looked into the gloom at his brother's scarred boots inches away from a rattlesnake, and the unfamiliar clothes hanging on a nail next to the bunk. "I wanted to be out here, with you, Cliff, doing something. To be, well, to be a cowboy, like you."

"Bad choice, Russell. You should be in school—not like me."

Rusty watched Cliff's eyes narrow just like their Pa's used to do before he took off his belt.

"Something we better get straight right from the git go," Cliff said. "You ain't staying out here. No way. Nobody asked you to come out here. There's nothing for a kid to do but school. And the only school you should be in is back in Kendallville. That's where you're headed after your short summer vacation out here in the Wild West."

"I ain't."

"Ain't what? Goin' back? You sure as hell are."

"You can't tell me—"

"I can and I will. You might not want to listen to Pa, but you'll damn well listen to me."

Rusty saw lines as rough as sash cord appear on the sides of his brother's neck. The muscles in Cliff's arms began to bulge as his fists formed into two dark tan-colored balls.

"Cliff, you sound just like the old man. Same crap. 'Cept maybe he was better 'cause at least he said I didn't need to waste time schoolin'."

Rusty could see pearls of sweat, held together by a string of dirt, form at the base of Cliff's neck.

"Listen kid—"

"I ain't a kid so stop calling me one. I'm better than fourteen years old, maybe fifteen. Damn near fifteen, anyway. I don't have to listen to you or no one. You think a kid could get out here on his own like I did? Huh?"

Cliff lowered his head. His voice was low and Rusty had to lean forward to be sure he heard all the words. "Russell, I'm sending you back. That's that."

Without looking, Cliff pushed past him and walked toward the house.

Rusty kept blinking his eyes to keep his vision clear. "We'll see about that. We'll see. If you don't let me stay and be a cowboy I'll—"

Cliff turned. "You'll what? And you better shut that damned door or we'll be sleeping with more rattlers than just old Ralph tonight."

"I'll run off and join the circus, that's what."

He heard Cliff snigger as he walked away. Rusty kicked at the rock that held the door open and launched it into the grass.

The silence at the dinner table was broken by the clinking of utensils on the plates, the wind, and the pounding of Rusty's heart. The piece of chicken and mashed potatoes on the plate in front of him had no taste. There was no talk of riding the range, rounding up the herd, or fighting off the bad guys. Occasionally, George broke the quiet to comment about how the baseball team would be better if they practiced, or how the crops would be better if it rained. Or how the country would be better if the Republicans didn't run things into the ground. Every sentence ended with either, "Wait 'til next year" or "If it rains."

Dinner was followed by two more hours of silence. Rusty's body ached. He wanted to go to bed. Les was seated at the kitchen table reading, as was George. Unwilling to enter the dugout alone in the dark, Rusty walked around the farm listening to night sounds. He found Cliff in the barn lying on a stack of hay bales, eyes fixed on the ceiling. Several chickens had managed to balance themselves on a thin piece of framing between two uprights in the rafters. He knew that Cliff was looking far past the chickens.

Rusty sucked in the rich smell of hay and fresh wood in the barn, cleared his throat, and said, "What is it, Cliff?"

Without looking at him Cliff said, "I'm just not meant to be a farmer, kid. I just ain't. This spring we broke our backs putting in kafir corn. What the wind didn't tear up in April, the hail pounded to death in May. Round here, corn don't grow over five feet tall. That's what being a rich farmer in Kansas looks like."

"But I thought you were going to be a cowboy and I'd ride the range with you. Maybe fight Injuns if need be."

"Not gonna happen. This here's mostly wheat and field corn country. Any real cow punchin' is over in Chase County, around Strong City, maybe down at Matfield Green, or Cassoday. Anyplace but here."

They both watched the chickens in silence. Then Cliff said, "Shit. I suppose we could go over there, Chase County maybe. You know, in a couple a weeks when they're shipping steers and see if anybody's hiring."

"Sure, we can both ride okay. And fencing, or riding fence, sounds like an easy enough job."

Cliff abandoned the chickens, turned toward him, and said, "How do you know about riding fence?"

Rusty threw himself onto the hay pile next to his big brother. "I've been studying cowboy ways, even watched them round up cattle in Kansas City on my trip out here."

Cliff grabbed a hand full of hay and tossed it at Rusty. "Humph. Must have been some trip."

Rusty sat up and said, "It was! Want me to tell you about it?"

"Nope. Can't imagine it was any fun."

"Well, I met these guys."

"Forget it. I ain't interested."

"But I nearly got killed a couple of times!"

Cliff slowly turn his face in Rusty's direction. His brother's eyebrows stood like two mountain peaks, nearly hidden by a shock of black hair.

"Killed? You mean, like dead? This I gotta hear."

Cliff and Rusty spent the next few days riding around Woodson County, meeting relatives and friends Cliff had made since arriving the previous summer. At each stop, Cliff encouraged Rusty to retell his harrowing tales of escape from railroad bulls, how he relied on the kindness of strangers for his survival, and how he didn't eat for days at a time. And at the end of each story he told people how proud he was of a fourteen-year-old kid who could make it, on his own, all the way out to Kansas—just for a visit. Rusty also talked about Jupiter, how the man was brave and, since he was a hobo, free to travel. He just left out the part about Jupiter being a former slave.

Of the relatives he met, Rusty enjoyed his Uncle Curtis, George's brother who had also run away from home with hopes of becoming a cowboy. Curtis always had a smile and said his current job of delivering newspapers was just temporary until something worse came along. It was while dining with Uncle Curtis the boys got their first lead on jobs. At the dinner table, Curtis said, "Ya know, you might want to stop over in Beaumont, south of Eldorado a ways there, and check with the guys at the Nation spread."

"Why's that, Uncle Curtis?" Cliff asked.

"Well, they still do some loose herding over there and I heard tell they were looking for some herd boys. They like youngsters like you uns 'cause they only have to pay about fifty cents a day."

Cliff let out a breath of air, mostly through his teeth. "I can earn that making rock fences up at the Spring Hill Ranch, and don't have to smell the cow manure. I heard old moneybags Steve Jones, since he started that place in the '80s, plans to put stone fence around the entire ranch, damn near thirty mile of it! They've already built a house bigger than the state capitol building, and a barn to match."

"Yeah, I suppose you could," said Curtis as he loaded more potatoes into his mouth. "But if you hire on with a cattle outfit you'll get your horse, your eats, and a place to bunk. You might want to think about that."

Rusty's eyes shifted back and forth with the conversation while his feet tapped quietly on the floor and the palms of his hands rubbed against his trousers. This sounded great. A chance to be a cowboy, nobody telling you what to do, or what to wear. Riding a horse every day. Chasing down cows that ran astray.

He asked, "So, what does a herd boy do when he's loose herding, whatever that is?"

"Well, it's not loose herding like it was in the days of open range," Curtis said, wiping his face with a napkin. "Those days are long gone from Kansas. What they do now, this time a year, is put a boy in each corner of the pasture, some on the edges if it's a big pasture, thousands of acres, ya know, and they all spend days riding toward the middle, rounding up the foraging livestock. Not as tough as it was when we first came out here in '92, is it, Mary?"

Rusty noticed that Curtis didn't wait for his wife's response as he reached out with his knife and speared another square of roast beef from the large platter.

The ride back to Uncle George's farm was quiet. Only the tapping sounds of the horses' hooves on the hard road surface mixed with crickets and frogs hiding in the grass along the edges. It was just the way Rusty liked it. A few birds still moved in the bushes looking for a safe place to spend the night, and the smell and promise of rain seemed far off to the west. Rusty glanced over at Cliff more than once. He recognized that same look he'd seen come over Pa when the old man was thinking about something unpleasant. When they reached the ranch, the brothers rode around back of the house and unsaddled and fed their horses.

Rusty watched how Cliff tossed his saddle over a rail in the barn and did the same.

"How's that, Cliff? Is that how cowboys do it?" he asked.

Cliff looked at him, then the saddle. "Yeah, it's okay. But if you don't stop grinning so much, people are going to think you're loony, like that old Irish guy who lived down the street from us back home."

From the barn Rusty could see George already seated on the back porch steps. He and Cliff walked to the house in silence and dropped into place next to George. The sky had turned from gold to orange with a promise of red joining the display from out of the dark grass.

Rusty listened to the quiet cacophony of insects.

"Nice night, eh Uncle George? Any rain coming?" he asked.

"Might be some. A bit. Remind you of Indiana?"

"Yep. Except for no lakes, no trees, hardly any cars, and none of the people I know, it's just like Indiana."

George and Cliff snorted in response.

The screen door opened and closed with a clicking sound nearly lost in the music of the insects. Rusty turned to see Belle wipe her hands on her apron and tether an unruly strand of hair behind her right ear before joining the men on the porch steps to watch the last of the sunset.

"You know, Russell, contentment is a matter of hoping for the best and making the best of what you get," Belle said.

Rusty was unsure of how he should respond. He looked at Belle, her face golden, her hair the color of flames in the waning sunlight.

George turned and looked at her, too. "That so, Miss Belle? Well then, I'm one happy and contented homesteader."

Rusty turned to Cliff, who seemed to be studying his dust-covered boots. His brother took a deep breath, rubbed his palms on the legs of his dusty coveralls, and said, "Uncle George, I was wondering if there might not be more, maybe better, opportunities for me elsewhere than Woodson County."

"Set on being a carpenter rather than a dirt farmer or plasterer, are ya lad?"

"Yeah. That or soldiering, maybe."

Rusty looked at Belle and George. Both stared at the back of Cliff's head. Belle broke the silence.

"No," she said.

"No what?" Cliff said. "No endless string of dead-end jobs or no soldiering?"

"First, carpentry is hardly a dead-end job like cowboying. Second, soldiering is the ultimate dead-end job. Besides, America isn't in this war, no matter what you hear in town or read in the newspaper."

"That's true, lad," said George. "America don't have a dog in this fight. Let the Brits and the Frenchies work it out with the Krouts."

"It's coming. I can feel it," Cliff said. "Me and Fritz Munck, we were talking about going up to Canada and joining their army. Canada's been in the fight since '14 and they need some help. And when this country wakes up and does its part, we'll be seasoned veterans."

"Or dead," said Belle.

Rusty turned to his brother. "Wait, Cliff. Ain't we gonna be cowboys? You were all ready to find us jobs as herd boys a couple hours ago. Now what's this about?"

"It's about you going home, to Kendallville, and me being over twenty-one years old and getting on with my life," Cliff said as he stood, jammed his hands into his pockets, and walked away.

The thud of boots pushed aside the rhythm of crickets. Rusty turned to George, still staring at Cliff's back, rubbed his hands on his sweat-stained trousers, then looked at Belle. She stared back at him and motioned with her head to signal that he should move away from George.

Rusty stood, slipped his hands into his pockets, walked to the far end of the porch, and dropped onto the rough boards of the porch swing. Belle ran her hands down the back of her skirt and settled next to him, her eyes fixed on Cliff's back. Her weight made the swing's boards give off a warning squeak.

"Russell, what you have to understand is that, anymore, not everyone thinks of what they currently do as being an anchor for their life," she said. "It's different here in Kansas than what you might have seen in Kendallville."

"But until Ma died it was pretty good." Rusty's voice was louder and higher pitched than he intended, and he saw George turn and look in his direction. Belle wiped her hands on her stained apron and dropped her eyes from the setting sun. Rusty leaned forward to get up. He was surprised at the strength in Belle's grasp on his arm as it held him in place.

"I gotta talk to Cliff," he said.

"Let him go. It's just the wind out here that sometimes does that to people," Belle said.

"What?"

"The damn wind. It just flattens everything out here, including hope. Even promises."

"But—"

"Wait'll tomorrow," Belle said as she rose and went back inside.

CHAPTER FIVE

Jobs

The sounds of their uncle talking to the horses and readying a wagon brought Rusty and Cliff to the door of the dugout. Rusty squinted against the brightness of the sun. "What's up, Uncle George?"

"Time's a wastin', lads. We can ride over to Cassoday and be back in time for a late dinner if we get a move on."

"What for?" Cliff said.

"For work for you two, for starters," George said as he slipped the bridle over one of the horse's heads. "Let's get a move on."

Rusty turned to Cliff. "Christ, does he always get this anxious before coffee?"

Cliff rubbed his face with his hands. "Must be some politicking he wants to do over there."

Cassoday smelled and sounded like cattle. There had been little conversation among Rusty, Cliff, and George as they traveled twenty-five miles west of the Hardy farm that morning, headed for the nearest cattle-shipping town. The sun burned Rusty's back and neck, and for the last hour, the pungent smell of cow dung, accompanied by a far-off moaning sound he could not identify, replaced his thoughts of thundering stampedes and wagon trains fading into the sunset.

The trio stopped at the top of a rise to look at the town spread before them. Corrals and cattle pens took up more space than buildings, and cowboys seated on fence rails took up more space than cattle.

"Seems to be a lot of smell and noise for so few cows," Rusty said.

"Call 'em steers or cattle," George said, "or they'll think you're from Indiana or someplace."

"I am from Indiana, Uncle George," Rusty said.

Cliff turned to his brother. "That's just the point, Russell. You're from Indiana, and wanting to be a cowboy in Kansas is the wrong thing to be just now."

George looked over at Cliff and asked, "You been eating nails or something this morning, young man? To answer your question, Russell, the heavy shipping season ain't started yet. It'll get a lot more busy in the coming weeks."

"But the shit smells so strong."

"That smell is just part of the earth in these parts. For those birds you see perched on the fence rails it's the smell of money," George said as he slapped the reins on the horses' backs.

As soon as they reached the corral, George parked the wagon and moved off to talk to men standing near the open boxcars. Rusty climbed to the top rail of the fence where he could best watch the action and keep an eye out for his uncle, who seemed to be talking with anyone who would listen.

Each time Cliff sat next to him on the fence rail, Rusty tried to move away. He balanced with his left hand and used his right to pull his straw hat further down to cover his face. There had been no discussion of the subject of Rusty's return to the east since the night before. He moved as far as he could and stopped next to a set post.

"Looks to me like the horse does both the thinking and working out there," he said to Cliff.

"You're mostly right," George said as he walked up behind the brothers. "Oh, be back in just a minute, boys. We'll get started home as soon as I talk to a man over there."

Rusty watched George walk along the corral fence, shaking hands and slapping an occasional cowboy on the shoulder. His uncle stopped for a longer discussion with one of the cattle buyers. Several times the two men looked back in his direction, before they resumed talking.

"Looks like Uncle George is serious about that idea of running for political office back in Woodson County. At least he's sure working this crowd like a politician," Cliff said.

George walked back to Cliff and Rusty. "Boys, I got some bad news and some good news for you."

Rusty and Cliff looked at each other.

"First, I promised Belle I'd try to find some work for Cliff here so's he wouldn't run off and do something stupid, like join the Canadian Army. So, I've been asking 'round to see if there's any work here for two inexperienced cowhands. Other than maybe some fence riding later in the season, there's not much need for two like yourselves.

"Now the good news, at least for you, Cliff, is that I got the name of a guy on the other side of the county, down in Yates Center, who might prove worth checking out. I'm not so sure I know him, but I will. He's a builder who could use an apprentice carpenter, someone with enough skill to know the difference between the walls of a house and the ceiling. Folks tell me he's putting up a lot of buildings and houses."

Rusty looked first at his uncle, then to his brother. "What about me? Can I just stay here in Cassoday and be a cowboy?"

"Well, first off," George said, "you should be in school. And since it's too far for a daily trip from the farm into Yates Center, maybe this guy, Frank LaFevre is his name, can put you two up for room and board. Then you'd be able to go to school there in town."

Rusty could feel the rough edges of the corral fence cut into the palms of his hands. "But I really want to be a cowboy."

Cliff jumped down from the fence rail, sending up a cloud of dust when he landed. He added more dust when he slapped his hat against his trouser leg.

"That's great news, Uncle George. It's just what I want to do!"

"But I wanna be a cowboy," Rusty said as he jumped from the rail, nearly pitched forward onto his hands and knees, then looked at the ground. He jammed his hands into his pockets.

"Yeah, yeah," Cliff said. "First you have to get an education, not stumble along like me. Look around you here. Which guys have the nice clothes, automobiles, and fancy girls? Is it the boys punching the cattle or the guys who own the steers?"

Rusty looked at two well-dressed men standing near a cattle car. Even in the midday heat they wore derby hats and dark suits, had no necks, smoked cigars, and looked like their stomachs were about to explode over the top of their trousers. He could not picture himself in a derby hat.

"But I wanna be a cowboy," he repeated, kicking at the fence post.

"Well, in that case, maybe it's best if you come on back to the farm with me," George said. "Cliff, here, could go on into Yates by himself and I could use another hand 'cause I have some plans to—"

"No!" Rusty ripped his hat from his head, threw it on the ground, and stomped on it. His face was red, hands bunched into fists, teeth clinched. "We ain't separating again. Okay, I'll go to school, but I ain't leaving Cliff."

"Look Russell, I'm about tired of you following me around like a puppy dog or something. Do what yer told, for a change. Maybe school in Kendallville."

"No!" Rusty said and turned to the activity in the corral.

Cliff and George turned their backs to him and walked toward the wagon. Rusty rested his forehead on his arm against the fence rail and studied the horse droppings inside the corral. Shouts and laughter coming from cowboys around him drew his attention to where a rider had fallen from his horse. Rusty wiped his nose on the sleeve of his shirt, released a long breath, and looked toward the railroad tracks.

As he watched, a steer slowly moved away from a group being herded toward a railcar. Each time the cowboys slapped it with a rope, it took a couple steps to the side. When the cowboys lost interest in the steer it would move a bit closer to the edge of the fence. Eventually it worked its way around the corral and came eye-to-eye with him.

Rusty could not move. He was afraid to breathe. He'd never been this close to one of these animals with horns that stretched wider than his arms could reach. The steer looked at him, snorted once, and swung its massive head as it turned and walked back toward the rest of its kind.

"Time for me to move on, too, I guess," he said to the animal's back.

Three days later, before sunup, the brothers saddled horses and began the three-hour ride into Yates Center. In town, Rusty headed for the café they had spotted and Cliff went to the railway station where they had agreed to meet his new boss.

Cliff looked at the train station sandwiched between the tracks and Main Street, elevated three feet above ground level. The building, surrounded by a weather-stained boardwalk, looked like an island floating in a sea of wood. The building had a single door on the Railroad Street side and another on the track side. Facing the tracks and Kansas Street, which ran parallel, a three-sided bowed window in the corner of the building provided the stationmaster unobstructed views in as many directions. Today, the station's lone bench was held captive by full sun at the end of the building facing Green Street on the east.

Cliff watched automobiles, trucks made from automobiles, free-roaming dogs, horse-drawn wagons, and pedestrians mingle in an undisciplined parade that moved up one side and down the other along Main Street. The endless activity generated a steady cloud of dust that drifted over him and the spot where he leaned against the side of the train station. A small patch of shade offered by the station's roof was the only cool spot on the otherwise glaring streets. He rubbed his shoulder blades back and forth against the rough planks of the building and felt heat dive down his throat when he yawned and stretched.

Cliff had not paid much attention to the town on his few previous visits, his thoughts more concentrated on the young lady who worked up the way in Corbett's Mercantile. This morning he took the time to examine the place he might soon call home. His first thought was that the town seemed to end as abruptly as it began, as if the whole place had been dropped from the sky and landed in one neat pile in southeastern Kansas.

The muffled sound of pounding, followed by the short screech of a window sliding open, broke through Cliff's daydream. He turned to his left and watched the telegraph operator lean through the now-open window. The balding man, who appeared to be Uncle George's age, inspected the track in both directions and checked the sky for whatever it was old men always checked the sky. The cuffs on the sleeves of his white shirt were kept safe from his wrists and hands by tight rubber bands cutting into his arms just above his elbows.

The stationmaster looked over at Cliff, dusted unseen specks from his right sleeve, and said, "Okay then, guess we're all set."

"Set for what?" Cliff asked.

"Why, set for the next day."

Cliff disliked people who were cheerful for no reason, other than being alive. He said, "Well, what about this day? Are we ready for this one?"

The telegraph operator's smile grew even wider. He cleared his throat. "Young man, it's too late to do anything about this day. Sun's been up for hours. Let's get ready for tomorrow."

"Humph. Maybe I just ain't had my morning coffee. I don't feel like today's started yet."

The clicking sound of a telegraph key interrupted and the man disappeared into a dark recess. Cliff could see in the corner of the cramped office a desk, file cabinet, and stacks of books.

Minutes later the man reappeared.

"You're not from around these parts, are you."

"Well, the easiest answer to that is yes and no," Cliff said.

"Best answer for most questions, I suppose. I meant, I've seen you around town a time or two, but I don't know your name. And I know just about everybody. Name's Slocum, Ed Slocum, stationmaster of this here patch of the planet Earth."

"You make it sound like a pretty big deal. I'm Cliff, Cliff Starke. Me and my brother are staying up at our uncle's spread. He's George Hardy."

For the next half hour the conversation between Cliff and the stationmaster centered on who knew whom and various baseball teams. Cliff had just about run out of relatives to discuss when Rusty rounded the corner of the building carrying a brown bag displaying a large grease stain along the bottom. In his right hand he balanced a mug of coffee. From the stains on the side of the white mug Cliff knew he would not be getting a full cup.

"This here's my brother, Rusty. This is Mr. Slocum."

"Good to meet you, Rusty. Your brother here and me have been having a good talk about your relatives."

"Good to meet you too, Mr. Slocum. Did Cliff tell you he's going to be a carpenter and I'm going to be a cowboy?"

"No, he didn't. A couple of ambitious jobs in this town, I'd say. But we're growing in lots of ways, so I guess we can always use carpenters."

"What about cowboys?" Rusty asked.

"Hmmm. That's another matter. See that building behind you? About a half block down? Tim Kilbane's place."

The boys strained to see the building on Main Street Mr. Slocum was pointing toward. When the motorcars and trucks passed, they saw a man sitting in a chair, smoking a pipe, cleaning his fingernails with a pocketknife.

"Ya mean the blacksmith's place?" asked Cliff.

"Yep. You don't want to choose a job like that, like being the last blacksmith in town. Kinda like cowboying, I figure. Something to think about. Always something to think about."

Rusty watched as Mr. Slocum disappeared back inside, softly closing the window. He joined Cliff at the edge of the station platform and let his legs dangle over the boards. In silence they sipped the now-cold coffee and finished the bag of donuts. The sun was almost directly overhead and the roof of the train station offered little shelter. Looking east, they watched a train crew finish filling the boiler on a steam engine idling on the westbound track.

"Wish someone woulda told me about that train into Yates a few weeks ago when I was trying to get here," Rusty said. "They must come out of someplace other than Kansas City."

"You did okay, kid, getting out here without getting killed. I rode a train all the way out on money I swiped from the old man's sock drawer. Took nearly a week. Seemed like a long trip doin' it that way. Can't imagine hopping freights."

"Looks like she's gonna start her last leg out to Hamilton," Rusty said. "I was talking to a guy in the bakery about cowboy jobs out here. He told me Mr. Raleigh, some guy with the big herd of steers out near Hamilton, is always looking for herd boys. This guy says I could maybe earn as much as $25 a month if I stuck with it."

"A cowpuncher is a dead-end job if there ever was one. Everybody says so," Cliff said.

"Shit. What does everybody know?"

Cliff didn't respond. Rusty watched his brother's eyes follow three young women coming out of the bakery on Main Street, past the black-smith's shop.

"I think we're going to like it here, Cliff."

"Oh, why's that?"

"Well, for one thing, they have some real pretty girls in that bakery over there."

Cliff responded with a snort.

"For another," Rusty continued, "it seems everybody in town knows this Mr. LaFevre guy who has the job for you. I asked about him."

"For all the building that's supposed to be going on here in the county seat, it don't look like much is happening," Cliff said.

Rusty was still looking west toward the central part of town. His eyes moved from the bakery and scanned two commercial banks further up Main. That left the harness shop, a mercantile across the street, and three other buildings he could not identify. Across Railroad Street, at an angle from the station, was a hardscrabble patch of grass people called the square. In the middle of the square stood the county courthouse, a three-story building made of sandstone. The lack of glass in the windows on the second and third floors gave the building a hollow look.

He turned and checked the other direction. Along Main Street, between where they sat and Washington Street, on the other side of Green Street, he counted three church steeples and an unkempt building that was no doubt the school. Yates Center looked like a fine place to live if you wanted to go to church a lot.

Turning back to Cliff, Rusty asked, "We're going to keep together now, ain't we, Cliff?"

"We'll see. You can go to school here and I'll work. Who knows, what with that war going on, maybe we'll get into that. I'm a pretty good shot, so maybe there'll be a place for me."

"School's a waste of time, Cliff. But I'll go if you want me to," Rusty said as he climbed back onto the platform.

Still hungry after the donuts, Rusty took his mind off the rumbling sounds coming from his stomach by looking in the direction of the weathered, clapboard school building two blocks away. It was dirtier and smaller than many houses back home. Three window frames were painted three different shades of white, but at least they had paint. The rest of the building, sand blasted by the wind, was gray and appeared never to have been painted. In front of the building stood a stanchion that in the past must have supported a bell. Now, guessing from the pile of horse droppings around it, it served as a hitching post.

Consumed by unpleasant thoughts of his future imprisonment in the schoolhouse, Rusty welcomed the interruption of a sputtering gasoline engine coming to a halt in front of them across the tracks on Kansas Street. Before the black Ford truck rolled to a complete stop, Rusty identified it for Cliff as the newest 1916 Ford TT. The vehicle's glimmering black paint offset the red spokes of the wheels. Gold lettering on the wood stakes surrounding the truck's bed announced, "LaFevre Construction."

A man tipped his head down to better see them and yelled, "Which one of you is the Starke kid?"

The man appeared to be Pa's age, Rusty thought. His dark hair was sprinkled with gray and sawdust. A thick layer of tan sawdust stuck to his arms and lay on the thighs of his blue strap coveralls. When the man leaned toward them, the sawdust drifted from his head like snowflakes. He wore no shirt.

"That's me. Or us, I guess," said Cliff.

"Well, I'm Frank and I'm looking for the one who wants to be the carpenter. Hop on up in here, you two, and we'll sort it out. Let's go see what Anna, that's the wife, has cooking."

That was all the invitation the boys needed as they scrambled to their feet, tossed their meager possessions into the back of the truck, and climbed in alongside Frank.

"I'm Cliff and this here's Russell."

"Glad to meet you, boys. Always like doing a favor for my friends. Especially politician friends."

When Rusty grasped the extended hand, he felt the familiar crushing grip and calluses he knew from lumbermen friends of his father back home. He also recognized the aroma of fresh-cut oak and the smell of dried sweat.

Just as Frank shifted into second gear and released the clutch, he slammed on the brakes and stalled the truck. Rusty and Cliff pitched forward and smashed their hands against the truck's windshield. Rusty grabbed for his cap that pitched forward over his eyes.

"Whoa," Frank said. "Don't want to run over the prettiest ladies of the town."

The boys looked up to see three young women stepping from the boardwalk into the street. All were frozen in mid-step, each with a hand holding her skirt out of the dust and horse dung, the other hand covering her mouth.

In a low voice Rusty asked, "Who's that one there, in the green dress? She's the lady from the bakery shop I saw a bit ago."

"That'd be Rebekah Kern," Frank said. "Her folks, from over in Hamilton, been out here a long time. Nesters, like mine. She's the book-keeper over at the mercantile store so I'm lucky enough to see a lot of her."

"Mighty pretty," said Cliff, looking down at his shoes. "I, aaah, seen her around town before."

"She is that," Frank said, his eyes on the women. "She's also the kind that'll leave ya cryin'."

Rusty looked from Frank to his brother, then toward Rebekah. Her eyes seemed focused on Cliff, who was looking straight ahead through the windshield. He watched Rebekah move her head back and forth as if begging for attention. Her right hand dropped from her mouth and its fingers rippled in a timid wave, then fluttered up to tuck at a stray strand of auburn hair that had escaped from under her broad-brimmed hat.

"Heck, she looks mighty pretty to me, too," Rusty said. "I can't see anything about her that would make you cry."

"Oh, someday you'll understand, Rusty," Frank said.

As Frank jumped from the driver's seat, gave the crank a quick jerk to get the truck restarted, and climbed back in, Rusty watched the women make their way across the street. He noted that only Rebekah acknowledged the vehicle's presence by dipping her head a bit, still trying to see who was riding in the cab.

"Some people still ain't used to motorcars out here," Frank said. "Seems that every week some fool walks out in front of me like that and nearly gets killed."

Rusty squirmed in his seat, trying to catch another look at the girl named Rebekah. Cliff continued to look straight ahead.

At the dinner table, Rusty asked questions about cowboy life. Frank's standard answer was that he was a carpenter and the only thing he knew about steers was that they tasted good with mashed potatoes. Cliff asked an equal number of questions about carpentry, to which Frank could offer more information. Frank was staring at his clean plate when he said they'd have to find someplace in town to stay since his house was too small.

"What about with the Slocums?" Anna said.

Anna was a small, energetic woman in constant motion, alternating between bringing food to the table and eating. "Since, well, you know, since their boys died, they have some extra room."

"You mean the stationmaster?" Cliff asked.

"Right. You know him?" Anna said.

"Well, sort of. We met him this morning while waiting for Frank. Seems like a nice enough fellow. A bit chirpy, but okay."

"Yeah, he sure talks a lot," Rusty said.

Frank glanced at the two newcomers, then at Anna. "Not a bad idea, wife."

To Rusty and Cliff he said, "One of those freak things that still happens out here. Last fall the grass was all dry and a brush fire got loose. Both of Mr. Slocum's boys we're out rounding up some strays over north of Cassoday and got caught in the fire. Them and four other hands. Worst fire people in these parts had seen in a long while. Maybe ever."

Rusty's fork halted midway between his plate and mouth as Frank told the story. Across the table he watched Anna wipe the corner of her eye with her napkin.

"Seems like a lot more ways to die out here in Kansas than back in Indiana," Cliff said.

No one spoke. Rusty watched an unspoken exchange between Frank and Anna as she stood, brushed her hands on her blue apron, and reached across the table to gather the plates.

"I'll cut you boys some pie, if you'd like," she said to the empty plates.

Frank cleared his throat, wiped at his mouth with his napkin, and smiled. "Well, let's skip the pie and go over to see what Mr. Slocum thinks about us making plans for him."

CHAPTER SIX

Friends

As the trio walked along Western Avenue, Rusty surveyed each house, all of which seemed in need of repairs great and small. While still a half block from their destination, Frank pointed to the Slocum house. It was a two-story structure like others on the street, blanketed with tan dust on its west side. Peeling paint on the south sides reminded him of fish scales in shades ranging from fresh white to black. As they neared the house, Rusty could see interior rooms of the first floor veiled behind neat, white ruffled curtains that hung in graceful arcs. Through the window on the left he saw the silhouettes of two people seated at a table near the back of the house. On the second floor, flat, sheer curtains hung behind rain-spotted glass in lopsided frames.

"Needs a coat of paint," Cliff said.

"Yeah, it does, for starters," Frank said. "I suppose I should do the neighborly thing and offer to do the work for these older folks, only we've been so busy, that, well … that's no excuse, I guess."

"Maybe we could offer to do it for them. You know, to sorta help pay for our room and board," Rusty said.

"Good idea, lad," Frank said.

"I can see there's a lot of scrapping needs doing, and then the paint. I bet it will take months to do the job," Rusty said.

"Months that would keep you out of school. Is that what you're thinking?" Cliff said, smiling at his brother. "Forget it, Russell. I said you're going to school."

Rusty watched Frank slip his hands into the pockets of his coveralls and examine the dirt path leading to the Slocums' front porch.

"We can settle that later," Frank said. "Since the Slocums lost their two boys the missus is still a bit, well, strange about it. Ed seems to be over it. Let's see what they think."

Through the door's screen and dim interior lights, Rusty could see that the two people seated at a large table appeared to be having an animated conversation. It was Mr. Slocum, still wearing his pillbox-shaped stationmaster's cap, who responded to Frank's soft knock on the weathered screen doorframe. He pushed open the door and said, "Well, look at this: friends old and new. How are you on this glorious day, Frank?"

"Fine Ed, just fine. I guess you already met the Starke brothers?"

"Indeed, indeed. And fine fellows they are, too. I bet the sheriff hasn't had to arrest them yet today, has he?"

Rusty heard a groan come from Cliff. His eyes roamed around the large furniture-less room that looked larger than their entire house back in Kendallville. The woman seated at the table did not move, not even to look up at the three people who entered the room. Her hands remained folded in her lap while her eyes examined her plate. The curtains next to her were drawn, cloaking her in shadow. It was August, yet she wore a sweater over the top of her dress.

After an awkward shaking of hands, Mr. Slocum said, "Well, come in fellas. Excuse the wife. Not feeling too good today. What's all this about? Need to get a telegram out to the world about winning a baseball game?"

"No thanks, Ed."

Rusty noticed that Frank looked over at Mrs. Slocum before he continued. She slowly turned her head and looked at the three visitors, not seeming to recognize her neighbor of many years.

"Well, these two young gents are in need of a place to stay. This here's Cliff Starke and his brother Russell. Well, you know that. Indiana boys. Well, you know that, too. They're kin to the Hardys up at the north end of the county. I suppose you knew that, too."

"Tell me something I don't already know so's I can get excited, Frank," Mr. Slocum said, lightly pushing against Rusty with his shoulder.

"Anyways, I'm hiring Cliff here as an apprentice and plan to pay his room and board. Rusty there will be going to school, mostly, but maybe we can find him something to earn a bit of money."

"Hmm. I could use an apprentice, too," said Mr. Slocum.

Rusty saw the stationmaster's eyes quickly shift to the back of the room, then to Frank before he leaned forward and said, "Ah, well, I'm not so sure this is such a good idea, Frank. Not right now. I mean the missus—"

"Yes," came a voice from the back of the room.

The strength of her voice from the shadows startled the men. All turned to see Mrs. Slocum still staring down at her plate.

"Well, that settles it, doesn't it?" Mr. Slocum said. "You boys can take the two rooms upstairs. There's a stairway on the outside of the house so, well, so you can come and go as you choose."

After another round of handshakes, Frank and the boys turned to leave. Rusty hesitated and looked back at Mrs. Slocum, who continued to watch her untouched plate. "Thanks ma'am, for letting us stay here, I mean. It'll be okay," he said.

The trio walked across the Slocums' porch and stepped into the bright sun on Western Street. Heat of late afternoon punched Rusty in his chest, stopping him in mid-stride. Frank smoothed his sweaty hair back with his left hand and crushed his straw hat onto his head with the right. "Whew. Well, still have quite a few hours of daylight, so I'll be heading back over to Wilson's place for a bit. You boys able to find your way around?"

"Sure, no problem," Cliff said. "We'll just grab our stuff from your truck. Do I start tomorrow?"

"Yep. Bright and early. My place. And Rusty, you mind what Mr. Slocum there tells ya. He's a good man."

Cliff and Rusty reached for their bags splayed amidst lumber and tools in the back of Frank's truck, then hesitated. Something moving in the shadows across the street caught their attention. A black man, head down, hands in his pockets, slipped through the few shady spots created by the sparse trees of the street. Even at a distance Rusty could see the whites of the man's eyes shift toward them. He knew the man was watching them from beneath the brim of his dust-covered straw hat.

"There goes the beginning of trouble in these parts," Frank said.

"Yep. First one comes in, then, like rats, you have more of 'em than you can handle," Cliff said.

"Lucius there is the second family of niggers to come here in the past six months. They ain't trouble yet, but they've been picking up work some of the others, white folks I mean, could be doing."

Rusty shuffled his feet and rubbed the penny in his pocket between his finger and thumb, trying to think of how he could get into the conversation. "Cliff, you remember me telling you about the guy I met in the train yard in Chicago that got beat up pretty good? His name was Jupiter and—"

"Yeah," Cliff said. "What's that got to do with what we're talking about?"

"Well, he was a, well, a black guy and he was real nice to me."

"When you told that story before you didn't say he was a nigger," Cliff said.

"Why does that make any difference?" Rusty said, removing his hands from his pockets.

"It makes a difference," Frank said. "I never met a one that gave a fig for a white man."

"How many colored guys have you met?" Rusty asked.

"That's enough, smart mouth," Cliff said.

Rusty looked at the stains on his newspaper boy's bag lying in the sawdust of Frank's truck and wondered if Jupiter had made it to the Promised Land yet.

In silence the trio watched the black man turn the corner onto Railroad Street, never looking back at them. Rusty waited for Cliff or Frank to say something more. He cleared his throat and said, "Well, I know—"

Frank turned in his direction and said, "You know what, Russell?"

"Oh, nothin'."

Late September. Hay harvest was finished, most cattle were shipped, and Rusty was out of excuses not to go to school. The cool morning brought relief from the heat and air not thick with dust. After a month of exploring town he was familiar with key locations like the harness shop, bakery, and Corbett's Mercantile scattered along Main Street. The schoolhouse, with its weathered wood, crooked shutters, and missing bell, loomed a block east of the railroad station. He'd made it a practice to turn his head in the opposite direction of the school, or not even look in that direction, if his travels took him near the building. Everyone said he could learn something new in there, but he didn't see how that was possible. Besides, he didn't want to learn something new, he wanted to learn something old—like being a cowboy.

This morning he walked around back of the buildings on Main Street until he was past Railroad Street, thus avoiding the schoolhouse altogether on his way to the barbershop. Even if it was Saturday, and school hadn't started, he didn't want to get too close. For the first time since coming to Kansas the air carried the anticipatory promise of fall. *Maybe the fishing will get better in the cooler weather.* His eyes followed the jagged row of cottonwoods that traced the gash cut by the river to a place he knew offered a lot more fun than getting a haircut.

When Rusty reached the door of the barbershop, he hesitated. He placed his hands on the sides of his head and pushed his hair back behind his ears. Maybe getting a haircut for school wasn't a bad idea. *Maybe I'll have the barber part it on the right like most men in town. Sure. Then what?*

He found his entry to the shop blocked by the smell of aftershave lotion. It was the same stuff old Mr. Swenson back home splashed on his neck after a haircut. It made him smell like an old lady for days afterward. Sometimes it was so bad he almost wanted to take a bath.

He filled his lungs with fresh air, his last for probably an hour, and walked straight for the refuge of a scarred leather chair at the end of the row along the wall next to the windows. As he moved over the hardwood floor, he felt the pressure from ten eyes turned in his direction. Safety waited if only he could get to that empty chair. From that spot he could gaze out and watch the endless stream of Saturday activity flowing in the street. The cracked leather of the chair's seat made squeaking, mouse-like sounds as he settled in.

Rusty glanced at the well-dressed man reading the newspaper in the chair next to him. He wished he had a newspaper to hide behind. He stretched his legs, crossed them at the ankles, and rested his shoulders against the wooden frame of the chair's back, like other men in the shop were doing. His eyes wandered around the well-lit room, and he tried not to listen to the usual talk of war in places he couldn't imagine. His hands stayed in their customary place, his pockets. Between his fingers he rubbed the quarter Cliff had given him.

It was not the first time Cliff shared what little money they earned. When they helped Pa cut and load timber their reward was always a nickel or a dime. Often, at the end of the day, Cliff would give him a few extra pennies for candy. And it wasn't just money Cliff shared. There were those times when they went sled riding in winter that Cliff would pull his sled up the hill for him.

Conversation in the barbershop grew louder and Rusty couldn't avoid hearing what the men said about the war. What bothered him was the way people talked about the Germans; what a race of rats they were, one man said.

I'm German—at least Pa is—so all Germans can't be rats. There had to be good Germans, too. Germans in Germany, not in America, caused the war. Those were the rats. And why should Americans get into some beef between the Germans and the Frenchies? Why would Cliff want to go to Canada to fight with them against the Germans? None of it makes sense.

"Looks like President Wilson is trying to keep us out of that mess," said the white-haired customer wrapped in the striped barber's cape. As he spoke, Rusty could see the man's eyes trace the pattern of cracks in the ceiling.

"Bullshit," said the barber. "He's a Democrat. Wilson just wants people, whole countries, to sign up for that league of his that he thinks will keep peace in the world. I'm tellin' ya, people like those Krauts and Eye-talians can't be trusted. They're sneaky, just like the niggers. They ain't got land of their own, so they want to take somebody else's rather than stop screwing and making more of themselves. They're goddamn papists, that's what they are. They get their orders from that Pope in Rome and don't give a damn about the rest of the world, that's my opinion."

Rusty felt the man in the chair next to him stir. He did not recognize the man wearing the clean, well-pressed, dark suit and stiff-collared white shirt. *Probably a banker.*

The man took a deep breath, quietly cleared his throat, lowered his paper, and looked over at the barber. "You know Roger, opinions are like assholes—everybody's got one. Some are just bigger than others."

The room was so quiet Rusty heard blood thumping in his ears. Ticking sounds from the pendulum in the wall clock at the far end of the room boomed. The only things that moved were dust motes floating through a beam of sunlight, trying to escape via the front window. When he stood, the well-dressed man appeared taller than Rusty expected. The man never took his eyes off the barber as he tapped the bowler hat he'd been holding on his lap into place. His shoes made a light tapping sound as he walked through the open door into the sun-filled street.

Rusty looked back at the barber. The man's mouth was partially opened, his comb in one hand, scissors in the other, hovering inches above the bald head of customer in the chair. Along with everyone else in the shop, Roger, the barber, watched the tall man in the black suit cross the street toward Johnson's Barbershop on the other side of Main.

The elderly customer in the barber's chair sniffed, laughed hesitantly, and said, "Well Roger, looks like you just talked yourself out of two bits."

The chatter in the shop slowly returned. Rusty tried to follow the war talk, but was distracted from the banter by someone standing in the middle of the street near the hardware store. He realized it was Cliff. He watched his brother dash across the street, avoiding cars and horse droppings. Cliff looked clean-shaven and appeared to be wearing a fresh white shirt. His hair was wet and combed back. When he reached the safety of the boardwalk steps, he seemed to hesitate, then bounded up to the door and stopped. Rusty watched Cliff turn to look in both directions, wipe his hands on his trousers, then reach for the door handle.

Minutes later Rusty saw Cliff and Rebekah Kern step out of the building into the bright sunlight, her arm looped through his. They seemed to be having a discussion, then both laughed as they headed west along the boardwalk. His eyes followed as the pair stopped near Regal's Diner at the next block.

"You want a haircut young man, or do you just want to stare out that window?"

A loud voice inches from his ear startled him. He pitched forward, thumping his head against the glass and biting down on his tongue. Hot breath so laden with the smell of onions caused his eyes to water.

"Oh, yes sir. I need my hair cut for starting school."

"Good. You've come to the right place then."

Rusty strained to get another look at his brother and Rebekah, now hidden by wagons and the few cars that moved through the dust swirling in the street.

Monday morning smelled like school. A memory, left over from Indiana, of chalk dust mixed with the pungent aroma of freshly sharpened pencils, settled over Rusty's bed and held him captive. Just moments before he'd been dreaming he was unable to mount a horse that stood laughing at him. He struggled to free his arms from the twisted sheets, then bolted upright, fully awake. He wiped sweat from his forehead and took three deep breaths.

Even the distant sound of bacon sizzling in the skillet in Mrs. Slocum's kitchen could not clear the dreadful thought of what this day might bring. The unmistakable smells of biscuits and coffee accompanied that of the bacon up the stairs, snaked under the door into his room, and made his stomach queasy. Yesterday, Sunday, had smelled like the end of summer: like harvest, like dew on fresh-mowed fields and buzzing insects. All that was gone now. Ahead lay only darkness. He fell back on his pillow and tried to erase the image of a teacher holding a stick of white chalk as long as her arm.

"Okay Russell, time to get up. Big day ahead. Promise fills the air," the cheerful voice of Mr. Slocum boomed from the bottom of the stairs.

Rusty agreed with his brother—Mr. Slocum was always too cheerful. How could promising to end someone's life, sending a hard-working kid like himself off to do something that should be against the law, make him cheerful? What could be worse than a day with people you didn't know, in a place so hot even the flies died in the windows? And you had to sit on seats harder than railroad tracks. *Well, maybe going to church could be worse.*

Rusty's slow pace came to a standstill as he reached the corner of Main and Green Street. His eyes surveyed the weathered schoolhouse with its gaping door. Its jagged edges reminded him of the mouth of the giant flesh-eating beast he'd seen in a book about Captain Nemo and sea monsters. Today, the building was festooned in red, white, and blue bunting. A man in strap coveralls wavered on the top of a stepladder nailing an American flag over the entrance. Clusters of boys and girls he didn't know stood in small patches of shade provided by a large wind-bent cottonwood to the left of the building. The tree leaned toward the schoolhouse as if dependent upon it for company.

Rusty took a deep breath and prepared to step off the boardwalk. As he did, a voice close behind him said, "Great day, ain't it?"

He spun around and looked into the eyes of a boy about his own age. A black boy with sparkling brown eyes surrounded by the whitest whites Rusty had ever seen. The boy's infectious smile made Rusty grin, too, in spite of this unhappy occasion.

"You going to school?" Rusty asked.

"Yes sir. And I can't wait."

Rusty looked more closely at the boy. The kid's dazzling clean shirt, as white as his eyes, was buttoned painfully tight at the neck. His too-short sleeves were buttoned at the cuffs. His black trousers were spotless. The boy wore no shoes. Slung across his chest was a gray canvas newspaper boy's bag similar to Rusty's own, only missing the red letters. The boy's bag appeared heavy with something.

"What's in the bag?"

"Oh, these is my pencils and stuff. Lunch. Some books we usually keep in the house. My name's Tom. Thomas Jefferson Washington, really. You can call me Tom for short, but not for long."

Rusty did not laugh at the joke. He looked at Tom and thought about Jupiter and how Jupiter had probably been a slave when he was this boy's age. He looked at his own scuffed boots and thought about rolling down his sleeves, maybe give his trousers a quick brushing off.

"So, you got a name or do I just refer to you as my new friend?"

"Oh, sure. Name's Russell Starke. You can call me Rusty for short, but not for long."

With a grin that matched Tom's, Rusty extended his hand. Tom looked at the hand and Rusty noticed the boy's hesitation before reaching out.

"Don't worry," Rusty said, "this white color won't come off on you."

Tom burst into laughter and grabbed Rusty's hand.

"We're gonna have some kind of fun in this school," Tom said. He nudged against Rusty's shoulder with his own and started to move toward the door where other kids were congregating.

"I ain't so sure. I mean, I'm going to punch cows the rest of my life and I don't think they teach that in this school."

"Well, that may be so. But my ma says there's something more important about going to school than just finding a way to keep kids from getting underfoot. You comin'?"

Rusty took a deep breath, lowered his head, and followed Tom across the threshold. Inside the room he stepped to his right and searched through the dim light and churning mass of bodies, hoping to find someone he knew. He was unsure if the room's smell of wet clothes and dirt came from the two dozen children running around, or the walls of the building.

"Hello there. I don't believe we've met."

Rusty jerked his head to the left. He was looking at his own reflection in two round eyeglass lenses only twelve inches away. Other than Doc Williamson back home, he'd never known anyone to wear eyeglasses. The glasses appeared poised to attack him; the lenses, joined in the middle by a piece of wire, and fixed to tiny, foot-shaped pads, pinched the bridge of the nose of a woman wide as she was tall. Dressed in a clean white blouse and black skirt that hid her feet, the woman, who had probably never smiled a day in her life, cradled a barrier of books and slates.

Her unblinking eyes, magnified by the glass lenses, froze him in place. He was trapped. He looked over his right shoulder. An unseen hand had closed the door to the building. Rusty cleared his throat, yanked his cap from his head, and said, "Morning ma'am. I'm Rusty, er, Russell Starke. I've come here for schoolin', from Indiana."

"Welcome Russell. Well, Indiana. You've come a long way to go to school, much farther than some of these children who only live here in Yates Center."

"Oh, I live here, too, now, I mean. But I'm here for just a short time until I learn to be a cowboy."

"Well, I'm Miss Zerkle and this is my school. And we'll have to see if we have any lessons about being a cowboy. Let's find you a seat."

Before Rusty could turn and run, Miss Zerkle peppered him with questions to get him seated with the right group of students. Fortunately, his age group was in the back of the room and he could sit next to Tom, the only person in the building he knew.

As Rusty slipped into the seat with its adjoining arm that would serve as a place to write, Tom looked up from a sheet of paper. "Well, we meet again, Rusty," he said. "Looks like you and me and two others are about the oldest kids in here."

"Glad you didn't say the smartest, Tom. I think the smartest kids have figured out how to avoid school."

Rusty looked at Tom's unsmiling face. "Did I say something wrong?"

"No, not wrong," Tom said. "It's just that I think schoolin's about the best thing that can happen to a person. You seem to think other ways."

Rusty looked over at the room's single window, so covered with dust on the inside and dirt on the outside, it appeared like a gray painting someone had hung on the wall. He turned back to Tom and said, "Just 'cause we think different about school doesn't mean we can't be friends, does it?"

Tom's smile returned. "Naw. How we think about school won't be the problem for us."

Like most people in town, Rusty welcomed the unexpected rise in temperatures for late September as a chance to prepare for fall. For him, however, on a Saturday with nothing to do, it would be a day of sitting on a rock, in the shade, tempting some big river fish to take the bait. As he walked toward the river, he let his shadow slide in front of him and lead the way south on Railroad Street. When he reached the river he scrambled over the rocks to get to his favorite spot. It was the only place he could easily cast a line upstream or downstream without getting tangled in tree branches. He sat on the familiar boulder, holding the rod in one hand, hook and bait in the other, staring into the slow-moving water. He liked the way the river smelled—better than spring flowers, better than fresh-cut hay. He wished he could see under the water to know where the big fish might be swimming. But that would take all the fun out of it, knowing where the fish were.

A twig snapped behind him. Rusty felt the hair on the back of his neck rise. His mouth felt dry and his hands damp. Another snap. Clearly, footsteps too heavy for an animal along this section of the river. He did not move or turn to look.

"Oh!" came a startled voice from behind.

Rusty whipped around so quickly his hat spun to the ground. A young black boy, mouth hanging open, held a large stick, a club, in his right hand. The two locked eyes. It was Tom.

"Rusty! Didn't know anyone was here. You fishin'?"

"What's it look like I'm doing, baling hay?" Rusty managed.

"Yeah, guess yer right. Stupid question. Be seeing ya then."

"Hey, wait. It's okay. Plenty of room on this rock, Tom."

Rusty swallowed hard, trying to get some moisture in his mouth.

"It's okay for me to be here, then, sir?"

"It is if you cut that 'sir' crap."

"It's a deal, Rusty." He reached out to shake hands.

Rusty hesitated as he started to reach for the bright pink palm held only inches from his face. Tom's hand reminded him of Jupiter's feet. As Tom started to withdraw his hand, Rusty reached up and grasped it.

Rusty looked at Tom's fishing tackle. What he first thought was a club was nothing more than a long branch from a willow tree with some string and a hook. He looked at his own metal bait-casting rod and new Shakespeare reel Frank had loaned him. Tom was looking, too.

"Mighty nice fishing stuff you have, Rusty."

"My friend, he's my brother's boss really, Frank, lent it to me. It's great."

Rusty watched Tom effortlessly flip the willow branch and its line into the water with an underhanded flick. "My dad always says it's more about the Indian than the arrow that ya gotta watch for."

"You seen Indians out here?"

"Naw. That's just an expression my dad uses when I tell him I need something better to do a job he's been doing for years with basic tools. He's a carpenter."

"Is he getting much work?"

"Yeah, some. It's tough for us colored folks, out here."

"I bet."

"So, you gonna fish with that fancy fishing tackle or just look at it?"

Rusty laughed and made a long cast into the middle of the river.

"Wow! I hope the fish are swimming in closer to the shore than that today."

"Is your pa Lucius?"

"That's him. You know him?"

"Nope. Just seen him around town and Frank told me his name."

"Yeah. Well, I guess we kinda stand out around here."

Rusty looked at Tom, who was looking at the end of his fishing pole, not paying much attention to where his line was drifting.

"You catch much here, Rusty?"

"Enough to keep me coming back. Not like at home, though."

"This not your home?"

"Nah. I'm from Kendallville. That's in Indiana. How about you?"

"Guess you could say we're from all over. I think we been on the move for as long as I can recall. But I like it here in Kansas and I hope my folks stay. Never know about Pa, though. He says, 'If God wanted us to stay in one place he'd a given us roots, not feets.' "

"My uncles are dirt farmers here in Woodson County. I'm gonna be a cowboy."

"So you say."

Rusty looked at Tom and resolved that on his next free day he was somehow going to start learning about cowboy skills, not waste important time fishing.

The two boys sat and listened to the river's conversation with the rock they sat upon. A quiet rustle of leaves and snapping of twigs drew their attention from the stream to a patch of woods on their right.

They searched for the noise. Tom was first to spot its source.

"There's trouble coming straight for us," he said, his voice quiet and high pitched.

Rusty could see sweat moving down the side of Tom's face and his friend's wide-eyed stare. He followed Tom's gaze into the woods until he saw the black-and-white shape, its nose twisting and probing along the ground. Its striped tail pointed skyward, the white tip bent like a signal flag. The skunk stopped, raised its head, and surveyed the two boys. It shifted its eyes from one to the other as if trying to make a decision.

Rusty's voice, just above a whisper, fought to leave his throat. "As long as he's looking at us we're okay."

Tom's voice was equally quiet. "Yeah, the bad business comes from the other end."

"My pa says you're never suppose to look a wild animal in the eyes," Rusty said.

"I think that applies to big animals," Tom said. "The kind that can eat you. Not the other way 'round."

It didn't take long for the skunk to lose interest in the fishermen. It went back to scratching and turning over leaves and sticks. The boys, however, did not lose interest in the skunk until it changed its course and moved to the right.

Rusty relaxed and said, "Ya know, Tom, that little guy over there might be useful for guys who like to go fishing."

Tom looked at Rusty, over at the skunk, and back to his friend. He scratched at the side of his neck. "Can't say as I get your drift."

"Well, what if we were to catch that critter and give him a new home, say a place like under the schoolhouse. He might not like it at first and do a bit of spraying."

"Hmmm. And Miss Zerkle would have to dismiss class for a few days to air the place out," Tom said.

"Exactly!"

Rusty watched Tom's smile grow as they both turned and watched the skunk move deeper into the row of trees that lined the stream.

"I think your plan has merit; however, it has a few minor hitches," Tom said. "Starting with, how do we catch him?"

Rusty looked to see how much progress the skunk was making. All he could see was the tip of the animal's tail. "Well, if we grab him by the tail and lift him straight up, he can't spray us."

"Which brings up another point," Tom said. "About the 'we' in that plan. Who is the 'we' and who is fast enough to grab the tail, not getting something in the face at the same time?"

Rusty looked down at the moving water, reeled in his line, checked the bait on his hook, then made a long cast into the stream. He turned back to Tom's expectant look.

"Well, I've given a lot of thought to that," Rusty said. "I think the answer is, you and me is the 'we.' And, if you're not brave enough to grab a skinny little skunk by the tail, then I guess it would be my job."

"Well, Rusty, it comes as a great relief to me to hear you're willing to make that sacrifice for the good of all the children in Yates Center, Kansas, United States of America."

Rusty looked at Tom's wide grin. "What's so funny?"

"How old did you say you were?"

"Fifteen. Why?"

Tom looked down at his trousers and wiped the palm of his left hand along the top of his thigh. He was no longer smiling. "Oh, I just happen to think that at our age we should be finding ways to spend more time in school, not less."

Rusty looked beyond the riverbank across from them. He watched the clouds drift east, gather, and change shapes. When he looked back at Tom, he noticed his friend was still not smiling.

"You have to admit, it's a damn good plan for getting out of school," Rusty said.

"That it is. Maybe you should work on it and we can talk about it on our next free day."

"Tom, do you think if I learn to rope and brand, it's the same as going to school?"

"Well, I suppose it's education. I just don't know how much it will help you in the future, is all."

"You're so interested in the future. The only future I want is as a cowboy."

Tom looked at him. "Ha. Sounds like you want a past more than a future."

Later that day shadows cast by the cottonwood trees stretched to the opposite bank of the river. The smell of food cooking in restaurants in town occasionally reached the boys, and they made a game out of guessing what the aromas might be.

Tom looked over at Rusty and said, "Is that a bear sitting over there next to you or what's that growling I'm hearing?"

Rusty smiled. "Naw. It's way past eating time for me, and whatever they're cooking up there at Sander's place is killing me."

"I hear that," Tom said. " 'Bout time I was getting home to get dinner started for Ma."

"You do the cookin' at home?" Rusty said.

"Sure do. Lots of times. And now, with Pa out looking for work most days, I get a lot of practice."

Long shadows from the stores in town hid most of the street activity and made it seem later than it was when Rusty and Tom walked into town. The boys were deep in conversation about baseball as they started up Railroad Street. Neither noticed Mr. Slocum and another man approach.

"Hey! Hey there, you two," Mr. Slocum said.

The boys stopped, looked at each other, then at the two men.

Tom lowered his head and in a low voice said, "We best not run."

"We ain't done nothing to run from, Tom," Rusty whispered.

"You ain't a nigger."

Mr. Slocum was smiling as he approached. "Just the two boys I was hoping to find. Thought you might be fishing. Any luck?"

"For us or the fish?" Tom asked, not looking up.

The man with Mr. Slocum, dressed in a black-and-white plaid wool suit, tipped his head back and laughed. His lips were shaped like the letter O and his rapid breathing reminded Rusty of the bass he'd earlier pulled from the river. Rusty could see that sweat from the man's face had mixed with dust and stained the edge of his shirt collar. He stared at the man's brilliant white teeth with their gold fillings that flashed in the dim light.

"I like the cut of your jib, young man," the sweaty man said. "You two are just the kind of lads I need to hire."

Rusty and Tom looked at each other, barely moving their heads.

"Well," Mr. Slocum said, "this here's Mr. Keir. He's an advance man for the Ringling Brothers Circus. You won't believe how lucky we folks here in Yates Center are going to be."

Rusty looked over at the always-cheerful Mr. Slocum. Now, however, he was really excited, dancing around like he had to pee. Rusty wanted to ask him if maybe he'd been eating grasshoppers.

"Why don't you let me explain to these fine young gentlemen what I am so willing to reward them for doing," Mr. Keir said.

Rusty glanced at Tom, who seemed to be showing interest in examining the scuffed toes of his mismatched shoes. His friend's eyebrows were pulled together, a frown on his lips and his hands jammed into his pockets. Rusty wondered if running away might still be possible.

"You see, boys," Mr. Keir said, "next week the circus train is going to need to lay over a day on its way from Kansas City to Wichita. We figured Yates Center would be the perfect spot. Our train is more than a hundred cars long, and because you all have that sidetrack over there, this will be the perfect spot for us to rest a bit and put on a little show for you fine folks. Now, what I need is two young, good-looking, strong boys like yourselves to nail up posters about the circus on every post and wall in town. We need to advertise so people will come out and see the world's greatest show!"

"And how much is this job payin'?" Tom asked, not looking up from his shoes.

"Right. What's it pay?" echoed Rusty, instead of asking what he really wanted to know—what kinds of performances there'd be. He straightened and hooked his thumbs through the empty belt loops of his trousers.

"Well, that's the best part," Mr. Keir said. "When you boys finish nailing up these posters here, I'll give you each two free tickets to the show!"

Tom snorted. "Can't eat tickets."

"No, you certainly cannot. You're a very observant young man. But you know, sometimes folks need to step out of their drab, daily world to see people fly through the air like birds, or fearless beautiful women stand on the backs of galloping white stallions, or this!"

With a sweeping motion, Mr. Keir bent and reached into a large box by his side. He pulled out a picture poster so terrifying Tom and Rusty staggered back, bumping into each other as their fishing tackle clattered on the ground.

A huge orange-and-black striped tiger leapt at them from out of dense green foliage. The animal's fierce eyes glowed yellow beneath its wrinkled brows. Three-inch-long claws on the animal's paws dripped blood and threatened to rip the boys to shreds. Its fire-red tongue looked as if it could lick the skin from their bones in a single slurp.

Rusty managed to push Tom in front of him as a shield. "Holy shit!" he said.

"Now, don't you think something like this will make your friends and neighbors want to enter the big top?" Mr. Keir said.

Rusty kept both hands on Tom's shoulders as he leaned forward, mouth open, staring at the poster. He could feel Tom's body shaking as much as his own. When he tried to step to the side, he realized Tom was standing on his shoe tops.

"And all we get is two tickets?" Tom managed after clearing his throat.

Rusty felt heat where his arm pressed against Tom's back. His friend's voice now sounded calm, no trace of the shaking he still felt in his own body.

"Young man, do you know how many other boys in this town would put these posters up for just a single ticket?"

"Yeah, they's one I know of, but he wouldn't know which end of the hammer to use," Tom said.

Laughter boomed from Mr. Slocum and Mr. Keir. Rusty feared the older men might quit breathing. When they stopped laughing, Rusty said, "Okay, Mr. Keir, we'll do it. But you have to give us the tickets up front. And one more thing: Can I have one of these tiger posters to keep?"

"Certainly, young man. Might I ask why?"

"Well, I'm gonna be a cowboy, but if that doesn't work out for me, well, I might want to run away and join the circus. I want to keep this as a reminder of what I might be getting into."

Rusty nailed the last poster to the side of the mercantile and looked back at Tom, who stood hands on hips, head tilted a bit to the right.

"Good job, Rusty. Nice and straight. 'Course its so dark out here that even that damn tiger could never see us."

"Thanks. Hey Tom, why don't you and your pa come to the circus with me and my brother?"

Thomas rattled his two tickets back and forth between his fingers. "Don't know as that's a real good idea, Rusty. Don't think they'd take to coloreds coming to a white person's show."

"What?"

"It's true. We coloreds don't know much, but we know our place."

Rusty watched Tom's dark hand extend toward him. His eyes followed the hand and he felt its pressure against his chest as the two wrinkled tickets were deposited into his shirt pocket. Without another word, Tom turned and walked up the street.

"Wait!"

"Waitin's what we do best," Tom said over his shoulder. "Thanks anyways."

Tom turned off Railroad Street onto West Mary Street. He could hear the willow branch he'd used as a fishing pole scratching in the dust behind him. He looked back at his tracks, two different size feet since he'd worn one of his and one of Pa's shoes. He thought about swishing the pole around to cover his footprints like he'd heard Indians used to do. Instead, he gripped the pole in the middle, leaned back, and threw it as far as he could, into weeds that looked like the frayed edges of Ma's tablecloth against the dark sky.

He looked around to see if anyone was watching, or might be within hearing. When he felt safe he stopped and looked at the chunk of moon that came out from behind a cloud. "If I was in Africa where my pa says our people come from, I'd use that spear I just threw into the weeds to kill a tiger. Then we wouldn't be so hungry as now," he said.

He lowered his head as he began walking toward home and thought about the tickets he and Rusty had earned for nailing up all those posters. Maybe Pa would like to go to the circus. Maybe he could sit with Rusty and his brother. Maybe he could watch people fly through the air like birds. *Can't do any of those maybes unless I get those tickets back.*

Tom turned back toward town. He knew where Frank LaFevre's shop was 'cause Pa told him to stay clear of the place. As he approached the building he heard someone whistling inside. Bending to keep from showing himself in the light coming through the window, he worked his way along the wall to where he could see through the partially opened door.

Inside, he saw Rusty cleaning the rod and reel. He opened his mouth to call out just as someone entered through the back door. *Must be Rusty's brother. They sure look alike.*

Rusty heard the door behind him open and turned to see his brother come in and lean against the wall.

"Whatcha been up to, kid?" Cliff asked.

"Fishing," Rusty said as he wiped off the rod and reel, preparing to put it back in place on the wall.

"Not like fishing for bluegills back home. Were you fishing alone?"

"Nope. Met a friend from school. He didn't have tackle like this, though."

"What kid?"

"Oh, just a guy I met on my first day."

"Who? I like to know who your friends are," Cliff said as he removed his hands from his pockets and took a few steps closer. "You know, 'cause I'm not always around and I just want to be sure you're, well, that you're okay."

"Just a friend. Tom's his name."

Cliff exhaled and pushed his hands into his pockets. He raised his head and looked his brother in the eye. "Russell, when I said you should find someone to go fishing with I didn't mean some nigger kid," Cliff said, turning away. "One of the guys on the work crew told me he saw you with a nigger this afternoon."

Rusty slowly turned to look at his brother. "He's a good kid."

"He's a nigger."

"So?"

"So? Look, kid," Cliff said, pointing his finger at Rusty. "There's something you gotta understand. We don't associate with them and they don't associate with us."

"Why's that?"

"Look smart ass, how about because I say so?"

"Not good enough, Cliff. Ma says—"

"Ma's dead," he said and turned to look through the darkness of the open door. "Get that through your thick skull. I'm responsible for you now since you followed me out here. If you don't like what I do or say, you can just get your smart ass back to Kendallville. Maybe that's the best thing for you."

"But Cliff, I want to be with you."

"Well then, start acting like it. Start thinking like me and other people out here."

"Okay, okay. You're right, Cliff," Rusty said and looked down at the floor. "He's just a dumb nigger like the rest. I'll find someone else to go fishing with."

Rusty could feel the heat of Cliff's eyes drilling into the back of his head as he hung the fishing rod on the wall.

"That's better. They're different, Russell. And they want to stay that way. Understand?"

The lump in Rusty's throat prevented him from answering.

"I said, do you understand?"

"Right. Right. I got it. Who wants to be seen around town or at a circus with any of those people."

"Right. And what's this crap about a circus?"

"Nothin'. Just something to say."

Rusty waited to turn around until he was sure Cliff was out of the workshop, taking the fun of the day's fishing and nailing up circus posters with him. He could still feel the place where Tom's hand pushed the two circus tickets into his shirt pocket. He pulled the wrinkled tickets from his shirt, and, along with the pair from his pants pocket, dropped them into the trashcan at the end of the workbench.

Tom leaned against the outside wall of the building and allowed his body to slide to the ground. As he moved, the rough planks of the workshop scraped against his back and splinters nipped at his hands. He sat in the dark considering what he'd just heard. Weren't he and Rusty supposed to be friends? *Maybe Pa was right—you can't trust any of those white people.*

CHAPTER SEVEN

Winter

With only a slight shift in the direction of the wind, fall turned to winter and daily routines focused on things indoors for the next few months. There was no hope of going fishing, and Tom seemed always too busy to talk before or after school. Rusty found any attempt at conversation with his friend met with a shrug of his shoulders and a mumbled excuse.

Rusty stepped from the warmth of the Slocums' parlor into the biting cold of the front porch. *This is the first week of April. I should be thinking about bluegill fishing, not searching for firewood.* He could see a few dark leaves still clinging to branches and heard them hiss and snap in the constant wind. He raised his nose to capture the aroma of coffee drifting past from somewhere to the east, probably the Johnsons' place. The Johnson kids always went to school and were usually up early. Between the empty gray house across the street and the one next to it, he could see a swath of snow-covered prairie that spread to the horizon like a tablecloth recently scarred by Sunday's dinner. Looking west he could peer down an enticing tunnel formed by snow-laden branches bent over the road.

He pulled his oversized coat tighter around himself and stepped from the safety of the porch toward another day in the one-room building adults called school and kids called jail. When he reached the corner he looked at jagged silhouettes created by cottonwoods lining the banks of the far-off river. The trees' limbs pointed east, as if pushing against the force of the rising sun. It took effort to remember why he'd come to Kansas, this foreign place with different trees, different animals, and different people. The bright spot was that the routine of winter would end soon. Cattle and springtime, both coming from the south, both pale and weak, were filled with promise. *Can't get here soon enough.*

For now, each day seemed the same. Cliff worked at the mercantile on days too cold for house building and often chose to sleep in the barn. They never seemed to have much time to talk. Rusty spent afternoons and evenings with Mr. Slocum in the railway station learning the intricacies of the telegraph. He couldn't understand the mystery of how it was the space, or time between the dots and dashes, that really carried messages. Mr. Slocum tried to explain that every telegraph operator's touch on the key was as individual as handwriting on a page and he could tell who was operating the key in Garden City, or Hamilton, or lots of other places.

When he thought about what he was learning in school and what Mr. Slocum was teaching him, school work seemed easier, but time in the station more fun. The best part was sitting in the warm bubble of the station's three-sided window where he could look in all directions at the same time.

Because of the pending war, coal was already in short supply in town. Rusty hoped maybe today would be a short day in school since there was so little fuel left to burn. This morning, however, school could wait. He had to find some firewood for the Slocums. His pace slowed as he walked south on Railroad Street toward the river. He looked off to the east, to see what was keeping the sun from rising. A gray curtain of snow-laden clouds was wrapped around the sun like a shroud, creating unfamiliar shadows, and holding it close to the earth.

Where his path crossed Main Street he lifted his shoulders against a sudden blast of wind pushing against his back from the northwest. To his right, lights from inside the hardware store cast yellow circles across the boardwalk and slid down the steps into the frozen mud of the street. The café to his left appeared to be closed, so he opted to head straight for the river.

Driftwood often became trapped in the dirt-laden ice and rocks on the riverbank. That's where he'd start. He just needed a few good pieces to supplement the remaining lumps of coal in the Slocums' wood box.

In the dim light he spotted a large cottonwood limb wedged between two rocks.

"Hey!"

"Aiyeee!" Rusty yelped like a dog and jumped to his right, pressed his legs together, and wrapped his arms tighter around himself. Shadows, and the person's black skin, combined to hide the caller in the trees.

"Jesus Christ! Hey Tom! You out here dreaming about fishing or what?" Rusty said when he caught his breath. "I haven't seen you in a coon's age. Where you been?"

Tom stomped his feet, slapped his arms across his chest, and stepped out from behind the tree. Rusty could see that his friend was not wearing a coat.

"I was hoping a log like this one might be here. What you up to?" Tom said.

"Same as you, I guess. Where's your coat?"

Tom turned away from him and rubbed his hand on the log.

"Oh, Ma has to wear it since we don't have much wood left for the fire."

The boys stared at each other, then at the log, then back at each other. Rusty knew something was different about Tom, something was wrong, but he couldn't figure it out.

Rusty studied the log jammed in the ice. "Looks like it's going to be a tough job, getting that log outta there. Too tough for one guy, I'd say," Rusty said.

Without looking at him, Tom said, "Yeah, well, one strong nigger could probably get it out. You can go back home now, sir."

Rusty's breath came out in a short laugh. He looked at Tom, who was looking at the palms of his hands.

"Well, guess we better get on with this, then," Rusty said. "Tell you what, Tom, when we get this thing out and broken up, why don't you take the bigger half since we have some coal left."

Tom looked up at him. "How's about if I just take it all since I was the one who found it?"

"Huh? What are you talking about? Let's get it out of here, together."

"There is no together, Rusty. It's just you or me. And I got the axe."

"I don't get it, Tom. What's up?"

"Wake up, Rusty. Your people don't scrounge around for wood. My people do. That's that."

Rusty could not see his friend's eyes in the growing light. Tom turned his back on him and started chopping at the frozen log. Rusty jammed his hands into the pockets of his coat and moved along the river in search of driftwood.

Rusty and Tom weren't the only ones out scrounging for heating fuel in the April cold. The Hoffner brothers watched from the shadows as the two boys examined the large cottonwood limb.

"Can you believe that shit?" Isaac said. "That punk kid and that nigger beat us to the best log that's been stuck here in days."

"Did ya hear what that boy said, about his ma not having enough heat?" Lloyd said. "Shit! What say we find a way to really heat up that nigger's house?"

Both men broke into spasms of coughing and laughter. They turned and covered their mouths as they moved away.

Two days later Rusty stood behind a cottonwood tree and watched Tom saw the log he'd hauled out of the river by himself. Tom cleverly wedged the stump between the bottom two steps of his front porch to hold it as he cut it into smaller pieces. The smell of fresh-cut wood reminded Rusty of Kendallville on those days they made crates to ship onions. It also brought back memories of the many cold mornings he'd spent in the forest with Cliff and Pa, the finest lumberman in northeast Indiana, or so he told everyone.

" 'Morning Tom. Got yourself a job, I see."

"Shit! Don't ever sneak up on a man with a blade in his hands! I coulda cut off my leg or something worse. Maybe even your neck."

"You'd have to be quick to do either, so I ain't all that worried."

Sun lit the sweat on Tom's black skin and steam rose in the cold morning air. Rusty shifted his books from one hand to the other. "It's getting late. You going to school today, Tom?"

"We ain't talking, Rusty," Tom said, not looking up from his work.

Rusty's attention turned from the log to Tom's face.

"What do you mean? We're friends, Tom."

Tom wheeled on him. He tossed the saw to the ground and stepped to within an arm's length of Rusty.

"We ain't, Rusty. I heard what you told your brother that night we hung the circus posters. I heard you say I was just another dumb nigger. Yeah, I thought we were friends, too. But friends don't talk like that. Get outta here."

"Wait! Wait. I didn't mean that. I just said that stuff—"

"I ain't listening to any more of your bullshit. I got work and you got school. Good-bye."

"But Tom ..."

Rusty couldn't finish because he didn't know what to say. He turned to leave, then looked back at his friend. Tom's shoulders were shaking. Rusty thought of what Ma had told him: "Sometimes it's best not to say anything when nothing needs to be said."

Later that evening as Rusty walked along Main Street toward the railway station, he thought about Tom, what Tom had said, what he'd said to Tom. He jumped at the sound of the motorcar's bleating horn, unaware that he had stopped in the middle of the street. He looked up at the closed door of the mercantile. Next door, two kerosene lamps stared at him from the darkened windows of Truman's Haberdashery. Rusty felt around in his pocket until he found his Indian head penny Ma had given him for his birthday when he was ten. She'd said the penny was born the same year as him.

When he got to the station, Mr. Slocum, coat and hat already on, stood waiting at the door.

"Rusty, can you mind the station while I run home for a bit? Have to see to Mrs. Slocum. She's not feeling too good and I want to make sure she's okay."

"Sure. I'll just sweep up in here. Nothing on the schedule?"

"Nope. Nothing coming until morning. Just the usual unknown coming our way. I'll be back in about an hour."

"Can I ask you something, sir?"

Mr. Slocum hesitated as he looked over Rusty's shoulder up the street toward home. "Sure."

"How long does it take to unlearn something? Maybe something like an idea or feeling you have or thought you had about somebody?"

Mr. Slocum made a grunting sound and pushed his wool cap tighter onto his head. "That's a tough one, son, without being specific, I mean. Best I can come up with is that you can never unlearn something that wasn't learned into you."

Mr. Slocum moved forward to step past Rusty in the doorway, pulled off his wool cap, and unbuttoned his coat.

"Okay, young man, what seems to be the problem?"

"Nothin'."

"That's probably what Nero said when somebody asked him what that red glow coming from the city might be."

"Huh?"

"Nothing. I can see you're troubled about something. Want to talk about it?"

"No. I guess it was something I said that maybe I shouldn't have said. To someone I really like, I mean. Well, not to him so much as about him and I didn't know he'd hear me 'cause it wasn't true and I didn't want to hurt his feelings but that's what happened and now I'm in deep shit."

When Rusty stopped to take a breath, Mr. Slocum jumped in. "Whew. Sometimes talking with you is like trying to get a drink of water from a fire hose. Slow down a bit and tell me what happened."

Rusty explained how Cliff had threatened to send him back to Kendallville if he didn't start acting like a grownup. And he thought being a grownup meant he had to say bad things about niggers, but he really liked Tom. And Jupiter had helped him and that it didn't seem fair to say all niggers were bad.

"Well, I think you're on the right track, lad. Not fair to judge all the apples in the barrel because of a couple bad ones."

"What am I gonna do, Mr. Slocum?"

"Well, first off, I think you owe Tom an apology. It's a problem, though. With words, it's just like that new-fangled dental cream from Colgate Company—once it's out of the tube you can't put it back."

"I suppose I can try."

"Good lad. You're both young fellas and I expect Tom's heard a lot worse than what you said."

"Do you think we'll be friends again?"

"Don't know. That's up to him, I suppose. Now I have to get on home to check on the missus. You okay?"

"Sure."

Frank LaFevre rubbed his eyes with the heels of his hands and released a labored sigh. He closed the ledger book, looked at the paycheck made out to Clifton Starke, and thought about how the week's work had gone—his apprentice scampering up the ladder with a load of bricks on his shoulder. He liked the guy. Hard working, did what he was told, and always showed up on time. As he slipped the ledger into the top drawer of his desk he heard a rattling sound coming from the far end of the workshop. He felt around inside the desk drawer, searching for the revolver he kept hidden. He felt the comfort and weight of the gun against his fingers and leaned back in his chair far enough to see past the office doorjamb. Before he saw anyone, his nose detected the smell of human sweat. Old sweat, followed by coughing, punctuated by the sound of boot heels on the shop's wood floor.

Isaac and Lloyd, the Hoffner brothers. Had to be. Two of the most mismatched people God ever created. One was tall and lanky, the other looked like a cut-off tree stump. People speculated on whether the boys had the same mother, and if their mother might have been a gorilla that had escaped from the zoo in St. Louis. About the only thing they seemed to have in common was their smell—an odor that could bring tears to a pig's eyes. Frank smiled when he thought about the time old Mr. Ritchey said the brothers' smell could knock the shoes off a horse.

What could they want at this time of night, other than to steal something? He slipped his hand back into the desk drawer, moved his fingers across the knurling on the grip of the gun, and questioned whether shooting them would be worth wasting the ammunition. Frank tipped his head back a bit farther and watched as two shapes shuffled down the center aisle of the shop, probably assessing the array of clean tools hanging in perfect order from pegs.

When the two men were within ten feet of the office door, Frank cleared his throat.

The taller man in the lead jerked backward and hit the short man in the face with his elbow.

"Shit! Oh, evening Frank," Isaac said. He cleared his throat and uttered a quiet laugh. "We seen your light was on and thought we might stop by and discuss a, well, a construction project with you."

"You seem a bit startled there, Isaac. Surprised or disappointed to see me in my own shop at this hour?"

No answer. Frank looked Isaac Hoffner over. The taller of the two brothers stood within a couple inches of the top of the doorframe, even when he removed the stained hat he twisted by the brim in his grimy hands. Isaac kept shifting his eyes toward the floor as if looking for rattlesnakes. The man's ears stuck out on the sides of his head like the open doors of a motorcar. And when he wasn't talking he seemed to either be spitting or coughing. *The only thing these two guys could construct is a bar bill at Jonsey's Saloon south of town.*

"Hmm. A construction job? Is that right? What might that be, boys?"

Lloyd Hoffner stepped from behind his brother. He appeared to be half the height but twice the width of Isaac. He slumped into a chair across the desk from Frank and leaned forward, resting his stubby arms on the desk. Lloyd always seemed to be out of breath. His black-callused elbows attested to hours spent in local taverns. Lloyd's mouth was open just enough for Frank to see a ragged ridge of brown-stained teeth. Frank's eyes began to water from the assault of the smell.

"Well, we're getting this here little problem in town," Lloyd said. Between breaths he licked his lips and looked around to see if anyone else in the room might overhear what he had to say. "And we thought solving that problem would best be done by someone with your expertise."

"Expertise? That's a big word for you, Lloyd," Frank said.

Lloyd blinked and scratched at some place between his legs below the level of the desk. Again, he licked his lips and stared at Frank as if waiting for a reply. His mouth hung open and Frank wanted to ask him if he'd ever had a full set of teeth when he was a kid.

"So, is this a problem that needs my expertise at the courthouse, or the jail in the county building, or something? Seems that's where you two characters spend a lot of your time these days."

"Nah, it's a bit further out on West Mary Street," Isaac said.

Frank straightened in his chair and glanced down to be sure the desk drawer was still slightly opened. "Excuse me, boys, but you seem to have me at a disadvantage here."

Isaac leaned down, putting his grimy hands on the neatly stacked papers of Frank's desk. He looked back over both shoulders and moved in closer to Frank. Frank's first inclination was to reach out and save his paperwork; however, he was forced to hold his breath, turn his head as if looking at the calendar on the wall, and lean back in his chair.

"Ya might want to think about taking a bath sometime before the year's out, Isaac," Frank said.

As the tall man straightened to his full height papers stuck to his hands and fluttered to the floor. "Listen to me, Frank. We're talkin' about niggers here."

"Oh?"

"Yeah, 'oh' is right. We heard that Washington family—"

"Can you believe they use a great name like that?" cut in Lloyd.

"Like I was sayin', we heard they was bringing up more of their should-be-slave relatives from Georgia. Carryin' 'em up here to Yates," Isaac said.

"I see what you're saying, boys. One nest of those vipers is one too many. Soon enough they'll be doing work I could be doing and at half what I charge."

"Exactly," Isaac said. "You hit the nail right on the thumb."

A paroxysm of laughter and coughing broke out between the brothers. They pointed at each other and slapped each other on the shoulders, sending up small dust clouds that Frank watched drift through the light of his desk lamp. The brothers' faces reddened as they coughed, laughed, and choked. When they finally stopped, Isaac's cheeks were swelled like two small balloons. Frank realized the man was looking for some place to spit. He used the toe of his boot to slide a spittoon from beneath his desk to a spot where the tall man could see it.

He was sorry he did. He had to turn his head away in disgust as Isaac released a chunk-laden stream of red and yellow liquid, most of which went into the spittoon.

Isaac wiped his mouth on his sleeve and mumbled something Frank understood to be thanks. He watched the tall man gasp for air, while the shorter brother resumed the conversation.

"So we was thinking, Frank, seeing's how we could use a bit of spending cash, and you, being in the construction trade and all, well, maybe we could sort of show them niggers they ain't welcome in this town and you could help us with some cash and a little something that might go boom."

Frank leaned forward, resting his forearms on the edge of his desk. His thoughts again strayed to the revolver in his drawer and the humane act of putting the coughing Isaac out of his misery. He waited until Isaac stopped hacking and wiping his mouth on his sleeve.

"Let's get this straight, fellas, I don't want to get into anything illegal. Nor something that's going to get somebody hurt. As for scaring the shit out of some people, well, that kind of plan I might listen to. Tell me what you have in mind."

Rusty smiled as he pulled on his coat. Some days, like today, you got lucky. Going to school on Saturdays in the winter meant school would end sooner in the spring to allow the boys to help with planting. All of the coal donated by families to keep the building warm enough had run out. Miss Zerkle had to release the prisoners before noon. She instructed all the children to bring at least one log to school on Monday.

Rusty left the schoolhouse and started down Green Street to take a look at the river. He looked toward the railway station and remembered Mr. Slocum had asked him to stop in at the mercantile and pick up some nails. *I guess the river will be there when I get back.*

He slowed his approach at the steps of the gray mercantile building. He wondered what the fading colors of the false front had been before years of sand and wind turned it into the spotted brown color of a Texas longhorn. He looked up and down the street. Cliff wouldn't be there because it had turned into a good day for house building, so he'd probably have to talk with Rebekah Kern.

He reached for the door handle and was nearly knocked from the top step as the door swept open. A bear-like shape brushed against him, causing him to stagger back so the man could pass.

"Oh, hey, Rusty!"

"Hey, Mr. Klien."

"How's school these days?"

"Okay, I guess."

"What's your favorite subject?"

"Sarah Tillman."

Mr. Klien laughed and slapped him on the shoulder like he was slapping one of the horses in his livery stable.

Rusty rubbed his shoulder and wondered if there would be a permanent bruise on the spot. He waited until the burly man reached the middle of the street before going in. He wiped his hands on the front of his trousers as he entered the cavernous store. The array of sleigh bells attached to the door announced his arrival. He could see what Mr. Slocum meant when he said the coming war was already claiming victims on the home front. Instead of neat rows of canned goods lining the shelves as there had been in the past, single jars were randomly scattered on bare shelves like crows perched in a tree. His eyes followed a string of unlit overhead light bulbs that led toward the back of the store. *When had the musty smell of mushrooms replaced the clean aroma of tack leather hanging on the walls?*

He shivered and grabbed for his cap when he saw Rebekah walk out of the office room in back. She paused and stared directly at him as if seeing him for the first time. Even the length of the room could not diminish the heat he felt coming from her eyes. He felt his chest tighten and reached up to unbutton his button-less jacket.

"Gosh, for a minute there I thought I had a real customer. You'd been about the second or third of the day," she said.

"Hello, Miss Kern."

"Rusty, you know me well enough, or leastwise your brother does, for you to call me Rebekah."

Rusty cleared his throat and pushed his free hand deeper into his jacket pocket. He looked at the floor, unsure of what might happen if he looked into her face.

"Right, Rebekah," he said.

"So, what brings you here, Rusty, business or pleasure?"

"Huh?"

"Did you want to buy something or are you just here to take up my valuable time?"

"Well, I came in for some roofing nails, for Mr. Slocum."

Rebekah smiled at him and turned to look behind the counter. "Isn't this a great coincidence? Why don't you make yourself useful and help me back there with these roofing nails that got spilled?" she said.

He looked over the counter top, following her line of vision. "Don't see any nails, Miss Kern, err, Rebekah."

With the toe of her right foot Rebekah reached out and tipped over a keg of nails onto the floor behind the counter.

"There, see?"

Before he could answer, Rebekah dropped to the floor behind the counter next to the overturned keg of nails. She sat, staring up at him, and slowly pulled her dress back from her parted legs.

Rusty felt the sides of his head begin to pound and all the air leave the room. His eyes were drawn past her black stockings, into the blinding whiteness of her legs above her knees.

She licked her lips and said, "Russell, why don't you come down here and help me with my little problem?"

Air whooshed from his lungs as his knees buckled. He felt himself falling, plummeting toward her, unsure if he should keep his eyes open. Too late he remembered both hands were trapped in his pockets. All he could think was *don't land on top of her*. As he twisted, trying to free his left hand, the underside edge of the counter came into view, then the ceiling. His freed left hand hit the floor and nails. Pain shot into his wrist and he smelled the fragrance of lemon drops.

"Ouch! Oh god!" he said. Rebekah's body absorbed most of his weight. The clean scent of soap filled his head as his face pressed against the pillow-like softness of her breasts. He fought for air and wrestled his right hand out of his pants pocket. His words of apology were lost in the fabric of her dress.

"Christ, Russell! Be careful. You'll mess up my hair and make me untidy," she said through clinched teeth.

Rumbling footsteps on the boardwalk outside made them both turn and look in the direction of the door. At first, Rusty was unsure if the noise was coming from outside the building or inside his head. He twisted his body from where he had landed between Rebekah's legs and gasped for air as he rolled into a seated position. He pressed his back against the wood counter and looked up at the tin plates of the ceiling. He knew he was probably going to die, right there in the mercantile, and no one would know what killed him. Only an arm's length away sat Rebekah, knees raised, head tilted to the right. She was looking straight at him, the first finger of her right hand with its bright red nail tapping against her smiling lips. Twice she shifted her eyes up and rolled them toward the front of the store as if signaling for him to do something. Rusty's eyes could not leave the red fingernail that matched the color of her lips.

He looked toward the ceiling to see what she might be pointing at. He wanted to run for the back door of the building, but was certain his legs would not move. Along with sweat, he smelled something metallic, like sharpened pencils, and he felt a warm dampness growing in the crotch of his trousers.

To Rusty, the small bells above the front door sounded as loud as the bells of the Catholic Church on Sunday morning. He knew by the coughing and loud voices it was the Hoffner brothers coming into the store. Without another look at Rebekah, he scrambled on his hands and knees toward the rear of the store, looking for a place to hide. When safely around the corner of the counter, he stood, and from between a pair of hand-tooled boots watched the Hoffner brothers enter.

Rebekah stood. She used one hand to straighten her dress, the other to tame her hair.

"Well, good afternoon, sirs!"

"Ah, hello, young lady. You weren't on the floor over there, was you now?" Isaac Hoffner asked.

"I was indeed, sir. Clumsy me knocked over a keg of nails and I was picking them up, one at a time. Fortunately, you two gentlemen have delayed that task, surely a fate worse than death."

She kept her eyes on the Hoffner brothers because she knew they would be watching her as she moved along the back of the counter. "Now, what can I do for you two?"

Isaac Hoffner leaned toward the counter. Rebekah knew the man's eyes would explore every wrinkle in the back of her dress.

"Well, we'd like to help you with those nails, but we're in a bit of a hurry. We need a dozen blasting caps," he said.

Rebekah's face began to redden when she noticed Lloyd's eyes exploring the tops of her breasts. She straightened a bit. "Kind of the wrong season for blasting, isn't it, boys? But that's not a problem. If you just step over to that counter, I'll see what I can do for you," she said, pointing with her chin.

As the Hoffner brothers turned, Rebekah looked back to where she knew Rusty was hiding and winked.

"We still have some of those fuse-type blasting caps over here. Is that what you're after? Please don't tell me you're after those fancy electric kind. The army has taken all of those."

"No ma'am, the old fuse caps is what we're after," Isaac said.

"And do you need any fuse line for those?"

"Nope. We're okay there."

"And boys, tell me you're not going to crimp that fuse and cap in with your teeth. I'd hate to think I sold anything that might damage a handsome man's looks."

She held her smile and watched both men's unshaven faces redden.

"Surely not, ma'am," Isaac said through fits of coughing. "You surely do know your stuff around fuses and all. Which means we could use a good pair of fence pliers."

Rebekah looked toward the back of the store, lowered her voice, and leaned forward on the counter. The two men bent over toward her as well. She said, "And you do know about the danger of trying to crimp those caps in front of you, don't you? You know to do it behind your back, just in case. Some injuries, like blowing off half his face, a man can recover from, but some other things can do serious damage. If you get my drift."

The Hoffner brothers sputtered, wiped at their mouths with the backs of their hands, and cleared their throats, enjoying the flirtation.

The short brother, Lloyd, said, "You're right, miss. Friend of ours crimped a cap too tight. Fortunately he had his hands in back of himself, like you're supposed to, or he wouldn't have no offspring. Couldn't sit down for a week, though."

Rebekah joined in the laughter as the Hoffner brothers coughed and sputtered at their own joke.

"So what are you boys up to, blasting in early April?"

Lloyd looked around the room. "Well, we got us a job, ya see. We're helping Frank LaFevre with a construction project. You might say it's more of a teaching experience we're giving some folks who are slow learners."

Rebekah knitted her raised eyebrows. She leaned forward, resting her elbows on the counter, and looked from one brother to the other. She followed their gaze, knowing they were looking down the top of her dress. She then straightened and reached up with her right hand to pull the front of her dress a bit higher.

"I don't quite follow you, boys."

Her head was tilted slightly to the right and her smile began to widen. The tip of her tongue appeared between her lips, moved from the center to the left corner, and disappeared. Lloyd's hands rattled the change in his pockets. He cleared his throat and looked toward the door. He brushed his tongue over his lower lip before he spoke.

"Well, ah, I guess we can tell you. You look like the kind of lady who knows how to keep a secret."

Rebekah smiled, showing the brothers a row of straight white teeth. She leaned on the counter top closest to Lloyd, pulled her arms tighter across her chest, and looked down through the glass countertop as if examining the dusty tools in the cabinet below. "Oh, I'm real good with secrets."

She glanced up in time to see Lloyd's eyes rake the top of her dress. He cleared his throat. "We're going to have a, well, I guess you'd call it a housewarming party, for some of the new niggers in town."

Rebekah narrowed her eyes, straightened a bit, and leaned toward the men again. She could see spittle forming at the corners of Isaac's mouth. His breath came in shallow gulps. In a low voice she said, "I know just what you mean. Especially the way they look at us white women sometimes."

"There! That's just what we mean," Isaac said.

"But, ah, you're not going to hurt anyone, are you? I mean, you're just going to, ah, well, do something to the house, right?"

"Right. We ain't exactly figured how we'll get them outside the place, but we will," Lloyd said.

Rebekah blinked her eyes several times and said, "You boys just be careful and come back. I'll put those blasting caps and pliers on Frank's account for you."

Rusty waited until he could no longer hear voices before he opened his eyes. When the clumping sound of the Hoffner brothers' boots disappeared, he stepped from behind the display of straw hats. He was looking for the store's rear exit and did not hear Rebekah approach. When he turned to look back into the store he was startled to see her, hands on hips, only a few feet away.

"Ain't you the brave one?" she said, a smile on her lips. "From all your brother's told me about you, I thought you were brave enough to at least stand in the same room as those two. Did you see the way they looked at me? The way they were trying to look here, down my dress? What if I needed help?"

Rebekah brushed at the front of her dress, exposing the tops of her breasts. Rusty couldn't look at her. He couldn't breathe. All he could do was lick his lips, bury his hands in his pockets, and look toward the front door, which appeared to be miles away.

"I think I better be going, Miss Kern. Honestly. I need a quarter pound of roofing nails for Mr. Slocum, if you don't mind. Well, maybe I should just come back later."

"It's your choice, Russell. But I have to warn you, I might not be in such good humor when you come back."

Rusty swallowed and without looking at Rebekah, said, "I think I'll take my chances, ma'am."

Rebekah watched Rusty stumble over his feet as he half-walked, half-ran down Main Street. She smiled at the thought of what she might be able to teach that boy. She also thought of her other problem that she knew was standing behind her.

"You can come out now," she said over her shoulder in the direction of the office.

Frank LaFevre leaned around the corner of the office door. "Well, that was quite a performance, young lady. I don't know which part I liked best—the way you almost made that Starke kid pee his pants or the way you sent those Hoffner brothers off in such a lather."

She pulled at the top of her dress and smiled at the man who had been her lover for the past month.

"I think it was a bit more than almost with that kid," she said and laughed until her face turned red. "Wasn't that the darnedest thing?"

Rebekah drew in a long breath. "But you know, it's not my fault, Frank. You had me so worked up before that kid stumbled in here. Did you see the way he nearly fell over himself trying to get away?"

She leaned against the counter in another fit of laughter. Frank walked up behind her and placed his hands on her shoulders. He began to massage her neck muscles with his thumbs as he looked out the window. She couldn't stop the soft moaning sound that came from her throat. She smiled when she thought how Frank had panicked, almost the same way as that kid, the first time she rubbed up against his tight butt in the bakery.

"Ya know Rebekah, I think we have another little problem we need to take care of here, too."

"You don't mean your wife again, do you?" she said, rolling her head and neck in circles.

"No. She doesn't really care about the things you and me like to do. I'm talking about Cliff."

Rebekah turned to face him and pressed her body against his. She smiled and reached up to brush a few wood chips from his hair as she'd done with straw in Cliff's the night before. "You don't need to worry about him. He just likes to take me to lunch. You're all the man I can handle, Frank. You know that. Besides, you said I had to do something so people in town might not get suspicious of us."

"Well, let's just leave it at the fact that I don't like competition when it comes to my business, or my ladies."

"Does that mean you're not being faithful to me?" Before Frank could answer, she said, "Sounds like the Hoffner brothers have something in mind to solve at least one of those competition problems."

"Yeah. And the way things are going, I think Mr. Thomas Woodrow Wilson in Washington is going to solve the other for me."

As Tom bent to pick up a large piece of bark, all that remained of the log he'd finished cutting, a gruff voice behind him called out, "Hey boy, c'mon over here. We got something for you."

Tom spun around and found himself face to face with Isaac Hoffner, all smelly six-plus feet of him, along with his stubby pigpen brother, Lloyd. The brothers were standing next to a large wooden box. Tom could see their faces were flushed and hands red from the pressure of the box's rope handles.

Tom dropped the leather wood carrier he'd been loading but held on to the saw as he walked across the grassless space to where the Hoffner brothers stood.

"It's a box a fire wood for your ma," Lloyd said. "Thought you might be needing it during this cold spell."

Tom examined the variety of dirt on the Hoffner brothers' clothes and wondered if the two men had spent the night in a barn, or maybe under the boardwalk at the end of Main Street.

"Well, sir, we do appreciate that. We surely do," Tom said, remembering to keep his head down and eyes on the box. "But we don't have money to pay you, sirs."

"Oh, no money's expected, young man. We just thought you could use it, is all," Lloyd said.

"Why don't you just carry it on up to the porch there. You might want to think about not taking it into the house, though. Might be bugs in some of that wood, ya know," Isaac said. "Might want to leave it outside a day or two, at least overnight."

"That's real thoughtful of you, sir," Tom said, finally looking up at the men. "We can really use this. All we had left was that old log I just cut up."

Tom reached for the rope handle and hoisted the box on one end. "This is really a full load. Where should I bring the box back soon as I get it empty?"

"Aaa, no, that's okay. We don't really need it for a while," Lloyd said.

"Naw, we won't be needing it for some time. You just keep it there on the porch 'til it's empty so's you won't have to haul it all into the house," Isaac added. "Bugs and all in the box, maybe."

When the men scurried off, Tom pulled and pushed to get the box up the steps and positioned next to the door on the opposite side from where he'd put the cut logs. He used his foot to push the box against the wall of the house and did not see the piece of thick string hanging from the back.

Rusty thumbed through Mr. Slocum's collection of magazines and books about Morse code, descriptions of rail gauges, and pictures of trains. When he heard the door open he glanced at the Regulator clock and was surprised to see almost two hours had passed.

"Sorry to be so long," said Mr. Slocum.

"Not at all, sir. I was just reading some of your books. I might like to learn more of that Morse code one of these days."

"Be glad to teach you. It'll fit well with your regular school lessons."

"Oh god, thanks for reminding me. I have to make a book report tomorrow and I haven't hardly read the book. How bad is it going to be to have to stand in front of the class and talk?"

"Better get on home, then. And Rusty, Mrs. Slocum is sleeping so kind of tiptoe up those back steps."

Rusty left the station and headed north on Railroad Street, then took a shortcut along the well-worn path that angled toward the house. As he approached Western Street he heard two men coughing, spitting, and arguing. He stopped. He knew it was the Hoffner brothers. From a distance Rusty could see skinny Isaac, his arms flapping like a bird, and

Lloyd, hands stuffed into his pockets making him appear almost round, both kicking at a tree stump.

Rusty held his breath. *I must be downwind of those critters.* He moved behind a large cottonwood tree to get a better view of what the brothers were doing. The rough bark of the tree he pressed against made a hissing sound as it scraped his cheek.

As the two men walked past, their unintelligible words reminded Rusty of one tree whispering to another. He could only decipher something about niggers being blasted all the way to Washington. The slurred words were followed by sputters of coughs and laughs.

Rusty continued toward home. Outside the house, in the dim glow of the oil lamps, he could see the silhouette of Mrs. Slocum pacing in the front room as she did every night. Rarely was she asleep as Mr. Slocum believed. Rusty thought about the book he was supposed to read for his report. Mrs. Slocum had probably read the book and could tell him enough important things so he could fake his way through a report. He also thought about Tom and what he might say as an apology to his friend.

Instead of going inside, he decided to make a third attempt at an apology. It wasn't all that late and Tom's house wasn't that far if he took a couple shortcuts. Ma would tell him there's no time like the present to do something—except go fishing, maybe.

As he moved along Elm Street he picked up the scent of the Hoffner brothers heading the same direction. He jumped from dark spot to dark spot as he moved among the shadows cast by the trees and houses.

Holy shit. Could the Hoffners be planning to do something to Tom's family? There were only two colored families in town and he'd not seen Tom's pa around for several weeks. Tom was probably taking care of his ma and sister. Rusty watched the brothers turn onto West Mary Street and decided to take a shortcut to Tom's.

He ran through backyards until he reached the dead end of West Mary Street. From there he could work his way to the side of Tom's house, relying on shadows to hide his approach.

He flattened himself against a tree nearest the Washingtons' house. He tried to take in as much air as possible with his mouth open so he would not make any noise. Where were the Hoffner brothers? They had to have been coming here. As Rusty stepped from behind the tree he saw Lloyd, the stubby brother, on his hands and knees crawling toward Tom's front porch steps.

Suddenly it got dark, as if someone had blown out a candle. Rusty looked up and watched a billowy cloud drift across the face of the moon, making the house and yard disappear. He waited for his eyes to adjust to the darkness. He blinked several times, unsure if the shape on the porch was still moving. Scraping sounds came from the area near the door. Dim window light from inside illuminated two rounded shapes on the porch pushing against a huge wooden box. They appeared to be moving it closer to the door.

Rusty licked his lips. His breath came in short gulps. He looked in both directions at the few houses on the street. None showed any light. The only light in the neighborhood, other than the little bit sneaking from the front window, seemed to be the dim yellow glow at the back of the house. *Tom must be working on his book report like I'm supposed to be doing.*

Rusty heard what sounded like a chicken scratching. A sudden burst of light sparked at the front of the house. He stopped breathing. In the flare up, he could clearly see Isaac holding a match and leaning down close to a long piece of rope that trailed off toward the box. The flash and brilliant pink-and-white glare, along with a distinct hissing, told him the men were lighting a fuse. The hissing rattle grew louder as the spark slithered toward the box. The men jumped to their feet and bolted from the porch, disappearing into the shadows.

Rusty ran to the house and jumped onto the end of the waist-high porch. His boots landed on loose planks that rattled and wiggled. He pounded his fist against the side of the house as he ran toward the box.

"Get out! Get out! Wake up! Tom! Tom!" he shouted.

Rusty froze. He could see the fuse wriggling, glowing, and slipping toward the corner of the box. He lunged for the menacing creature's scarlet head. As he did, something slammed into his right side. He'd not seen the door open. Its thin frame smashed into his ribs, causing him to fall away from the fuse. His head crashed against the box as his hand searched for the fuse in the smoke-filled darkness.

The odor of sulfur filled Rusty's nose. He sneezed and blindly grabbed for the fuse. He felt the heat bite into his hand and pulled at it with all his strength. A crashing sound came from behind him and he rolled onto his side. He stared into the double barrels of a shotgun.

"Who's there? Who's, what—" Tom said.

"Get out, Tom! Get out!"

"What? Rusty?"

Rusty jumped to his feet and yelled, "Tom, get your ma outta there! Get out the back. The Hoffner brothers are trying to blow your house up!"

The picture of Tom, calmly standing with a shotgun across his chest, made Rusty stop yelling.

"Don't think that's gonna happen now, seeing's how you're holding on to that fuse," Tom said.

Rusty looked down at the foot-long piece of still-wiggling fuse in his hand. He felt the heat and tossed the fuse into the empty yard, the direction the Hoffner brothers had fled.

An odor like rotten eggs hung in the air. As they studied the shadows, the boys heard a voice say, "Shit!" followed by the sound of feet running. Then quiet again.

From inside the house Rusty heard a woman's voice ask, "What's going on, Thomas?"

"Nothing, Mama. You just go back to bed. Everything's okay, now."

Together the boys pushed at the large wood box and moved it along the porch until it fell over the side. Two sticks of dynamite lay among the scattered pieces of firewood.

"Step in here and warm up a bit," Tom said. "What you doing in this neighborhood this time of night, anyway?"

Rusty looked out into the darkness. "No thanks, Tom. I, ah, got that damn book report for tomorrow so I better get home."

He turned toward his friend as he brushed dirt from his trousers. His eyes moved beyond the shotgun, into the small living room behind Tom. The smell of cooked onions and something medicinal replaced the sulfur smell of the burning fuse.

"What? You just happened to be out for a stroll and saw two guys trying to burn down a house?"

Rusty blew air from his lungs, took a deep breath, and looked into Tom's eyes, so big and white they looked spooky to him. He felt his insides get squishy. There was no smile on his friend's face.

"Well, Tom, a while back I said some things about you that weren't true. Things I didn't really mean, and I want to apologize for what I said. My ma always says you should treat others the way you want to be treated and I didn't do that and I'm sorry and I still want to be your friend, or for us to be friends, I think I mean."

Tom lowered the shotgun as he looked over his shoulder into the small room, then back at Rusty.

Tom released a breath. "Well, it's past that, Rusty. We're moving on from here. Going over to Nicodemus with the rest of the colored people, our own people, so you won't have to worry about us niggers bothering your town."

Rusty felt his throat tighten, blocking any more words. Tears began to well up in his eyes and his vision blurred as Tom turned and walked into the house. He heard the click of the lock when Tom closed the inside door. The odor of sulfur returned to replace the smells of his friend's home.

CHAPTER EIGHT

War

Rusty stood, hands in pockets, watching a small, brown bird hunt for insects in the dark crevasses of the tree outside his window. He looked at his cleanest white shirt lying on the bed, one of two he'd brought from Indiana almost a year ago. The shirt fit then. Now it felt tight across the shoulders, plus the sleeves seemed to be getting shorter. The collar had always been too tight. Now it was impossible to button. He groaned when he thought of the struggle it would be to put the shirt on in the day's heat. The upside was that the shirt's material had gotten thinner after so many washings, so it might feel cooler.

It was just past noon and already a part of the day he enjoyed—lunch with Mrs. Slocum—was over. It was several months since Tom moved away. Other boys his age who lived in town during the winter months had gone out to farms to help relatives. Because of that, Rusty discovered he had more time for quiet conversations with his landlady. He smiled when he thought about Mr. Slocum saying, "The missus never has much to say anymore." While she, in turn, said their conversations should be kept as their own little secret.

Through the window screen he watched hazy images of neighbors walking south on Railroad Street heading for Courthouse Square. His thumb pressed against the Indian head penny in his pocket and he wondered how things in Yates Center were about to change. He knew the rest of his day would be consumed by a celebration on Main Street he did not want to attend. What's to celebrate when a bunch of guys volunteer so they can go off to war? He checked the tree branch again. The bird was gone. Time for him to go, too.

When he reached the last step of the Slocums' front porch, he paused in the shade, thinking how he'd rather be down at the river fishing. He twisted his head, trying to find comfort in the shirt's collar. The sun burned the back of his neck as if someone were pressing a branding iron against it. Not that he'd ever had a branding iron on his neck or even in his hand. But he thought about branding irons—a lot. Once, he even sketched designs in the sand with a stick. His favorite, the one he'd use someday when he became a big cattle rancher, was what he called the Flying S. It looked like the letter S, tilted to the right, with wings like a bird.

He stopped at the first tree that offered some shade and rolled his shirt sleeves to the elbow after using the left one to wipe sweat and dust from his face. When he saw the men in the street he began to regret his decision to leave his hat in the room. Any shade produced by that floppy straw hat would have been welcome, even through his thick shock of sandy-colored hair. God, he hated Kansas. If it wasn't hailstones big enough to kill a cow, it was tornadoes ripping up the farmland. Then it was the heat that made you feel like bacon in a skillet. Or you froze your butt off when all that other stuff wasn't happening. And no lakes to go fishing. He kicked the trunk of the nearest tree and continued toward town, stopping to examine a strange-looking bug that was eating one of Mrs. Jones's purple flowers.

He continued along the shade side of Railroad Street in the direction of Main Street. Even from a block away he could hear music coming from the square where the ceremony would be held. He stopped and looked at the pile of rubble that had been the Farleys' house. A twister had ripped the whole place from the Earth two weeks before, scattering pieces as far as the river. God, that was a scary day with the damn hail the size of baseballs, black sky, dogs running around town like crazy. *Poor old folks never had a chance.*

"I should get out of Yates while I'm still alive. Probably too damn late," he said to the hole.

"What's that?" Mr. Slocum said.

Rusty jumped. He'd not seen his landlord standing behind the upturned root ball and stump of a cottonwood tree. Mr. Slocum was also looking at the pile of debris that had once been a family's home.

"Oh, howdy, sir. Nothin', just talking to myself."

"Well, smells a bit like rain, don't you think?"

Rusty looked at the clear blue sky, noting the lack of any kind of breeze, and thought the day smelled like wet socks. He said nothing.

"Well then, going to the ceremony?"

"Yes sir. I guess I should, since Cliff's part of the group."

"Too bad about Roland and Nedda Farley, there. I knew them since they came out to Yates, probably twenty years now. That's the funny thing about twisters, or fires."

"What's so funny about it?"

"Oh, I don't mean funny, ha ha. I mean strange how bad things just seem to pick out good people, that's all."

He and Mr. Slocum continued to look at the fallen tree. Mr. Slocum said, "Mighty proud of you boy, mighty proud of the way you helped that Washington family a while back. Mighty proud. Did I tell you that before?"

Rusty's throat began to tighten as he waited for Mr. Slocum to finish. All he could do was tip his head a bit, tug at the collar of his shirt, and turn away. In the distance he could see a crowd gathering in front of Corbett's Mercantile.

"Yes sir," he said. "Thanks. Just doing what I had to do, is all." He did not need to remind Mr. Slocum that it was about the one-millionth time he'd praised him for helping Tom's family. Nor that he didn't even want to think about Tom anymore.

"Come along then, son. Come along. The boys will be moving out any minute now."

Rusty found a place to stand in the exact middle of Main Street, midway between two groups of men. There was something about standing in the middle of the street, knowing you did not have to watch for horses or cars, that seemed to create a holiday atmosphere. Women gathered in small clusters, backs to the sun, while men walked from group to group, shaking hands and slapping each other on the shoulder. Rusty counted the people in the crowd whom he knew. Not many. *Not like if this was Kendallville. And they're all dressed like, like what? There's something about going into town when the mayor decides to close Main Street that makes these folks think they should dress up and try to look their best.* He shook his head and watched a group of Civil War veterans across the street, some in blue, some in gray, talking among themselves.

Mr. Slocum walked up next to him and looked over at the same group. "Now there's some boys that could tell these young fellas what they're in for," he said to Rusty and anyone else within earshot.

"What do you suppose those old guys are talking about, Mr. Slocum? They were on opposite sides of the fence at one time, now they act like buddies."

"Yeah. I think now all they do is swat flies and swap lies, trying to make sense of it all," Mr. Slocum said. "Damnedest war if there ever was one. What a waste. Brothers fought each other for five years, for what? I suppose the colored families think differently, though."

Rusty twisted his neck in hope of finding some relief from the stranglehold of the stiff shirt collar and loosely tied necktie. Even with the sleeves of his white shirt rolled above his elbows he felt hot. He kept his hands safe in the pockets of his baggy trousers and, with his thumb, rubbed the Indian head penny.

He looked around. No kids his age or anyone else in the crowd he wanted to talk with. He examined the fresh layer of dust that covered his shoes. Not his shoes. They were an oversized pair of black boots he borrowed, like all his clothes, from Cliff. A wave of hushing sounds swept through the crowd, bringing all conversation to a halt. Rusty watched as men removed their hats and covered their private parts, women bowed their heads, and little children refrained from poking at each other while some preacher made promises no one would keep.

Rusty kept his head down and shifted his eyes around to see who else in the crowd might not be praying. He used the toe of his boot to draw circles in the dust. He did not want to think about what would happen to him now that Cliff was leaving for the army, or now that Tom and his family had left for the Promised Land.

"I won't be needing these things for a while," Cliff had said that rainy day last week, the day he told Rusty he'd enlisted in the army. Rusty had felt, not for the first time, like he wanted to rip his brother's heart out just to show him what it feels like when someone breaks a promise.

Instead, he said, "What? You mean you joined the army? And you're leaving?" It was all he could think of to say.

"Yep. Gotta do it. Gotta put those Dutchmen in their place. Besides, with me and the boys all signed up, the country meets its quota and there won't be a draft of boys who don't really want to go. It's my duty."

"What about me, your brother. Ain't I your duty?"

"Look, I told you," said Cliff, unsmiling, looking him in the eyes. "Stay back at George's, or even go back to Kendallville. I told you to go home. You seem to do nothing but go from one scrape to another out here."

"You can't leave, Cliff. I hate it here. I hate the twisters and no friends and everything. Without you here I'm just stuck. I got nobody I care about to go to."

"Stop it kid, and grow up, will ya? I'm getting real tired of this little-kid crap you pull all the time, crying just when you want something,"

Cliff said, turning away. "Besides, it's just temporary. I'll be back soon and it'll be just like old times. Remember?"

That had been their last conversation for more than a week. Rusty looked across the street at his brother standing alone near two dozen young men milling around, most with escorts of friends. Like the recruits, he paid no attention to the preacher's words. They wouldn't be the words he wanted to hear, anyway. He felt relieved when the drone of the man's voice abruptly stopped. He watched as others in the crowd lifted their heads and mumbled, "Amen." Across the street, in the shade of the blacksmith's shop, he saw Aunt Belle. Apparently, like most people in Woodson County, she and Uncle George must have taken a day off from the farm for this big event.

Farther down the street, away from the crowd, he could see George and Frank LaFevre, backs to the crowd, locked in conversation. No one was paying attention to the mayor, who stood on the hood of an automobile to make his speech. Belle's face was hidden by her bonnet and Rusty could see her handkerchief, probably used to wipe her eyes, on the ground in front of her. She appeared to be looking in Cliff's direction.

Rusty blinked sweat out of his eyes and looked across at his aunt. She turned and stared directly at him. Her eyebrows were pulled together, showing lines on her forehead he'd not noticed before. She appeared to be trying to tell him something with her eyes.

Rusty swallowed and searched for something interesting on the ground. When he looked back across the street, Belle was gone. In her spot stood Rebekah, also looking at him, but with a smile, not the angry, questioning look of Belle. Rusty lowered his head and walked toward the group of people where Cliff stood, still searching through the crowd.

"Looking for me?" Rusty said.

Cliff did not respond.

Rusty thought about the lecture Cliff had given him last week: how Frank said it was the right thing for Cliff to do, join the army, and that there would always be a job waiting for Cliff when he got back.

He stepped closer. "Where they going to take you, Cliff?"

"Huh? Oh, well, first we go for induction, up to Fort Larned, I think, then down to Fort Sill, in Oklahoma, for basic training."

"I'll take really good care of these boots and those shirts you gave me."

"Don't worry, little brother. I'm gonna get a whole new wardrobe. One just right for hunting the Dutchmen."

"Why Dutchmen? I thought the war was with the Germans."

"Oh, that's just what they call 'em. They're Germans, all right. And if you wonder if they're mean sonsabitches, just think about the old man back in Kendallville."

Rusty looked west along Main Street, his hands rubbing his legs through his pockets. His eyes followed the road until it intersected the railroad tracks, then angled south, disappearing behind buildings that would probably fall over in the next good wind.

"Should we ... could we ever forgive him, Cliff?"

"Huh? Can't say as to how or why, Russell."

Cliff bobbed on his toes, scanning through the crowd of well-wishers. Other recruits began to hug women and shake hands with men in the crowd.

"Ya know, Cliff, you promised you wouldn't—"

"Now Russell, don't start in on that again. I'm doing what I have to do. Listen, I have one word of advice for you and I want you to promise me you'll abide."

Rusty felt the sharpness of the sun slice into the back of his neck. He shifted his eyes toward Cliff, then looked to the left to watch a wagon pass through the crowd.

"Besides staying away from the pretty girls, 'cause I know you're old enough to notice 'em, I want you to go to school every day, okay? And if you don't like that school here, or you have some problems here, get on back to Kendallville. There's always some kin who'll take you in."

"Right."

"Frank says maybe he can use you driving his truck this summer. Or if your heart's set on it, you might be able to hire on at some spread, punching cows. The pay's probably the same, but you'll learn more from Frank. And if things get tough for you here, Frank says he'll see to it that you get back to Kendallville if that's what suits you. You'll know best when the time comes. Understand me?"

"Right, I heard you the first time. I'm beginning to think I don't care much for what Frank thinks. He thinks about Frank, first. Did you ever notice that?"

Cliff paused his crowd search and looked at Rusty. "Well, the Slocum folks are real nice. That Mr. Slocum sure has skill as a telegraph operator, don't he? I guess you could work as an apprentice for him."

"Yep."

"Okay now, I have to go. I'll try to get back here on leave, maybe in the fall, and maybe you and me and Frank can go hunting or something. We'll see how it goes."

"Right, but Cliff, you know—"

Rusty never finished. He looked down at his empty outstretched hand, raised his head, and saw that his brother's attention was fixed on the parade of cars and wagons that stretched in uneven lines behind the clusters of army recruits. It all reminded him of the funeral procession after Ma died.

Cliff exhaled as he walked away from his brother. He concentrated on finding Rebekah. She had to be here someplace. Two nights ago she promised she'd come and say good-bye. He approached a group of men he knew. There, in the middle of dusty, horseshit-strewn Main Street, was a flowery scent he recognized. And there was a high-pitched laugh that floated above the male voices. He knew the scent and the sound. It was Rebekah and her irritating cackle—that characteristic way she had of ending every other sentence. He thought of those first few times in the hayloft when he asked what she found humorous in what they were about to do, or were doing. Her response had been to turn her head and giggle.

Now here she was, talking and laughing with men, most of whom were going off to the army like he was, probably to war—some to die, maybe. Frank had been right about her—she was the kind of woman that could leave a man crying, but that didn't seem to keep Frank, nor anyone else, from taking every opportunity to talk with her.

Rather than approach the group, Cliff turned and walked toward the line of waiting cars that would transport him and the other boys to—to what? Occasionally, he paused to cut some lines in the dust with the sides of his shoes. When he reached the lead car and could no longer hear Rebekah's giggle, he stopped. His legs felt heavy, rubbery, and he knew this was the wrong place to cry for the first time since Ma's funeral.

"Cliff? No, don't turn around," came the soft voice.

Even her giggle was hardly more than a whisper. That scent of flowers—*lavender, that's what it is*—made his chest tighten. Turning to look into her face was all he wanted to do. He felt a wave of heat wash upward from beneath the collar of his sweat-stained shirt, a blush so painful and dark he thought the color might make Rebekah turn away.

"Rebekah, I was, well, I was hoping you could get off work and maybe come say good-bye," he said to the radiator of the empty Packard touring car in front of him.

His breath quickened and he felt an erection begin when she breathed on his neck and her hand brushed against his trousers. He wanted to remove his hands from his pockets but was afraid to move.

"Oh, it's not good-bye, Cliff. It's like those Mexicans are fond of saying, '*hasta luego.*' You know, until the next time, or whatever it means."

"Rebekah, I saw you just now and, and well ..."

"Please, don't say anything. I was just talking with those men, waiting to get a chance to talk to you, alone, before, well, before you go to training."

"Can I turn around now?"

"No. I'm trying not to be conspicuous. We don't want the whole town to know, you know, what we've been doing. You remember, don't you?" she said, and rubbed her hand against his buttocks.

"Rebekah, Frank says he'll look in on you from time to time. And if there's something you need, well, maybe Rusty could fetch it for you."

He listened to her quiet laugh, trying to ignore the pounding of his heart.

"What's so funny?" Cliff asked.

She pressed her body against his back. "God, Cliff. Why do you have to ask me that all the time?"

"Why do you laugh all the time?"

His back felt cool as she straightened and leaned away from him.

"God, can't you be civil, especially today?" she said.

An order he barely understood, barked by a tall man in civilian clothes wearing a campaign hat, sent the other soon-to-be soldiers scurrying. The recruits looked more like circus clowns than fighting soldiers as they scrambled to arrange themselves in three ragged rows. The scene brought laughter and cheers from the crowd.

Cliff ran to find a place in line. He did not turn to look at Rebekah. He did not say good-bye, or even hear her parting words. He halted in the middle rank of men. His breathing was rapid, his eyes forward, locked on a small bug that searched for a way under the shirt collar of the man in front of him. The man reached up to swat the insect.

"Eyes forward! Hands at your sides, soldier!"

The gruffness in the sergeant's voice made all the other men turn and look at the tall fellow and his strange brown campaign hat.

"Eyes forward!" the man shouted. "You're in the army, now. From now on I'm your mother, father, and girlfriend. You pay attention only to me."

Rusty's cough to clear dust from his throat was lost in a cacophony of street sounds. He had moved along the boardwalk into a patch of shade near the corner of the railway station. He tried to blink away the stinging caused by sweat in his eyes. He had seen the group of men surrounding Rebekah part, allowing her to pass through. He had no doubt about her direction as her head turned from side to side and she stopped behind his brother. What were they talking about? Why didn't Cliff turn to look at her?

Now his attention, like everyone else's, was drawn to the rag-tag procession of running recruits. The new soldiers, in old white shirts and ties, scrambled from their ragged assembly to the long dark line of motorcars where drivers waited.

Cars coughed into life as men from the town pulled or kicked at the starting handles. Plumes of dust and exhaust rose and trailed after the noisy lineup as it moved south on Railroad Street and exited town east on Kansas Street, knifing into the open prairie. When the sound of engines lost its battle with the sound of wind, and the sky returned to its deep blue color, Rusty removed his left hand from his pocket and wiped dust from the corner of his eye.

"Penny for your thoughts."

"Oh, hi Rebekah. Gosh, you sure can give a fellow an awful surprise, sneaking up like that. They should make you wear a bell or something so we'd know you were coming."

"Oh now, Russell, are you saying I'm a cow or a goat or something?" she said and tipped her head, looked at the ground, and smoothed nonexistent wrinkles from her green dress.

Rusty could see her eyes peering out at him from beneath the edge of her bonnet. He knew he should not stare at her lips. *Just ignore that scent of lavender.*

"Oh, heck, not hardly. Not hardly, Rebekah. I just meant, well. Oh, nothing, I guess." He cleared his throat twice. "Say, that's a mighty pretty dress you have on. It's the same green one I saw you in for the first time when Cliff and I came to town nearly a year ago."

"Hmmm. That must have been the day of my seventeenth birthday party." She turned and looked in the direction of the thinning dust plume. "And now he's gone."

Rusty forced his eyes to follow her gaze. "Sure, but he'll be back. Don't worry."

His attention returned to where the line of cars had been parked. With his right hand he twisted the penny in his pocket, making it click against his pocketknife.

"I think that was maybe the biggest line of cars Yates has ever seen, least since I've been here," he said.

Standing still in the shade he could feel sweat crawling from his armpits down his sides like an army of ants. The stiff shirt collar and necktie, even loosened, restricted his breathing. He felt heat coming from all directions, as if he was wrapped in a wet, hot blanket.

His neck felt too stiff to move. He twisted his body and looked directly at Rebekah's unblinking green eyes locked onto his face. Perfect curls of thin red hair escaped from beneath her bonnet, creating a frame for her pale face. He realized he was slightly taller than she, not counting the dark green bonnet she wore.

Rebekah turned to look at a group of townsfolk that included Frank LaFevre, gathered around the small bunch of Civil War veterans where flasks were passing from hand to hand.

"I hope your brother'll be back, Russell, I sure do hope so. I hope you're right. But so many boys die in wars, don't they."

Because she was no longer facing him, Rusty had to lean toward her to catch all of her words. When she unexpectedly turned in his direction, he found his face only inches from her lips.

"Oh, well now," she said.

He felt weak. He backed away and wanted to lean against the side of the railway station to keep from falling. His right hand reached up to fumble with the already unbuttoned collar of his shirt.

Rusty cleared his throat. "Well, I have to be getting home now." His words, barely above a whisper, struggled to escape his throat. "I have to change to my work clothes. I think I still have to make some deliveries for Mr. LaFevre. I think."

He shifted his eyes to look at Rebekah, who had lowered her head and seemed to be examining the handkerchief she laced through her fingers. As she tipped her head back, the edge of her bonnet lifted like a stage curtain and revealed her growing smile.

"Well, wonderful. I'm going off that same direction myself. Why don't we walk together?"

As they started to walk north on Railroad Street, Rebekah worked her left arm through Rusty's right, making his bare forearm feel like it was on fire. He stumbled and nearly stepped off the boardwalk. He looked down at Rebekah's arm, puzzled at how the strange coolness of its silky fabric entwined with his unprotected, dust-covered arm could start a fire that dried his mouth and made sweat run down his back.

He could feel his throat tighten. He swallowed twice, licked his dry lips, and looked down at her arm hooked through his. "Ah, Rebekah, do you think it proper to do that?"

"Oh my, you mean a big hero like yourself, having saved that colored family, is afraid of something? Anything?"

In mid-step, Rebekah halted. She reached up with her right hand and placed it on the back of his left arm, forcing him to face her.

"I mean, you're sort of Cliff's girl and all. I mean, that's what people say, anyway," he said. To him, his own words sounded as if they were coming from some faraway place.

Her grip on his bicep increased as she pulled him closer. Their faces were inches apart. She tilted her head a bit to the right and gave him a long, unblinking stare.

"Tell you what, Russell, why don't you just call me Edith? That way, I'll be a different person to you, and it won't seem like I'm Cliff's girl."

Rusty's eyelids twitched as he fought the urge to cut and run. He held her gaze. His tongue felt thick and trapped in his dry mouth. He was sure the scent of lavender was making him dizzy.

"Okay, I think I can do that," he managed.

In his own ears he sounded more like a frog croaking than a human speaking. He cleared his throat and tried again. "Sure. I mean, okay."

They resumed their walk and Rebekah turned to him. "How old are you, Russell?"

He knew her eyes were about to set the side of his face on fire just like he and Cliff used to do to ants using a magnifying glass. For a moment he thought he might not be able to respond. Her smile never seemed to change, and he knew her eyes could see inside his brain. He cleared his throat and hoped an answer to her question might appear on the tops of his dusty shoes. "Well, nearly seventeen, I guess."

He would really be sixteen in a couple months, but he didn't think it would matter to Rebekah. *And anyway, Ma wouldn't think it was a lie. She always says age is more of an attitude than a number.*

"Why you asking?" he said.

"Oh, just making conversation, I suppose," she said, giggling without looking at him.

Rusty tried to stop licking his lips. His breathing returned to normal as they turned onto Western Street and approached the Slocum house. He leaned toward the path that led to the back steps. There was no lessening of Rebekah's hold on him.

"Ah, this is where I live, Rebekah."

"Call me Edith. My name's Edith to you. Surely you haven't forgotten already?"

"Aaa, okay, Edith. This is where I live."

She did not move. He watched her sidelong glance survey the Slocum house.

"Russell, why don't you walk me all the way home?" Rebekah said. "I live just up the way there on Green Street."

Rusty watched her lick her lips, the pink tip of her tongue halting at the left corner of her mouth. He looked east toward where Green Street crossed Western and on to empty rail tracks in the distance, sure that a train must be coming because of the painful roaring in his ears.

"Russell? You look a bit pale. Too much heat?" Rebekah asked.

His mouth opened but no words came out of his dry throat. He could feel his knees shaking and knew he was going to fall, probably dead before his head hit the ground.

"Hey, Rusty! Hold up a minute."

A man's voice cut through Rusty's confusion. He turned in the direction of the caller and saw Frank LaFevre and another man approaching. At the same moment he felt Rebekah disengage her arm from his.

"Thank you for coming this far with me," she said without looking at him, and was gone.

Rebekah moved away from the approaching men as quickly as she could without making it appear like she was running. Home was the last place she wanted to be; however, it was safe. And besides, father would be full of questions about the ceremony in town, and his chamber pot would probably need to be emptied. She'd leave out her conversations with Cliff and Rusty, and just give him the details of who and what. Anything to talk about with him was welcome since she became his handmaiden two years ago.

As she'd done every day since her mother died, Rebekah kicked her mother's chair as she passed through the parlor on her way to her ailing father's bedroom. The invitation to Cynthia's wedding, propped on the mantel, caught her eye, and she wondered if she'd be free of her father's grasp long enough on Saturday to attend. Cynthia was the last of her friends to marry—not counting herself, of course. Her quartet of friends often joked about who would be the last to marry and the first to bear a child. More than once Rebekah feared she might be both.

"Is that you, daughter?" came the raspy call from the back of the house.

"Yes, father," she said and tossed her bonnet onto an empty chair. She avoided looking in the mirror next to the bookcase. Softly she added, "Who else would be wasting her life to care for you? Certainly not your other daughter."

As if he'd read her mind, or possibly heard what she said, her father called out, "I don't know what I'd do without you, daughter. Since your mother died and your sister—"

"I know Pop, I know," she said to cut off his apologies that at times ran on for five minutes. She paused before entering his room and held her hand across her mouth to muffle her habit of giggling at the wrong moment.

"Let me tell you about all the brave and excited young boys going off to war," she said.

Before she was halfway through her description of the ceremony he was asleep. Even when he relaxed she thought his face looked tight as a laced-up shoe. She took a deep breath and leaned over him, her hair creating a tent over her father's face, and gave him a kiss on the forehead.

Rusty watched Rebekah's swaying back go up the street.

"Rebekah Kern, huh?" Frank said.

"Yes sir. She, ah, wanted me to walk her home. That's all. Honest."

"I bet. Well, Rusty, this here's Mr. Gorham, Granville Gorham," Frank said, introducing the tall man at his side. "He's the ranch manager out at the Raleigh spread over near Hamilton. We were talking in town, and when he found out I knew you, well, he said he had to meet you and shake your hand."

"I don't get it," Rusty said, looking from one man to the other.

With no explanation, Granville reached out with a right hand as big as a pie plate and grabbed Rusty's. As the grip tightened, Rusty heard his knuckles crack, felt his fingers curl into a ball, and winced as pain shot into his elbow.

"Son, we've all heard about you saving that colored family from those crazy Hoffner brothers," Granville said.

"Oh, wasn't nothing, sir," Rusty said, looking first at Frank, then the ground. His lifeless hand hung at his right side.

"Right, I'm sure it wasn't," Granville said.

"Tom's my only friend around here. Well, he was."

"And a good one, too, I bet," Granville said.

"Yes sir."

Rusty could feel his mouth getting dry and tried to guess what this man, big enough to blot out the sun, might be thinking. Each time Granville moved, a flashing glare over the man's shoulder made Rusty squint his eyes and shift his feet a bit. The yellow straw of the cowboy's hat seemed to glow. Granville's mouth was hidden behind his huge mustache. When the man spoke his words seemed to float out of nowhere, making Rusty want to laugh. It reminded him of a ventriloquist he'd seen who never moved his lips, yet the words seemed to come out of the puppet he had on the stand next to him.

Granville said, "Ya gotta horse, son?"

"No sir, I mean, yes sir, I don't have a horse, now, or well ... I'm not real sure, is what I mean."

Granville removed his hat and ran a callused hand through his matted white hair. Rusty could see the man was smiling.

"Well, you might want to think about having a horse if you want to be a cowboy."

"What? How did you know I wanted to be a cowboy?"

Granville said nothing. He put his hat back on and looked down at Rusty.

"Mr. Raleigh owns the spread, the Rocking R," Granville said, "but I'm the ranch manager. My wife and daughter take care of Mr. Raleigh's house and the hands, I take care of his cattle. We heard about a young man here in town asking every soul there was about cowboy work, and we got plenty of that. Let me give you a word of advice: what you done here in town, with those colored folks, was the right thing. I know it and Mr. Raleigh knows it. Some of the other boys out there at the ranch might not think so, if you get my drift."

"How'd you hear about that?" Rusty said.

"We got telephones, you know," Granville said. "The ranch's not like some old dirt farm where the news takes a week to find its way under the front door. Now, about that horse?"

"Well, she's up at my Uncle George's place, George Hardy, so I'd have to get her, well, borrow her, from Uncle George first. If he lets me, I mean."

"So, you're part of the Hardy clan? George is the kinda fellow who'd stop and talk to horses if they had the right to vote. Now, Belle Hardy, she taught my daughter in school. She's one of the finest women you'll ever meet," Granville said.

Rusty leaned forward, rocking up on his toes. "Are you saying I have a job, sir?"

"That's what ya come west for, wasn't it?" Granville said.

"Of course! I mean, yes sir. Thank you, sir. Thanks much. You mean I'm going to get to be a cowboy?" He wanted to reach out and shake hands again, but the pain in his right hand flashed in his mind. His hand retreated to the safety of his pocket.

"Well, we'll start ya out kinda slow for the first few years, then see how ya work out," Granville said.

"Years?" Rusty said, his voice louder than he meant.

"Take it from me, son, and I been out here since the '80s, cowboyin' ain't something you want to rush into. More than oncest I wished I was back in Indiana, farming—"

"You from Indiana, too?"

"Yep. Came out here with my brother John and family in '82, from Windfall. Know of it?"

"Nope, but I'm from Kendallville. Came out to Woodson County with my brother, Cliff, back in '16 and—"

"That's hardly more than a year ago, kid," Granville interrupted, silencing Rusty.

He cleared his throat and continued, "Well then, you best be gathering up that mare of yours and talk to the trail boss, Sam Hancock, down at the bunk house about where you can toss your stuff, if you have any stuff. Good luck to ya, son."

Rusty held his breath and tightened his butt muscles when he thought of the bone-crushing handshake he knew was coming, then extended his hand. He knew to not offer his hand would be considered impolite.

Through clinched teeth he said, "Yes sir. I'm glad, for lots of reasons, to be getting this chance."

CHAPTER NINE

Cowboyin'

"Well, well. Would you look at what the wind uprooted and blew all the way to this end of Woodson County?"

"Hey, Aunt Belle."

"Hey yourself, stranger. What brings you up here? Or maybe I should ask, how you'd get up here?"

"Shank's mare, mostly."

Belle smiled. "Good way to wear out a pair of boots."

Rusty stood facing his aunt, hands in his pockets. A balmy wind ruffled his hair and pressed against his chest, making him sway toward, then away, from Belle. He looked up into his aunt's face. The sun behind her created an auburn halo around her features. Her hair was so thick he wanted to reach out and touch it. He pushed his hands deeper into his pockets and watched chickens busy themselves beneath the porch steps. He drew in a deep breath.

"Gosh, this place sure smells better than town," he said.

"Heard about what you did a couple weeks back, Russell. With that Washington family, I mean."

"Yeah."

"It was a good thing, Russell. The right thing."

"You're one of the few people in the county that thinks so, then."

"No, I think the Washingtons are thankful."

A slight gust of wind flapped the sleeves of his shirt, making a sound like pigeons rising from the ground.

"Maybe. Tom's family's left Yates. Heading north to be with their own people. A place called Nicodemus. I heard of it before from Jupiter, my friend from the trains."

Belle tilted her head and looked away from Rusty, west to where the land dropped toward agreeable rolling hills green with the promise of tallgrass.

"Too bad," she said.

"I'm about the only one in the county that would agree with you, Aunt Belle. Tom is the only friend I have in this place—had."

"Hmm. Bet they'd made good neighbors if someone gave them the chance."

He couldn't answer. His throat felt closed, his tongue trapped against the roof of his mouth.

Rumbling sounds of a wagon replaced the susurrations of the wind. Rusty turned to see George leading a team of horses up the lane toward the house. He looked at Belle, her eyes locked on her husband's face.

"Afternoon, young man."

"Hey, Uncle George."

"Just heard from Frank LaFevre that the sheriff arrested those Hoffner brothers for that business out on West Mary Street."

"It wasn't business, Uncle George. They tried to burn down the house with Tom, his ma, and baby sister in it. What kinda business is killing?"

Rusty saw George shift his eyes to Belle, who stood, arms crossed, still looking at her husband. She broke off her stare and looked at the ground as she slipped her hands into the pockets of her apron.

"Bad business, son. Bad business," said George. "But you have to understand how some folks feel about niggers."

"I'm sort of catching on to the idea that not everyone has to feel the same about some things," Rusty said.

"Yeah, well, Frank told me about you meeting up with Granville Gorham, boss over at the Raleigh spread, too," George said and looked up at Belle.

Rusty released his breath. "Mr. Gorham offered me a cowboy job. A real cowboy job, if I have a horse. Which is why I come out here to talk with you about Sandy."

"Russell, are you sure Kansas is the right place for you? Maybe it's time you thought about heading back east, back to Kendallville. Just for a while, I mean. Until you get your schooling and until this war's over and Cliff gets back and the two of you—"

"Ain't gonna happen," Rusty said, cutting off his uncle. He licked his lips, cleared his throat, and forced himself to look at his uncle's lined face. "I'd appreciate it, sir, I would, if you could loan me Sandy. I'll figure some way to pay you. Please?"

"Sure. We'll figure it out," George said.

George watched Rusty walk toward the barn. The familiar honking of geese overhead drew his attention skyward. He said to Belle, "He'll get over it. He'll wake up some morning and smell the bullshit of cowboy life, not the coffee."

Belle looked at her husband, then turned her eyes on Rusty's back as the young man entered the barn.

"That's mighty poetic for a guy I have to tell to remove his boots just about every time he comes into my kitchen."

"Humph."

"But I'm not so sure about him, George. He might not give in as easily as some I know."

George released a short laugh. "In that case, I'd say he does not have the makings of a politician."

Belle looked at him. "Again, not like some I know."

Sun was in Rusty's eyes by the time he rode through the entrance gate of the Rocking R Ranch the next day. He slowed as he reached out to touch the left set post as he entered. He brought Sandy to a halt at a watering trough just inside the gate. The smell of creosote bush filled the air. Birds, buried deep in the grass, sang unfamiliar songs. In the distance loomed the largest house he'd ever seen. From the ground up he counted four rows of windows. Two front doors and a porch that stretched the length of the house made all of stone. From this distance, in the heat of the afternoon the sandstone house seemed to float above the waving tallgrass, shimmering as if alive.

He looked at his dusty trousers and scarred boots. His saddle creaked as he twisted to take in the view. Nothing but grass, some just barely poking out of the ground and some in the far-off pastures that appeared as tall as himself. Nothing else. No cattle. No cowboys. Just the conversation insects were having with the wind.

Sandy suddenly stopped drinking and jerked to the right, and Rusty's attention was quickly brought down from the rolling sea of green.

"Whoa, girl."

"Looks to me like she's already whoad there, young man," came a friendly voice.

Rusty turned and looked down at the widest mustache he'd ever seen. Twisted strands of gray-black hair reached out beyond the borders of the man's face in curves so large they reminded him of handlebars on a bicycle. A pointy nose equally divided the halves of the mustache. Two dark eyes looked straight at him out of skin the color of saddle leather. A wide-brimmed, dust-laden black hat produced enough shade for the mustache and the man attached to it. The cowboy was braced against the wind, feet apart, thumbs looped behind his belt buckle.

"Where'd you come from?" Rusty managed.

The cowboy just smiled, then said, "You want me to have Minnie bring you your meals up there or are you going to climb down from that saddle and join the rest of the hands at the bunk house table?"

"Oh ... oh, sure," Rusty said, wrapping the reins around the saddle horn as he dismounted.

"Name's Sam," the cowboy said. "Around here you'll answer to me until I'm dead, which could be any minute now, and then you'll answer to someone not half as nice, or half as good lookin'."

"Oh, I'm, ah, Rusty, err Russell Starke, that is," Rusty said, reaching out to shake hands, remembering too late Granville Gorham's crushing handshake.

"Yep. I know who you are and I'm glad you're here."

Rusty's hand stopped moving when he saw that Sam had only three fingers to shake with.

Sam looked down at his own hand. "Don't believe what these lazy cowboys around here tell you about where my fingers went. I got froze up one winter and the doc had to cut them off. I really didn't eat 'em. Best close your mouth now and take your horse there down to the corral for some feed. Got a name?"

"Yes sir, it's Rusty, I thought I said—"

"I'm not talkin' about you, son. I'm talkin' to the horse there."

"Oh, yes sir. Her name's Sandy. But she's shy around strangers so I have to do the talking for her."

Sam laughed, clapped his hands together, and lashed out with his right hand, slapping Rusty on the arm so hard, the boy spun around and struggled to keep from falling.

"You go on ahead down to the barn, Rusty. I have to check the gate here. Be along shortly."

Sam Hancock watched the new kid move down the path toward the bunkhouse. He looked at his hands, as weather-beaten as the set post he pressed them against. When the boy was out of sight he turned toward the setting sun and gasped for breath. He pressed his right hand against his chest to slow his pounding heart and wondered if this was how a heart attack would feel.

It's just not possible. Jeff's dead and buried and this is just some punk kid from Indiana who happens to look exactly like him. That's all it is. Can't be anything else. Cowboys might be superstitious but they don't believe in ghosts—not live ones anyways.

Most of Sam's life had been saved or directed by simple negligence. Ever since his father died from some disease he picked up helping out on the battlefields during the war, and his mother passed on a few years later, Sam had been a drifter. He did what needed to be done since he was ten years old. Even if tragedy had engulfed most of his achievements, he felt he was a fair trail boss and didn't deserve to be bothered by ghosts or haints.

He closed his eyes and tried to make his son Jeff's image disappear. Sam had been hunkered down while waiting for the kid to show up, lost in the pungent aroma and examination of the yellow flowers he'd mashed with the heel of his boot. What had Jeff told him people back east called these yellowy-orange flowers? Then the clatter and clack of horse's hooves on flint rock cut through the silence and reached him before he'd seen the rider—this new kid.

Heat pushed against Sam's back. He wiped sweat from his forehead with his shirtsleeve and tugged on his hat to keep it from becoming hostage to the wind. He stepped on several more prairie marigold blossoms with the toe of his boot and wondered why otherwise savvy cattle would eat them and get sick. *Another question I'll never know the answer to. Just like why does a boy, smart enough go to Harvard College, want to be a cowboy and wind up dead.*

Sam felt air from his lungs race to beat his throat's constriction. This Rusty's sandy-colored hair, blue eyes, and small scar above the left eyebrow were the same as Jeff's. He could feel the sweat start down his back when he thought of how this kid looked at him with that same big smile.

The worse part, the thing that made his mouth go dry, was the way the kid got off his horse. Jeff was the only person he'd seen dismount by swinging his right leg over the horn of the saddle rather than the cantle, then drop to the ground.

Movement next to him on the road caught his attention. He realized he'd been thinking too much about things past. A rattlesnake lifted its triangular head out of its circle of coils. It lay no more than two good steps away. The tallgrass had offered the animal some shade and concealment. Now what it perceived as danger had moved too close.

"Apparently you were smart enough to stop and examine the road ahead, then?" he said to the snake.

The snake's dry, hiss-like rattle sputtered and tapered to blend with the sound of crickets hidden in the grass.

"Good idea there, buster," Sam said. "Stop and check for danger before you stick your neck out too far, and stop talking after you've made your point. Any suggestion of how I'm going to handle my current problem?"

The snake's head did not move, its eyes locked on Sam. Its tongue flicked in the air and its warning rattle sounded again. Sam stood motionless and took in the smell of marigolds mixed with the odor of his sweat.

"So what you're telling me is, I say my piece, warn this kid about cowboy life, then back away. That live and let live crap my pa used to talk about. Thanks for the help, sir," Sam said and kept his thumbs looped behind his belt buckle as he cautiously stepped back and to the side, never taking his eyes off the coiled snake.

The canvas newspaper boy's bag bounced on the wire springs of the narrow cot, sent up a cloud of dust, and made a clanging sound that echoed in the cavernous room. Two dozen beds in all stages of being unmade lined the walls. An assortment of men's pants, shirts, and underwear hung from nails. A collection of scarred boots in two shades, black and muddy, lay between the bunks or spilled into the middle of the room. A large soot-stained wood-burning stove, shaped like a metal pumpkin, sat at the far end of the bunkhouse. High along the side walls dirty windows filtered the only source of light. A scarred wooden table, guarded by two dozen unmatched chairs, divided the room. A single bunk at the far end of the room was the only one neatly made up by its owner. Next to that bunk Rusty could see what appeared to be a small table and a hairbrush.

Sam entered the bunkhouse while Rusty unrolled the white-and-gray striped mattress on the only unclaimed cot. As he did, three mice scurried out and down the leg of the bed and across the floor.

"Don't worry about them mice," Sam said. "They only eat what the hands drop on the floor. The smart cowboy, if he doesn't want mice in his face all night, doesn't bring biscuits or anything away from the table."

"I lived in a dugout for a while," Rusty said.

"Then I needn't tell you about mice."

"This will be perfect, Sam. Perfect. I can't believe I'm going to be a real cowboy."

"Yeah, real enough," Sam said, looking down the length of the room to the made up bunk nearest the far door.

Rusty's eyes met Sam's. He thought the trail boss was waiting for him to say something, he just didn't know what.

Sam broke the silence. "Well, the hands will be coming back from their day in town shortly. I won't stick around for introductions. Best you do that yourself. Try and get some sleep tonight. Don't let these cowboys keep you up with their card playing when they come in. We'll get you to work first thing. Minnie'll be down here with coffee and toast. We get bacon and eggs on the weekends if things go well."

"Right, sir." Rusty's face hurt from smiling and he knew sleep would be a long way off.

Rusty woke but could not sit up. The silence in the oven-like bunkhouse hurt his ears. His arms and legs would not move. He looked down the length of his body. During the night someone had tied him to the bunk. *Oh, god!* He looked left and right. There, on the middle beam near the ceiling, he saw his clothes. They'd been stuffed with newspaper and hung with a hangman's noose. *Holy shit! My first day as a real live cowboy and I'm going to be late. Oh shit!*

The rope wrapped around his right arm was loose. He worked his hand free and was able to untie the knots around his left hand

and feet. When he tossed back the sheet he saw that someone had painted pictures of Indian teepees, buffalos, and horses all over his body. When had this happened? *How come I didn't wake up while all this was going on?*

He freed his clothes from the hangman's noose, dressed, and ran from the dinginess of the bunkhouse into the glare of the morning sun. He halted on the porch, trying to shade his eyes and button his shirt. *No time for that.* With his head down, he jumped from the steps toward the commotion in the corral, unaware of the young woman coming around the corner of the bunkhouse carrying a tray of coffee cups. Rusty's left foot landed in fresh horse droppings. As he slipped, he caught sight of the woman and spun to avoid crashing into her. They passed so close that his open shirt brushed against her sleeve.

"Hey!" she called out, also spinning in a circle to prevent the tray from spilling.

"Sorry ma'am," he said without looking back.

He got as far as the watering trough near the corral gate, dropped to his knees, cupped his hands, and drank, splashing tepid water onto this face.

"I'll toss ya a bar of soap and you can finish the job," came a voice from overhead.

Rusty gasped and looked up at a man on horseback smiling at him.

"Sorry, mister. I just needed a drink."

"Take all ya want, kid. Looks like you could use it. Don't mind a bit. Just save some for the horses. 'Course, ya know, most horses do spit some back when they take a drink from that trough."

As the rider moved back into the corral, Rusty looked down at bits of straw, bugs, and things he could not identify floating in the water.

Thirst forgotten, he scrambled along the fence toward the roiling sounds of bawling cattle, thumping horses' hooves, and shouting men. Dust clouds floated in the corral, hiding the action on the far side. The faint jangle of rowels on the cowboys' spurs brought back memories of sleigh rides with his sisters back home.

Another shadow fell over Rusty. He shaded his eyes enough to see a cowboy looming on the other side of the fence. The man's wrinkled, sunburned skin looked as dark as his caramel-colored saddle. White scars on the right side of his face looked like three fishing worms trying to crawl into his sideburns. Three equally spaced scars on the left were as straight as shooting stars. Rusty watched the cowboy's gnarled hands struggle to pull a tobacco pouch and rolling papers from his left shirt pocket. The man cradled the rolling papers between the first and second fingers of his left hand because he was missing a thumb. He tipped the tobacco pouch, spilling more than he loaded onto the paper. Rusty could see the little finger of his right hand was frozen at an angle pointing away from the rest of his crooked fingers.

When the cowboy finally got his smoke rolled, the paper licked and lit, a cloud of smoke exited his mouth and reentered his body through his nose, igniting a paroxysm of coughing. The smoke rushed back out, making him look like dragons Rusty'd seen in picture books. The man cleared his throat and spit in the direction of the fence post close to Rusty's feet.

Rusty cleared his throat, spit on the ground, and without taking his eyes off the action of the working cowboys, said, "Ya know mister, back home we have ready-mades now. Sure would be easier for you than rollin' a smoke."

No answer. Rusty took a deep breath and looked up at the cowboy. The man faced him, his eyes so squinted that Rusty couldn't determine their color. Mud spattered rivulets coursed down the man's face and disappeared into his mustache. Circling the crown of the cowboy's pearl-gray hat was a band of alternating colors—red, yellow, white, and black—a snake's skin. The snake's head had no eyes and its teeth were biting into its own tail.

"Yer not from around these parts, are you, kid?" the cowboy said.

Rusty lowered his head, unsure if that was a question. "No sir, but I'm gonna be. I just hired on."

"Shit." The cowboy released a long-held breath, shook his head, and sent a clucking signal to his horse.

Rusty watched this man with the busted hands ride back into the herd, cigarette dangling from the corner of his mouth, ashes dropping onto the front of his black shirt. Even though he heard Sam's approach, he kept his eye on the cowboy.

"There's good cowboys and there's bad cowboys, and then there's cowboys like old Snake over there," Sam said, following Rusty's gaze.

"Morning Sam. Well, I'd choose to be a cowboy just like whatshisname, then."

He waited while Sam surveyed the action in the corral.

"Decide to get a few extra winks your first day on the job, did you?" Sam said.

"Oh, I'm sorry, sir. It wasn't my fault, honest. The hands must have tied me up sometime during the night and painted pictures all over me. I never knew it was going on. Honest."

"Yeah, sure. That's what they all say," Sam said, kicking at the ground and looking to his left to hide his smile.

A snorting steer drew Rusty's attention back to the corral. "Why's that guy—did you say his name was Snake?—cough so much? Does he have that name because of his hatband?"

"Yep. It's a coral snake. Deadliest sumanabitch God ever made. Story goes that Snake there used to ride herd down in Argentina. One night, fueled by alcohol I'd wager, he bet the other hands he could catch a snake with his teeth."

"And he lived through it?"

"Well, it would appear so, doesn't it," Sam said as he tapped his fist against the rail and again looked away from Rusty. "You won't learn anything by watching. We should get you out there in the action."

Rusty looked back at the corral, put his hands into his pockets, and said, "Well, great Sam. But I think I'm already picking up on some of the cowboy ways."

"Oh, what's that, now?"

"Well, it seems that the horse does most of the work in getting those cows—"

"Call 'em steers, son, or the hands'll think you're from Indiana or someplace."

"I am from—"

"What else ya learning?" Sam said, and again had to turn away so Rusty wouldn't see his smile.

"Well, it seems most cowboys are missing something, you know, like ..."

Rusty hesitated. He looked at the calluses on his palms and the dirt trapped under his finger nails and thought about Sam's missing fingers when they shook hands the day before. He decided enough had been said.

"Yeah, well, most cowboys come furnished with only half a brain so God gave 'em ten fingers so's they could at least count to nine."

Rusty looked over at Sam's right hand still jammed in his pocket. He swallowed hard and turned his attention back to the action in the corral.

"Is Snake a bad guy?" asked Rusty. "He sure looks and rides like he's a real cowboy. Like the ones I seen in the magazines back home anyway."

"Bad? Guess that depends on who you ask. I say he's neither good or bad, same as a gun's not good or bad. I once heard someone say that Snake was the kind of guy even the police were afraid of. Around here, he's the best there is. I've known him a long time and we put him on a while ago to help with the younger—" Sam stopped.

"Maybe I could partner with him and learn something," Rusty said. "I bet if we worked together I could learn all about being a cowboy."

"Maybe you could son, maybe you could. Go get your horse and we'll see."

Later in the week Sam stood with his forearms against the top rail of the corral fence and rested a boot on the bottom rail. He watched Rusty hold back from two aggressive steers, but was pleased to see the kid's eyes follow every move of the experienced hands as they sorted out the herd. His attention was on the activity in the corral and he did not hear Granville approach.

"Morning Sam," Granville said. "That kid afraid to step between two 1,500-pound beasts with killing on their minds?"

Sam looked to his right. Steam from the ranch manager's coffee cup rose in a tight swirl and was momentarily trapped beneath the brim of his hat. His boss was carrying his usual long list of things that had to get done written on the back of an envelope.

"Morning Granville. Yep, the kid hasn't gone stupid on us yet. But it's still early."

"How's he working out?" Granville asked.

"Been on the job three days now, pays attention to what's going on around him, hasn't fallen off his horse, and shows no signs of quitting. Guess he's off to a good start. Damn, that coffee smells good, boss."

He turned his attention back to the action in the corral and listened as Granville sucked in a long drink. After twenty-five years of friendship, he knew without looking that Granville would be examining the dirt on his jacket. He'd probably get a lecture about being too old to be punching cows.

"How'd ya get dirt on that jacket Minnie spent hours washing for you?" Granville said.

"Don't know, boss. Must have brushed against an alligator or something."

"Humph," Granville said and bumped Sam with his shoulder. "The kid there remind you of anybody?"

"Nope," Sam said, looking down at the ground. He could feel Granville's eyes on him.

"Not even that scar above his left eyebrow? The hair? Or the way he gets off a horse?"

"Nope. Nobody, Granville. Not even my dead son. Nobody."

"I thought the same thing first time I saw him, Sam. He looked so much like Jeff I nearly shit my pants. Fact is, when we spoke, I nearly called him Jeff a couple times."

Sam examined the dust on top of his boot. "Scary, ain't it? It's almost like Jeff has come back to the ranch. He's smart like Jeff was, too. Too smart to be wasting time out here learning something that probably won't mean much in a few years."

"I could fire him just as easy," Granville said.

Sam turned and dropped his head a bit to see beneath the brim of Granville's hat. The ranch manager was a head shorter and always wore the widest brim hats Sam had ever seen. He grinned when he thought about the fistfight they'd had twenty-five years ago in a bar south of Wichita—when he said Granville was all hat and no horse.

"You better be smilin' when you say that, Granville. I plan to bring this young one up right. That means a short, sweet career as a cowboy."

Granville returned the smile, cleared his throat, and said, "You didn't do anything wrong with Jeff, ya know. College was the right idea. Cowboying was the right idea, too."

"So you say. Martha didn't see it exactly the same way before she took off with that drummer after the accident. What I did wrong was give the boy too much time in the saddle."

Sam looked toward the loading chute and the bull board that spanned the gap between the end of the chute and the floor of the cattle car.

"It *was* my fault, Granville. I shoulda told him he had to stay in school and not come back for loading that year. It *was* my fault, but I'm fixin' to change that kinda attitude with this lad."

Granville watched the corral action through steam curling up from his coffee. "Care to share your plan?"

"I'm gonna partner him up with old Henry Ellsworth for the rest of the season. A month or so of that, come roundup time, I think our young farmer from Indiana will be so sick of cowboying he'll be running to catch the next train back east."

"Partner with Snake? Sounds like a hell of a lot more grease than what's required to stop the squeaky wheel, Sam. I'm not sure who it will be toughest on, the kid or Snake."

"Don't worry, boss. Snake has already threatened to castrate me if I let that kid get within fifty feet of him. I think they'll make swell trail buddies."

Sam thought of all the years he'd known Henry Ellsworth, from their first meeting at Gettysburg to their chance meeting in a bar in '98, to the day he hired the man who had come to be called Snake someplace in Argentina. Whatever the stories, when it came to moving cattle, Snake rode like his pants were stitched to the horse's hide.

"Ever wonder if the stories they tell about old Henry are true?" Sam said.

Granville shook his head, drained the last of his coffee, and examined the bottom of his cup. "Well, I got a ranch to run. All I really care about is how he manages the herd today. What he did in the past, where he goes in the winter, and what he plans to do with the rest of his miserable life is no concern of mine," Granville said. "Now I'm heading up to the house for more coffee. Want me to bring some back for you?"

Before Sam could answer, both men caught sight of Minnie walking toward them carrying a tray with two steaming cups of coffee and two large slices of bread.

"Morning gents!" she said.

"An angel without the wings," said Sam as he reached for the coffee with one hand and a slice of bread with the other.

"Morning daughter. Didn't know you could read my mind from that far away," Granville said.

"It wasn't your mind that I read, Dad. I just watched until the steam stopped coming out of your ears and knew you needed a refill."

Granville gave a soft laugh. "Tell me, Sam, are these young people getting smarter or are us old dogs just slowing down some?"

Sam had his eye on Rusty struggling to unfurl his rope. "Speak for yourself, old dog. Meanwhile, looks like I'll have to teach that new pup a few old tricks."

Sam turned to Minnie and asked, "How's your mama doing this morning?"

Minnie smoothed the front of her apron and looked back at the house before answering. Sam noticed she glanced at her father out of the corner of her eye. "Oh, I guess she's about the same, Sam. Says she'll be up and at 'em in a day or so. We're not counting on it though, are we Dad?"

Granville straightened, looked at his daughter, and cleared his throat before answering. "We'll see what God has in store for her today. Don't you have chores to get to, daughter?"

Minnie ducked her head to look between the rails of the corral fence. "Oh, there's that new kid I had to work into the meal plan."

"Yep. Name's Rusty," Granville said. "I don't think you've met him. The kid seems to have more guts than brains, but Sam here has a plan to break him of the cowboy habit in only one season, then send him packing back to Indiana."

"Huh. I think I nearly ran over him a couple days ago. Reminds me a bit of Jeff for some reason."

The two men continued to watch the action in the corral. Minnie said, "Sam, how long's Jeff been gone?"

"It'll be seven years this fall," Granville said before Sam could answer. "Seems like yesterday. You were what, only about ten then? You weren't sweet on him, were you?"

"Come on, Dad. I hardly knew what a boy was good for back then."

"And now?"

"And now I read a lot," Minnie said as she turned and moved toward the house. When she reached the back porch she stopped and looked back toward the corral. She could see that the new hand was off his horse talking with Sam. He appeared to be paying attention—always a good sign.

Henry Ellsworth opened his left eye while the right stayed buried in the rolled shirt he preferred to use as a pillow. He surveyed the length of the bunkhouse, its two dozen snoring men and one kid. His gaze moved to the dirt-encased windowpane. A hint of daylight pushed against the glass, trying to enter and change the look of the walls and floor hidden beneath scattered shirts, pants, underwear, and boots.

Mornings had never been the favorite part of the day for Henry. He thought about how other cowboys looked forward to morning and a strong cup of coffee. Or how that damned kid down there in the middle row said he liked mornings because that's when the birds sing loudest and best. Shit.

For Henry, ever since Gettysburg, morning was a time for guilt: a time when he could not wash away personal losses no matter how much hot water and Lava soap he used. He tossed back the thin blanket and looked over the edge of the bunk to check the floor for scorpions before he rested his bare feet. He rubbed his face with his gnarled hands and looked, again, at the brightening window. Sunrise was a curse to him, not some fancy planetary event when the birds sang.

As senior cowhand, Henry had privileges the regulars had not earned—a bunk nearest the door, and more space between him and that fat Reynolds guy who was about as useful as pockets on a shroud. He looked at the chicken crate he used as a nightstand. It held nothing of value, except the hairbrush that never looked as clean as it did that day the woman in Argentina gave it to him. He sat as he did most mornings when sober, waiting for the sun to burn away the shadows in the room and better define its contents. He waited as long as he could, to see which demon, the one quieted with a cigarette, or the one that demanded he take a piss, would grab him and force him into his boots and out the door.

He halted on the bottom step of the bunkhouse searching through the morning gloom, knowing the cough would start. God, he hated this day before it even started. His eyes examined the shadows of the house, the barn, the posts of the corral as he walked to the nearest fence post to pee. Shadows felt like friends, protecting him from the glaring parts of the day.

"Great morning, ain't it, Mr. Snake!" Rusty said as he walked up next to Henry and fumbled with the buttons on his trousers.

Henry shook his head and looked off across the still tallgrass, its tips signaling the arrival of the sun. He said nothing. He sucked in a stream of smoke and tried to preview what positive thing might happen next to give him reason to get dressed for the day.

"I mean, just look at that big old red rubber ball of a sun over there. And smell that air!"

"Christ kid, don't you ever shut up?" Henry said. He dropped his lighted cigarette into the puddle he'd just created and tipped his head back, enjoying the hissing sound it made.

"Sorry sir, just making conversation."

"Well, talk about nothing or something other than morning. No tweeting goddamned birds."

"Oh, well, my ma always likes mornings. Says that it's the start of a whole new day of possibility."

"Shit. First off, I hear tell your ma is dead. Right?"

"Yes sir."

"Second off, morning is nothing more than a bad time that'll pass if you don't let it get its hooks into you."

Henry felt the kid's eyes boring a hole into the side of his face. The longer the kid looked at him the more conscious he became of standing there in his underwear and boots, not even wearing his goddamned hat, for god's sake. He looked down and met the kid's stare.

He cleared his throat and said, "I heard a bad rumor last night, kid. Sam's got me and you working together, starting maybe tomorrow or the next day."

"Yes sir, it's a true rumor. Of course, it may be just plain bad luck on your part, I guess."

Henry turned in the direction of the bunkhouse, hiding his smile from the kid. "Shit then, best we get on it."

Three days later Rusty got his first taste of what cowboy life would be like. He couldn't tell if it was early morning or late night as he stood on the top step of the bunkhouse stairs waiting for his eyes to adjust to the dark. He looked at the stars overhead, trying to imagine pictures of animals he'd seen in books at school. *Dumb pictures. There's so many stars up there, no way can you draw lines and see bears or lions or whatever it was Miss Zerkle said the ancient people drew.*

This was going to be the greatest day of his life. He and Snake were going to ride fence, all day, just like real cowboys. The light of a half moon was enough for him to find his way to the barn. Stillness filled the area around the building. Coming from inside he could hear movement in the back corner. *Probably Snake getting the equipment.* They had agreed to leave before sunup, so to be sure he'd be ready, he slept in his clothes as he'd seen Snake do most nights.

"Kid?" came a growl from the dark interior.

"Yes sir. And it's Rusty. I ain't a kid. I hopped a freight—"

"Okay, Rusty. Let's get this straight from the git go: no talking when we're riding."

"But sir, that's most of the day."

"Right. And no talk before sunrise in case we ain't on our horses by then."

"But I—"

"Look kid, err, Rusty. God gave you one mouth and two ears for a reason. And he pointed your eyes the same direction as your toes for the same reason."

Rusty looked at his feet, then in the direction of the voice, and strained to see what Snake was doing.

"Shit, Snake, you ain't making this sound like it'll be much fun."

"None of being a cowboy is fun. It's work, unless they hired you for some other job," Snake said. "Well, I guess the shipping of the steers is fun since we know that the work part is over."

"What should we do first?"

"First we do the boring stuff, patching some fence down near the Carter place."

"Okay. Then what?"

There was a long pause before Snake said anything. Rusty heard cattle grunting and moving in the nearby corral.

"Then, how about we rest? Another thing," Snake said. "By the looks of that bag you're carrying, you have too much stuff."

"But, I—"

"Listen, if you have more stuff than you can roll up and stash behind your saddle you're not a cowboy. You're a goddamned tourist. And this won't be some kind of vacation we're going on."

He heard Snake release a long breath. The scrape and snap of a match told him Snake had been rolling a smoke and was lighting up. Next would come the long cough and lots of spitting. Rusty watched the tip of the lighted cigarette moving among the saddles on the rail. Occasional flares in the smoke were enough for him to see that Snake was wearing his black shirt, as usual.

"With my first pay I'm going to buy me one of those black shirts, Snake," he said to the darkness.

"Shit," came the reply.

He heard Snake walk toward him and realized the man was carrying two saddles, bits, and bridles. "You coming or do I have to send you a special invitation so you'll be dressed properly?" Snake said from the corner of his mouth.

With each word Rusty could see the red tip of the cigarette bounce up and down, swinging like the far-off lantern of a trainman.

"Oh, yes sir. I just have to get—"

"I got it, whatever it is you think you need. What we need to get is going."

"Yes sir. I'll go up to the house to see if Miss Minnie has coffee we can—"

"We're leaving. Now!"

They didn't leave, however. Snake started hacking and coughing. In the dim light Rusty could see the older man stagger under the weight of the saddles and tack. He reached out to grab the saddles as Henry's knees started to bend. The saddle hammers and staple pouches Snake held under his arm hit the floor, staples spilling in all directions.

"Christ almighty," Snake said through spasms of coughing.

Rusty dropped the saddles and tack on the floor and with his bare hands began sweeping the staples back into the pouches. He did not look up at Snake, now resting his forehead on his arm that pressed against the barn door frame.

Rusty waited until the coughing stopped before he said, "You know, Snake, you should have the doc give you something for that cough."

"Kid, we don't talk about nothing until after the sun is up and never when we're in the saddle. Understand? You already broke enough rules to get yourself shot by someone not as nice as me."

Rusty looked at the mix of straw and sawdust that covered floor. It felt soft under his boots. In the stillness he listened to Snake's slow breathing. The rich aroma of cigarette tobacco mixed with the smell of new-cut hay.

"Snake, maybe there's things you should tell me about cowboying—before we head out, I mean."

No answer, just the sound of deep breathing mixed with a soft rattle coming from Snake's chest. Rusty thought of the rattling sound Ma made when she slept. And that last time when the rattle lost its rhythm and got really loud. In the dim light he saw Snake sit on a bale of straw. The man was looking down at his boots and rubbing his two disfigured hands on his jeans.

"Did Sam ever tell you about Jeff?" Snake asked from the darkness.

"Huh? What? Who?"

"Jeff, Sam's boy?"

"Ah, no sir. I didn't know he had a boy."

"He don't, anymore. The kid's dead. Been dead maybe seven years, now."

Rusty scratched at the side of his neck. As his eyes adjusted to the darkness of the barn, he could see the row of saddles silhouetted along the rail, stacks of straw bales falling apart where cowboys had rested on them, and chickens still roosting in the rafters. Even though there were no animals in the barn at this time of the year, he could smell cow piss and manure that had soaked into the stalls and floor over the years.

He turned toward the low moan of a Mourning Dove and the rustle of Snake's shirt.

"Dead?"

"Yep. Died trying to be a cowboy, like you. He was about your age, maybe a bit older since he was in college. It was an accident. Nobody's fault, really. Least that's what Granville said and I want to believe."

As Snake told the story it seemed simple enough, one of the many ways a cowboy could get hurt if he didn't pay attention to what was going on around him. It happened during loading season. Snake had seen the bull board, a panel that spanned the gap between the railcar and the loading chute, start to slip. He ran under it to push it back into place and Jeff had followed. The board slipped, a steer crashed through and landed on them, killing Jeff and leaving a few more scars on Snake.

A fit of coughing ended the story. Rusty waited for Snake to continue. When he finished wiping his mouth, Rusty realized the conversation was over. Snake turned and walked out of the barn into the gloom of the morning.

"Snake?"

"We don't talk before sunrise and not when we're in the saddle. Let's get saddled up before the sun shows its chicken-yellow face. And the name's Henry."

"Okay, Henry. But if you don't teach me about being a cowboy, how do I learn?"

"Just keep your mouth shut and your eyes open," Henry said and spit into the darkness.

"But I—"

"Mouth shut. Eyes open. *Comprende?*"

It was two hours before they stopped to examine some sagging barbed wire that should have been stretched tight between the fence posts. Rusty watched Henry look in both directions at the sagging wire. Without dismounting Henry said, "Goddamned devil's hatband, we used to call that stuff. I'd rather we just cut it all down, make it like the old days, and let the damned steers eat whatever they sink their rotting yellow teeth into."

"I guess Mr. Raleigh thinks otherwise," Rusty said.

Henry swung off his saddle, landed on the ground without making a sound, and said, "Shit. That he does, lad. That he does."

Rusty looked more closely at the post and realized it was stone, not wood like all the other posts he'd seen. "Henry, that post is a rock. How we going to staple the wire back on?"

Henry had removed his saddle hammer from its leather keeper and was digging a staple from his pouch. "Well, there's not much difference between those hedge posts there and these old stone posts except that the stone posts are easier to drive a staple into," he said. "Now get down here and pull that wire taut."

For the next few days Rusty was up each morning long before the sun and not back in the bunkhouse until after dark. By the third evening he thought his arms would fall off if he had to pull one more strand of barbed wire while Henry drove in staples. Occasionally, while working in the pasture, a long-horned steer would walk over to examine the job.

"Henry, do those steers ever get angry at cowboys and, you know, try to hurt you?"

Henry looked up from the debris caught in the water gap they were repairing and said, "I've seen a few take exception to being hit with a whip. I suppose they'd all be a bit upset if they were smart enough to know where the next stop was going to be. Now, you going to get down here and hold this fence panel back or worry about what some dumb animal is thinking?"

Rusty waded into the water and leaned his back against the swinging panel of the fence that spanned the creek. He could feel his boots digging into the mud as Henry pulled and pushed debris that had clogged the stream. When the dam of debris was released, water rushed past him and he lost his balance, falling back into the stream. He came up from under water and grabbed his hat as it started to float away. Henry was doubled over, coughing and laughing.

"What's so damn funny, Henry?"

When Henry caught his breath he said, "Rusty, you look like those Baptists I see in the river now and again over near Cottonwood Falls. Let's say you've atoned for your sins."

Air and sun dried his clothes as the pair rode back to the ranch. When the ranch house came into sight, Henry halted his horse to roll a smoke. Rusty examined the darkening sky in the east and waited. When the cigarette was lit and the coughing ended, Henry said, "Well Rusty, I think you've learned enough to go out on the trail for a few days without killing yourself."

"What? You mean you're sending me out by myself?"

"Not hardly," Henry said. "What I'm saying is that I'll tell Sam we should take a couple days and head for the far end of the ranch to start moving any strays this way."

"Oh, sure," Rusty said. He wanted to take off his hat and toss it into the air.

On the first day of the ride away from the ranch, not a word passed between the two for hours. All morning Rusty kept glancing over at Henry, trying to emulate the way the older man rode straight in his saddle. He noticed that Henry rarely looked directly ahead, always taking in what was happening to his left or right, depending on the horse to follow the cut through the tallgrass or path along a ridge. At mid-morning Rusty pulled back on Sandy's reins and said, "Henry, I gotta pee something awful. We gotta stop."

"I ain't stopping you, Rusty. And I ain't going to hold it for you either, so do as you please."

Rusty jumped from his horse, unbuttoned his trousers as fast as he could, and watched as Henry kept moving south and west along an animal track through the tallgrass. Henry seemed to know exactly where he was going. Rusty got back on his horse and caught up.

"Where we going? We're supposed to be looking for strays, so how do you know they ain't over yonder?"

"We're going out around the Widow Shaw's place."

"I mean, you're following this cut in the grass as if this is the direction the steers went."

"It's the direction they went."

"But how do you know?"

" 'Cause I'm a cowboy."

Rusty was silent. After a pause he said, "Wow. I guess I got a lot to learn."

"I guess."

Henry pulled back on the reins of his horse and mumbled something Rusty realized was not instructions for him so much as they were for his horse. With no effort on his part, Sandy stopped alongside Henry.

"Rusty, one of the first things you have to learn is that rounding up steers, no matter how many times you do it, is never the same. Once this batch is sent off to the slaughterhouses, next year's bunch is just as dumb or just as smart. Never the same animals you have to deal with, but still with the same bad habits."

"Sort of makes sense, Henry."

"Sort of. But it's always a new adventure."

Rusty looked over at Henry, who was facing away from him. "Have you been a cowboy all your life, Henry?"

Without turning, Henry said, "I suppose I have."

"Ever wanted to do something else?"

Henry looked at him, made a clucking sound to his horse, and said, "That's another story you don't need to know."

The second morning Rusty woke with a start, unsure of where he was or why. Grains of sand trickled into his shirt collar and down his back as he sat up in the bed molded by his body into the earth during the night. He wiped his hands on his pants, rubbed his face, and looked over at Sandy. Her coat blended with the drying tallgrass. She was still asleep on her feet, standing like a statue in the golden morning light. He listened to the sound of wind sliding through strands of barbed wire. It sounded like distant music coming through the open door of an unseen barn. His eyes followed the line of the wide gravel bar on the Cottonwood River where the night before they'd stopped to let their horses drink. This was the first open spot with access to the river they'd seen in hours of riding, and Henry seemed to know exactly where it was.

Sandy pawed at the ground and snorted, as did Henry's old palomino mare he called Fred. He looked around the campsite for Henry. Off in the tallgrass he heard the hacking and coughing noises that had become so familiar. No way was he going to say anything about Henry seeing a doc like he did the other day. One lecture about a man choosing to die just like he chooses to live was enough for him. *Let the old fart hack away if that's what he wants to do.*

"Lookin' for your morning drink, are you, girls?" he said to the horses.

He walked over and released the lead lines from a hedge fence post, removed the hobbles, and led the pair to the water's edge.

"Well girls, looks like today's lesson of cowboyin' is that there's no more open range. No more short cuts between here and there. I suppose the bright spot in all this fencing business is that it makes steers easier to catch, and it gives us cowboys something to do—fixing all that fence, I mean."

Sandy shook her head, never lifting it from the water. Rusty looked beyond the horse to the changing colors of the landscape. Cloud shadows chased each other, all running the same direction after something. Gullies and ravines, the work of streams struggling to get to the big river, sliced through shades of green. Low rocky hills to the north poked up through the ocean of grass. No trees, none, other than the few cottonwoods along the edges of the river. South and west, the direction they were traveling, the earth faded from dark green to the color of Sandy's coat.

"This sure ain't like home, Sandy. Sure ain't. Makes me think that if the wind had its way out here there'd be no trees at all. Just tallgrass and some bushes the fires miss."

"You're about half right," Henry said, emerging from the tallgrass.

He heard Henry's boots crunching the flint rocks as the cowboy approached. He'd not noticed when the man's coughing stopped. He was unsure if Henry was getting more friendly in the days they'd been riding, or if it was since they'd struck the unspoken deal that he'd stop calling him Snake if Henry would stop calling him kid.

" 'Morning Henry."

The evening before they'd finished looking for steers when the air got so thick you could almost wear it and the sun was just dipping into darkness. Henry told him the story about Gettysburg and the war. They sat, staring at the coffeepot balanced on rocks in the fire. Henry had been with the Ohio 8th Infantry and, with the help of some civilians, he'd just walked away from the war when he realized how stupid it was. Just walked away, Henry said, like a lot of other soldiers were doing. Then he got caught up in another fight in Texas and lost his thumb. *Maybe tonight I'll ask him about Argentina like the hands back at the ranch talk about and how he got the name, Snake.*

Earlier in yesterday's ride Rusty'd discovered that silence wasn't all bad. It made him focus on what was happening, or not happening, around him. He also learned that even though Henry said there'd be no talking while they were in the saddle, the old cowboy didn't mind conversation, as long as he didn't have to turn around to do it.

"Well, horse," Rusty said to Sandy as he rummaged in his canvas bag for something to eat, "meal planning is another cowboy skill I'll have to learn. Two days on the trail and we're nearly outta grub. I can't eat this tallgrass like you, so maybe it's time to get off our butts and find our way back to the ranch house."

"This is not hardly on the trail, and no need to worry about food, son," Henry said. "We're a couple hours' ride from the Widow Shaw's place. I'm sure she'll be more than happy to feed some hungry cowhands."

"Oh, great. I didn't know you knew the widow, Henry."

"Yep. You might say we know each other in the biblical fashion."

"What's that mean?"

"Nothing. Just an expression used by god-fearing people."

"You go to church?"

"Rusty, you've about used up your questions for the day and it's hardly sunrise. Let's see if there's enough coffee left to help chase away the morning."

Henry felt in no real hurry this morning. He had things far from stray cattle on his mind as he rummaged around in his saddlebags. Would she welcome him back?

"No need to start off in a rush," Henry said as he stoked life back into the fire from the night before. "Gather some water and any more dry wood you can find, and we'll try to get this morning to slip by as only a vague annoyance."

When Rusty returned with a few sticks, Henry offered him the steaming tin coffee cup. He noticed the boy flinch, but not cry out. He wasn't all that bad, just young, a problem he'd outgrow. *Like those damned white shirts he wears. Probably too smart to be a cowboy, but then, smart doesn't trump nothing sometimes. I should probably tell him about why black shirts are important.* He recalled the day Jeff showed up in a black shirt and Sam nearly shit himself yelling at the kid about wasting money on a shirt he couldn't wear back at Harvard.

He looked over at Rusty and met the kid's puppy-dog stare. "How'd you get out here, Rusty? From Indiana?" Henry asked.

"Well sir, I just looked at the setting sun and hopped a freight going in that direction. A lot of freights, really. Met some good people, some bad people. Got lucky. Got beat up."

"Ha. Probably says it all."

"How about you, Henry? If you fought at Gettysburg you must have come from someplace else."

Henry watched the tallgrass above their heads sway back and forth. He poked at the ground with a stick and spit in the general direction of a flat rock. He hadn't told the full story about going to the Argentine and coming back up to anyone since that first night with Lucy Shaw, too many years ago. *No need to stir those ashes again.*

"Look at that ground yonder, beneath the grass. See all those odd plants growing amongst the tallgrass?" Henry said, pointing with the stick in his hand.

Rusty looked closely at the base of the grass where prairie dogwood, burdock, and other plants he could not identify hid among the roots of the grass.

"Yeah, lots of odd stuff in there, I guess," Rusty said.

Henry tapped the stick on the ground in front of him and stirred the dying embers. "Some of that useless stuff gets delivered out here by the wind like those fluff-blown seeds. And some of the seeds get shit there by the birds. Sort of the same way you and me got here."

Rusty waited and held his breath as he watched Henry struggle to roll a smoke. The missing thumb and bent fingers all seemed to know what to do. When Henry had the smoke lit and finished his fit of coughing, Rusty asked, "Ever had to fight Injuns?"

"Nope. And some things I did do are best forgotten. Anybody ever tell you that your eyes are in the front of your head for a reason?"

"Yes sir. I've heard that from you."

"Good. Stop asking questions about the past then, and start looking ahead."

"Like patching up some more fence today? Maybe even finding a stray on our way over to the Shaw place?"

"Well, not exactly what I had in mind, but it's a start," Henry said and ground the butt of his cigarette into the soil with the heel of his boot.

"Henry, are you going to tell me anything more about the war?"

"Not much to tell. It happened. Thankfully it's over—for most of us."

"But what was it like?"

"It was somebody's idea of a contest to see who'd die first and who'd die second. The have-nots fighting the have-nots."

"People seem to be getting all excited about the new war in Europe."

"Only 'cause they haven't been in a war and don't know shit about getting killed," Henry said as he rolled onto his knees and pushed himself to his feet. "Now I think it's time to drop the subject of ancient history and move on to something more pleasant."

The seasonal wet weather seemed to have forgotten vast open sections of the arid land southwest of the ranch. Ahead, Rusty could see where prairie brown ended and sky blue began. The far-off dull green tops of cottonwoods defined the path of the river or some creek that had dared to break the pattern of the prairie. He noticed that Henry was no longer looking at the miles of open land to the north or south. His eyes seemed focused on something a thousand miles to the west.

As they rode, Rusty's head filled with images of fast-moving cutting ponies and even faster steers. The animals thrashed and ran in all directions. The air was filled with the smell of blood and the sound of sizzling branding irons. Blood oozed from puncture wounds in the steers' sides, caused by a giant tiger with blood dripping from its tongue as it sprang from behind stands of tallgrass. His head snapped forward, causing his hat to slip over his face, and he realized he'd dozed off. They had halted next to a well-tended garden at the top of a rise. His shirt was soaked with sweat. He looked over at Henry, smoke rising from the cigarette about to burn the crooked fingers of his right hand. His partner's eyes seemed locked on what must have been the Widow Shaw's sod house. The whisper of the tallgrass had stopped, or was hidden by Henry's unsteady breathing.

Like most dugouts and sod houses, the Shaw place, cut from the soil around it, blended with the endless prairie: brown walls and grass roofs, probably with flowers in the right season. You just rode along and suddenly they'd be there, little huts that popped out of the ground. Same with the people who lived in them, stained the color of the earth by the sun and wind.

There was no fence around the property, nor much of a road to mark the entryway. He could see outlines, no more than deep scratches in the earth, of a ditch the Shaws must have dug as was the custom, to plant Osage orange bushes for a windbreak, or maybe a fence. Rusty wondered if the fence was to keep domestic animals in the yard or wild animals out. Either way, it didn't seem to do much good. Without rain those plantings would soon become part of the soil.

Henry cleared his throat and spit off the left side of his horse.

"I was just thinking, Rusty. It's been a tough couple days for us out here and Mrs. Shaw has a couple boys who might like to go fishing at the creek over yonder. Do you know anything about fishing?"

"Do I? I'm from Indiana, remember?"

"How could I forget? Well, I'm thinking maybe the widow would appreciate you taking her two boys fishing while she and I sort of catch up on old times."

"Yes sir, if you think we can spare the time," Rusty said.

"You can take all the time you need. Cowboyin' is tough work and we need to rest every now and then," Henry said and made a clucking signal to his horse.

As they approached the dun-colored structure, two boys, younger than ten years old, he guessed, unmolested by water for weeks, bare feet unaffected by sharp stones or animal dung in the yard, rushed toward them. Rusty's thoughts were on fishing as his eyes searched the distant prairie for the telltale line of bushes or trees that marked the passage of a creek.

"Hi kids. Guess it's been a while since you seen your uncle," Henry said.

Rusty could see the older boy grinning up at Henry and Mrs. Shaw leaning against the doorframe, a smile on her lips. He wanted to ask Henry what this uncle stuff was all about, but held back.

"I should say," came her greeting. "Henry Ellsworth, what brings you out this way?"

Rusty watched how Henry smiled and reached up to touch the brim of his hat with his crooked thumb, then give a slight nod of his head. "Morning, Widow."

"Morning, ma'am," Rusty said, imitating Henry's gestures as best he could.

"And who's the young lad?" she asked, looking at Rusty.

"New hand. Name's Rusty. I'm showing him some of the old tricks," Henry said.

Rusty watched Widow Shaw's smile widen. "Not all of them, I hope."

"No ma'am," Henry said. "Young Rusty here has volunteered to take the boys there down to the creek to do a bit of fishing while you and me do the boring stuff, like talk about the good old days."

"Well, I do appreciate that sacrifice, Rusty," she said, licking her lips. "You boys can take all the time you need to catch us some dinner."

Rusty looked at her red, roughened hands as she rubbed them against her stained apron. She looked away from him as she tried to tuck errant strands of dark hair flecked with gray behind her ears. When she pushed her hair back he could see the whiteness of her forehead in contrast to her prairie-colored cheeks, chin, and neck.

Rusty started to dismount, but stopped when he noticed a soft, gray scar angling east across the blue face of the sky. The thought of fire made him pause. He rose in the stirrups to follow the length of the scar. It appeared blackest close to earth, fading to white, the color of summer clouds, as it widened and rose.

"Looks like fire up north of here," he said. "That's not where we're headed, is it Henry?"

Henry and Mrs. Shaw shaded their eyes with forearms and turned to look in the same direction. "Sort of. This wind from the south should keep it headed the other direction. Should be someone else's problem by the time we get up there," Henry said.

Rusty sat and watched Olaus and George, the Widow Shaw's two boys, ready their fishing gear, which amounted to nothing more than cottonwood branches, some string, and a straight pin bent in the shape of a hook.

"What do you expect to catch with this?" Rusty asked.

"Better than not goin' fishin'," Olaus said in a low voice.

"I guess you're right about that. Let's go see what's swimming in that creek of yours."

As they headed for the stream, Rusty looked over his shoulder at the line of smoke miles in the distance.

"Glad that fire's someone else's worry," he said to the two youngsters.

"Don't have to worry 'bout nothing when Henry's around," Olaus said.

Rusty turned to the older of the two boys, "You know Henry?"

"Sort of," Olaus said and turned away from Rusty. "Used to see him maybe once a year if Pa was out working. A while back, after Pa died, he began to stop by more regular. Comes by a couple times in the spring and fall for sure. Always says he's looking for strays out this way. We haven't seen him in a while."

As the three walked to the creek, Rusty glanced back toward the soddy. He could see Henry and Widow Shaw talking and looking in his direction.

Henry rubbed his back against the doorframe and watched the trio of boys move toward the line of cottonwoods. "How you and the boys doin' out here, Lucy?"

"Fine. Same as usual. How's that Rusty fella working out?"

"Okay."

"Where'd he come from?"

"Hopped freights out from Indiana."

"Did he run away from home?"

"Oh, he's not a bad kid, if that's what you're thinking. Reads too much of the wrong stuff and thinks there's something glamorous about being a cowboy."

"You mean being a cowboy ain't glamorous?" Lucy said as she leaned her shoulder against his arm.

Henry looked down at her. "Not a bit, Lucy, not a bit."

"Will he get over it or is he condemned to a life of wandering, like some men I know?"

Henry slipped his right arm around her waist and pulled her closer. "Not real sure. He's just a bit at loose ends in his life. He sort of reminds me of a kid's ball that gets lost out there in the tallgrass."

"I don't suppose that reminds you of anyone—close by—does it?"

Henry looked up and could just see the tops of the three boys' heads as they dropped down over the other side of a rise. "Maybe a bit too much."

"C'mon cowboy, let's get in out of this heat. I have something here I want to show you."

Leaning back against the warm bank of the creek, Rusty's mind filled with thoughts of similar days in Kendallville and fishing with Cliff. He laughed when the two young boys landed a catfish, then a gar, a strange-looking creature he'd never seen. They were using the unlikely bait of balls of dough, more appropriate for catching mice than fish.

He'd not noticed the wind shift and was looking at a small catfish the boys landed when he heard a strange crackling sound. He smelled something burning. Prairie grass. He scrambled to the top edge of the creek's bank and froze when he saw the new color of the once tan-and-yellow land. Smoke and sparks filled the sky a half-mile away. Slithering toward them, stretching to the horizon in both directions, was an orange-red tongue of flames less than a foot tall.

"Drop that stuff and run for the house," he shouted to George and Olaus. "We gotta get to your ma and Henry."

It took ten minutes of running and stumbling over uneven ground for the trio to return to the house. Both boys were panting, crying, and screaming by the time they reached the safety of their mother. Mrs. Shaw stood at the door of the house struggling to button the collar of her dress. Rusty could see water dripping from a blanket lying next to her.

"I'll ride someplace and get some help," Rusty shouted, gasping for breath and grabbing at the pain in his side. He bent over and used his right hand to try to push the pain deeper into his body where it might hurt less. He was unsure if his legs could carry him even as far as the horses tied around back in the shade of the house.

"No time," Henry shouted from somewhere deep within the soddy. Rusty could hear the pounding of the man's huge strides before he appeared carrying two winter coats and some blankets.

"Here, Olaus, grab your brother," Mrs. Shaw yelled. "You boys run over there into that plowed field. Lay down in the middle of it. Dig in. Cover yourselves with dirt. Go!"

"Rusty, take this coat," Henry said through a fit of coughing. He handed Rusty the waterlogged wool overcoat. "I'm gonna set this one afire and run up along that ditch yonder, on the other side."

"That's stupid, Henry. It'll just start more fire," Rusty said.

Rusty looked down at the heavy coat Henry was carrying and the box of matches he held with the remaining four fingers of his left hand. He looked back at the fire crawling toward them. He could hear Mrs. Shaw inside the house banging pans as she gathered more water from the rain barrel.

"I'm gonna start a backfire. You two follow up. Or do you want to be with the boys?" Henry said, turning to Mrs. Shaw.

"Go Henry, just go!" she shouted.

Rusty turned toward the howling monster now a hundred yards away. Its growl blocked out any last instructions. All he knew was that somehow, in this wind, Henry had to light the matches. Rusty waited and watched Henry's hands tremble. The man's right hand couldn't steady the matchbox. The left hand, what there was of it, struggled to strike the match while the man held the coat with his knees. Four times he saw Henry break the heads off matchsticks when he pushed them against the striker on the side of the box. Each time a spark emerged from the wood matchstick and burned Henry's fingertips before it was devoured by the wind.

Rusty dropped the water-soaked coat and ran over to Henry. "Widow Shaw needs help getting water on the other blankets. I ain't strong enough to help her. Let me get the coat burning and you help her!"

Henry stared at Rusty and hesitated. "I see what you mean, Rusty." Henry handed him the coat and matches, gave his shoulder a squeeze, and ran back into the sod house.

The coat would not ignite. Rusty needed paper. He searched his pockets and found nothing. He dug through the coat's pockets and discovered a crumpled piece of paper—a whole dollar bill—enough to probably buy groceries for a week!

"Oh god! Oh god!" Rusty yelled as he struck more matches. On the fifth try the dollar bill caught fire. He carefully pushed it into the coat's pocket and watched to be sure the heavy wool material was burning.

He looked back toward the house for Henry or Mrs. Shaw to tell them the coat was burning. Henry's back was to him. He could see him dumping the bucket of water they'd drawn for the horses onto another coat and his clothes.

Henry turned to him and waved as if he was heading off to a store. Rusty ran alongside the ditch where Osage orange bushes had been planted amid the dead grass. The smoldering coat followed him, as did the small orange snake of fire he started.

On the opposite side of the ditch, Henry and Mrs. Shaw leapt back and forth, beating out any sparks that managed to jump the furrow. When Rusty reached the corner of the field and looked back, the house appeared as a speck of dirt on the hazy horizon. He could see that the horses had broken loose and were running well ahead of the fire.

He stopped and tried to swallow away the taste of ashes in his mouth, placed his hands on his knees, and coughed until his breathing turned into dry heaves. Again he looked back toward the house. Henry was doubled over on his knees, hacking and coughing, while Mrs. Shaw beat the flames. As Rusty watched, Mrs. Shaw helped Henry to his feet and the pair headed for the open field where the boys had dug in.

In the opposite direction, the dancing wall of orange and red flames appeared to him like rain against a windowpane. Rusty's vision blurred and his eyes burned with smoke and sweat. He looked down at what was left of the wool coat—one sleeve and the collar. All the hair on his arms was singed. Sparks hammered against his back and felt like that nest of stinging yellow jackets he and Ralphie had gotten into one summer back home. He had to run.

Through the smoke he could see Henry and Mrs. Shaw stumbling away from the soddy. She had one arm around Henry's waist and with her other, beat at sparks that managed to cross the ditch or land in her hair. Finally she dropped the wet blanket and started to drag Henry by the collar of his shirt.

Rusty checked the backfire he'd been setting. It had widened in the direction of the main fire. Soon the two fires would mingle and in a short time, the life of one would bring death to the other.

Above the roar he thought he heard Mrs. Shaw's high-pitched scream. Through the dense smoke he saw her vague shape, arms waving, pointing toward Henry lying on the ground near her feet. Rusty dropped what was left of the smoldering coat sleeve and jumped the narrow ditch. When he landed, he heard a soft click and felt a jolt of pain race from his left ankle up his leg. His body pitched forward on the uneven ground, and his face and right hand smashed into a rock. He thought he was going to faint. He knew he should get up and run, except the world was getting dark. Maybe if he could just lie here and rest for a bit, just until morning ...

A shower of embers landed on him. He rose to his feet and pitched forward as a burst of pain shot through his leg. He thought about the beating he'd taken from the bull in the Chicago stockyard and how he had wanted to run that day. This time he was free to run and angled through the smoke to where he'd last seen Henry and Mrs. Shaw.

Rusty stumbled to Henry's side, hesitant to interrupt what appeared to be a man in prayer. He ignored his own pain and slipped his right hand under Henry's arm to try to lift the man to a standing position. Mrs. Shaw crawled over, struggling to get to her feet. She screamed, "Just grab under his arms. I'll get his feet. Get to that open field." Together they dragged the coughing Henry toward the open place where the boys huddled in a heap of mud created by the wet blankets and coats. Henry's weight suddenly increased, causing Rusty to drop to his knees. He looked back. Mrs. Shaw was lying on her face in the ashes and soil.

She waved for him to keep going as she rose to her hands and knees and continued crawling in his direction. Rusty waited but Mrs. Shaw continued past him toward her children, silhouettes to him through the smoke and ashes.

Rusty yelled above the roar of the fire, "What do I do?"

"Dig in and pray the best prayer you know," she screamed, making digging motions with her hands before spreading her arms and settling her body over her children.

Rusty scraped at the hard soil to create a shallow hole for Henry's face, relieved that Henry had stopped coughing. He looked at the unmoving shape of his friend and wished he knew some prayers that might stop this rain of fire coming down all around them.

What sounded like a small dog whimpering woke Rusty. Morning sun warmed his back and the soil he thought was a pillow warmed his face. He drew in a long breath and started coughing to spit the ashen taste from his mouth. To his left, Mrs. Shaw sat, rocking back and forth wrapped in a still-damp blanket. The two boys stood, throwing clods of dirt at where the fire must have headed to become someone else's problem, though he could no longer see smoke in the sky.

Henry lay to his right. During the night his friend must have rolled onto his back, laced his bent fingers over his stomach, and crossed his legs at the ankles. Henry seemed to be watching clouds change patterns overhead. An arrow of pain passed through Rusty's left ankle when he tried to stand. He forced his right hand and arm under Henry's back. He could feel heat and saw the back of the cowboy's black shirt shredded with burn holes.

Rusty raised the quiet man into a sitting position, trying not to get dirt into the cuts. The cowboy's forehead was the color of the ashes they were lying in. Henry opened his eyes and what appeared to be a smile came to his lips, coated with blood and mud. A fresh, crimson line crawled like a worm from the corner of his mouth, down his chin and into his still-buttoned shirt collar. The pearl-gray cowboy's hat was missing. Rusty scanned in all directions but did not see it. Thirty feet behind them he recognized the red, yellow, and black stripes of what looked like a dead coral snake.

"Sorry Henry," Rusty said. "Seems your hat must be chasing after the fire or something. But, unless I'm mistaken, I can see either a hatband that got loose from a hat, or a coral snake that got caught up in this fire."

Rusty watched Henry's eyelids flicker and his eyes shift back and forth as if following a flight of birds. He felt Henry's back muscles twitch against his arm as his friend took in small breaths through what Rusty wanted to believe was a smile.

"I know you told me a cowboy only takes off his hat for two reasons, Henry. I sure hope this ain't one of them," Rusty said. He felt tears starting and tried to brush them away with the singed skin of his left arm. The lump in his throat felt huge, threatening to cut off his breathing. He sucked in air through his mouth so he wouldn't have to smell the fire.

Lucy crawled to where Rusty cradled Henry. She placed her hand over Henry's scarred forearm and brushed away burned prairie grass stuck to the man's skin. Without looking at Rusty she said to Henry, "How ya doin' fella? You know, we didn't quite finish what we started back there in the house."

Rusty saw the corners of Henry's mouth jerk into a smile then relax as the man's eyes searched the woman's face. Henry released a shallow cough and whispered, "In the next world, then."

"Okay by me," said Lucy as she slipped her hand into Henry's, staring at it as if examining his crooked fingers for the first time.

Rusty looked back and forth between the two. "Henry, will you be okay while I ride to get us some help?"

"Save your time, kid—I mean Rusty. I'm finally done. Next ride I'm on my own. Time for me to get on with it."

Rusty leaned forward to hear the weak voice.

"What? Where you goin'? You ain't going anywheres without me. We're partners."

"Not this time, Rusty. Not sure where I'm heading, but maybe we'll meet up."

"How? Where you goin', Henry?" Rusty said, trying to swallow and fight back tears.

"Second star to the right and straight on 'til morning," Henry said.

Rusty looked up from Henry to Lucy. He could see her body silently heave; her face remained buried in the crook of her elbow.

"What's he mean, Mrs. Shaw? What do you mean, Henry?" Rusty's words were louder and higher pitched than he intended.

"It's a line from a book, Rusty," Lucy said and reached out to touch his shoulder.

Henry closed his eyes and said, "If you go to school, Rusty, to learn something other than cowboyin', you'll understand."

CHAPTER TEN

Ashes

Rusty was unsure if it was day or night, or if he was alive or dead. *Maybe I'm with Henry.* All he knew for sure was that he did not want to open his eyes.

"Looks like his cowboyin's done for this season," a voice said.

Is that Sam? Where am I? Rusty's eyes remained closed because it would take too much effort to open them. Everything seemed wrong—bed too soft and clean, no more fire smell. And were those women's voices?

Rusty blinked his eyes to be sure he was awake. Yes, two women stood behind Sam, looking down at him. Sam's hat was missing and Rusty realized he'd never seen him without a large felt or straw hat. Sam looked like he'd been caught in a rainstorm, but from the odor, it had to be sweat.

Rusty closed his eyes. "Huh? What ... what happened?" His lips felt too big. Swelling and pain combined to muffle his words. His tongue explored the unfamiliar edges of a ragged front tooth. When had he broken a tooth? He wanted to spit the taste of copper pennies from his mouth.

Sam shifted to face him and Rusty felt his body slip on the clean sheets. "Well, you sort of survived a prairie fire," came a voice.

Rusty turned his head. Granville was leaning against the wall, arms across his chest, staring down at him.

"Sorta?"

He could feel Sam's hand resting on his arm. He tried to listen to the explanation of what happened when other cowboys from the ranch spotted the fire and started riding out toward the widow's place because they knew he and Henry were looking for strays out that way.

"You and Henry and Widow Shaw and her kids were still in one big heap in the middle of a plowed field," Sam explained. "You looked like you were kicked in the face then stomped on by a mule. Mrs. Shaw and her young ones are a bit singed but okay, and Henry..."

"What about Henry?" Rusty asked.

"I'm afraid he's dead, son," Sam said.

When Sam's words stopped, Rusty saw the women nod in affirmation. The younger one's hair swayed like grass on the open prairie. He wanted to pay attention to Sam, but the ringing in his ears, combined with the distraction of the women's stares, made it impossible.

"... so that's why I think you'd best stay out of the saddle till that ankle and hand gets mended and those cuts heal. Doc will be here shortly to look you over."

Rusty's eyes drifted from Sam's face down to his own right hand. Someone had wrapped it in what looked like a bed sheet. Rusty could see that a dark flower of blood had blossomed under the sheet next to his arm, but that wasn't what made his legs go stiff. His breath stuck in his throat when he realized his clothes were missing.

The odor of horses, prairie fire, and rich earth were gone. He'd been scrubbed and smelled like lavender, not like dust and ashes the way he remembered Henry had when he'd been holding him. He closed his eyes and shook his head, trying to clear away fog. When he moved, pain grabbed him by the neck and throat.

"Henry helped," Rusty said.

"Helped," Sam said. "And he probably saved the bunch of you. That man knew more about prairie fires, hell, and disasters in general, than anyone you'll ever meet. I'll miss the guy, Rusty, I surely will."

Rusty looked up but Sam's face was turned toward the wall, his forearm pressed against his eyes.

Sam cleared his throat and said, "I've seen about every way there is to get hurt in this business, but not many survive a prairie fire."

"Great," was all Rusty could manage.

"Most often, injury involves a woman or an animal. Usually a mule. Those critters are the most patient beasts God ever made. They'll wait fifteen years just to get in one good kick at you."

"Sam!"

Rusty opened his eyes in search of the sharp voice. A woman he did not know stood squinting her eyes at Sam. Her arms, crossed over her chest, matched the wrinkles of her forehead and downturned corners of her mouth. Her skin was so pale her face blended with the wallpaper. An aroma of peppermint candy mixed with horse liniment seemed to drift from the woman's clothes.

"Yeah, you're right," Sam said in a softer tone. "I seen this before, couple times, usually when boys got tossed off their horses."

"Sam!" The woman's voice cracked like distant lightning.

"Oh, right. Doc probably can't do much to help ya out. Injury's just part of being a cowboy."

"Sam, would you just calm down and let this boy have some peace? You wear me out just being in the same room with you. I need a chair," the older woman said.

Rusty paid no attention to Sam's words, and only a little to the words of the older woman. He was starring at the young woman, who slipped a chair beneath the older one, then moved out of his line of vision behind the trail boss. She was Minnie, the cook. He'd seen her around the ranch. Rusty swallowed a couple times and felt his tongue scrape against a chipped tooth.

"Sam, who's the ladies?"

"Oh, excuse my manners," Sam said. "Thought you knew. This here's Mrs. Gorham, Granville's wife, and their daughter, Minnie. Well, you probably already know her. They offered to scrape the mud and crap off you so's we could find your injuries. You've been sleeping a full day now."

Rusty looked down at the outline of his body and felt the sheet get heavier. The thought of the younger woman possibly looking at his naked body made him shudder. He wished for the pain to come back to his ankle and hand so he'd have an excuse for shaking.

As the women began to leave the room, Rusty watched Sam stare at the ceiling and run his fingers around the brim of the remains of a hat he held. It was Henry's old gray hat, minus the snakeskin hatband. The stillness in the room filled with the sound of Sam's ticking watch and cattle bawling out in the corral.

"You're a mess, kid, the kind of mess cowboys get into way too often," Sam said. "You might want to give some further thought to this line of work."

"It's what I want to do, Sam," Rusty said.

"Nobody wants to die all alone in some prairie fire in the middle of nowhere like Henry did."

Rusty closed his eyes to hold back the tears, but it did no good. He felt their warmth as they ran over his cheeks into his ears. He gasped for air. When his breathing felt normal he said, "Henry didn't die alone. He died with me at his side, and a good woman holding his hand."

Rusty opened his eyes. The cracked plaster ceiling hovered above him, threatening to collapse. He listened to the sounds coming through the window and knew which cowboys were working that afternoon by the various shouts and whistles mixed with the sounds of the cattle. A light breeze moved the curtains and carried with it the sound of a motorcar engine. The curtains waved hello and good-bye, and he thought of how he'd never again hear Henry's sharp whistle in the corral.

A light tap on the door distracted his thoughts from the pain looping between his ankle and his wrist. He brushed his eyes with the corner of the sheet.

"What?" He swallowed and tried to speak again, but only a croaking sound emerged.

Another tap, then a soft, clear voice cut through the dense silence. "Are you awake, Mr. Starke?"

Oh, god. It was Minnie. He pulled the sheet closer to his chin. "Ah, yeah. I'm here," he managed, his eyes fixed on the cracks in the ceiling's plaster. "Ain't going anyplace soon."

The raspy sound of door hinges signaled an opening and a closing somewhere to his left. Using his uninjured hand and arm for leverage, he attempted to rise to a seated position to greet his visitor. As he rose, the sheet began to slip down his chest. He grabbed at it with his right hand, causing pain that straightened his entire body. His head hit the brass frame uprights of the bed's headboard and set off clanging bells that echoed around the sparse room.

"Aaaaaa, shit."

"Mr. Starke, please don't try to sit up. Oh, are you all right?"

His head came to rest on the pillow and he was unsure if he was hurt or embarrassed. He kept his eyes closed until his breathing slowed.

"Christ, whatta baby—"

"You're not," Minnie said.

He tried to lift his head to see her. "I'm sorry, ma'am. Hope I didn't say any rough words."

"You're not to worry, Mr. Starke. This is a working cattle ranch. I might be only seventeen, but I've heard all the words in the English language, and a few some people say are French."

The image of half a face covered by a golden drape, a blue eye, and a crooked smile floated into his line of vision. He tried not to move. "I'm grateful for all you did, ah, and your ma done."

She tipped her head a bit to her right and leaned forward. He watched hair the color of fall wheat sway to the side and surround her face. Now he could see that her eyes were two colors, one blue and one brown.

"Are you having trouble breathing, Mr. Starke? Is your nose okay?"

"Huh? No ma'am. I mean yes. I mean, why?"

"Well it looks like you're breathing awful quick through your mouth, not your nose, is all. Plus, you do have some nasty scuffs and it looks like you chipped a tooth."

Rusty was unaware that his mouth was open. His eyes were busy searching her face. When the moment he was hoping might never end, did, her image moved out of his line of sight. Her voice, however, remained in his head like the whisper of grass undulating on the prairie.

She broke the silence. "Call me Minnie, not ma'am. My real name is Wilhelmina, but that's too long to say, so I shortened it. Mama was against me using the name Minnie, like she's against most things I want."

Minnie stopped talking and Rusty was unsure if he was supposed to say something.

"So, Mr. Starke, I'll just put this tea Mama made right over there on the table for you to reach with your good hand."

Determined not to blink, he kept his eyes focused on a crack in the bedroom ceiling plaster. Fearing she might leave, he looked in her direction and said, "It's Russell. Rusty, my ma calls me, I mean when she ain't mad at me for wanting to be a cowboy. But she's dead and ..."

Movement behind Minnie interrupted him. He turned his head to see a man wearing a dark suit and white shirt with a stiff, buttoned collar move in behind her. Minnie turned to follow Rusty's stare.

"Oh, this here's Doc Campbell," she said. "When he ain't tending to sick steers, he's patching up broke cowboys, of which you seem to be one."

"A sick steer or a broke cowboy?" Rusty asked.

Minnie lowered her head and covered her mouth with her right hand, trying to stifle a laugh as she turned to leave. Doc Campbell made no such pretense. He laughed hard as he tossed his hat onto the chair where he'd already dropped his black bag.

"Jesus, that hurts!" Rusty said as the doc first twisted his ankle then his wrist.

"Well, it's supposed to hurt, young man. You broke it, plus the fire almost cooked you, as I hear the story. You're lucky you wasn't killed from what Sam tells me. Looks like the ankle is only a sprain. I can't hear any broken bones. Hand and wrist probably have some broken bones, though. Lots of little bones in there to break. Should heal okay. Just don't use it for awhile."

Rusty turned to the open window. Now in a seated position, he could see weathered wallboards of the near-empty bunkhouse below the gray sky. *The ramshackle place needs a coat of paint. Why hasn't anyone mentioned what they did with Henry after he died?*

"You might want to be thinking about a place to spend the rest of fall and winter. You have any family near by?"

"Sorta. I have a couple uncles, farmers over in Woodson County. I might be able to stay there 'til next season. Maybe Yates."

"Hmm. Well, okay," Doc Campbell said. "You might also want to think about a different line of work. Cowboyin's pretty much a dying occupation, if ya know what I mean. Not much of a future now with barbed wire keeping the strays in and trains taking over the hauling. Cattle are changing, too. We won't be seeing those Texas longhorns much longer."

Rusty said nothing. He looked at the door and wondered if Minnie was listening to the conversation.

"Say, did ya know they're not going to be making those longhorns any longer?" the doctor said.

"Huh? No. What do you mean? They—"

"Nope. Those horns are plenty long enough already," Campbell said and burst into laughter so hard it hurt Rusty's ears.

The doctor ended his laughing spell with a throat-clearing cough.

The corners of Rusty's mouth turned up. "Thanks doc. Now I got some real news to tell the folks back home in Indiana."

Doc Campbell cleaned his various scrapes with something Rusty thought smelled like the stuff they used on horses that brushed against barbed wire.

The doctor looked at Rusty's hand again. "Least you won't be a cripple, like some. Henry Ellsworth had bent up fingers similar to this, but I think you'll get most of the use of yours back."

Rusty thought about all of the things Henry could do with his injured hand. Henry told him that last day on the prairie he could do anything he had to do, but not what he really wanted to do. *I wonder what he wanted to do. Maybe when I'm feeling better I'll ride out to Widow Shaw's place and talk with her. She might know what Henry was talking about.*

As the doctor wiped his hands on a towel from his bag, he said, "You just have to take it easy, son. You're young and you'll heal up just fine, less than a month or so, I expect. Just relax."

When the doctor reached the door he said, "Say lad, if you need a ride down there to Yates, let me know. I'm up here often enough and travel down that way a couple times a week. I'd welcome the company. It's not as long a trip with the automobile as it was by horse and buggy, but it's still nice to have someone to talk with."

"Thank you, sir. I just might take you up on that. There's a couple things I should take care of here, first."

"Get your rest and think about your future. It's the best medicine for that broken hand."

What future? Images of the tiger poster picture he had rolled up in his bag in the bunkhouse came to mind. The doc's hand was on the doorknob when Rusty said, "Hey doc."

"Yeah?"

"Well, I was wondering, do you know if circus people ever get eaten by their animals?"

The doctor looked at him, his eyebrows furrowed into a single line above his nose. "That's about the strangest question I ever heard. I really don't know. I suppose they get bit now and again. Not eaten. Why?"

"Oh, just wondering. Thinking about my future, I guess."

Three days later Rusty was feeling well enough to limp down to the corral. His movement was hesitant, as if his left foot was unsure if it should follow his right. Sandy was standing there, her head over the top rail, watching him approach. He rubbed her face with his good hand. Sandy snorted and pushed her muzzle into his face, knocking him off balance. Nearby, an upturned crate provided an easy way for him to climb up and sit on the top rail of the fence. Sandy walked over and made huffing sounds, trying to tell him something.

"No girl, we're not going out there today. Doc says I have to rest this hand."

From this vantage point, for the first time he could see the kaleidoscopic sea of longhorn steers cowboys had been gathering for weeks. Small streams of cattle merged into a large river that the cowboys and their ponies narrowed and channeled toward the corral. The large corral alongside the spur from rail tracks Mr. Raleigh had paid the railroad company to build was reconfigured to accommodate the expanding herd, plus cattle from neighboring herds in the area. The pungent aroma of marigolds growing in the pasture and crushed by the cattles' hooves filled the air. He pushed back his stained, broad-brimmed hat and said, "Wow girl, would you take a look at that."

Sam Hancock, dust sticking to his sweat-stained shirt, rode up next to him and scanned the scene. "Quite a sight, isn't it, kid? Not many herds of these Texas longhorns left. Everybody wants faster-growing cattle now. Damn foreign cows. That and all the crossbreeding is doing away with these beasts. Pretty soon they'll find a way to crossbreed the beast out of cowboys, too."

He looked at Sam, who was following the endless lines of steers moving toward them. He was glad to see that during the few days he'd spent in bed, Sam's mustache had returned to its curvy shape.

"Sam, I have to ask you something."

He waited for the trail boss to turn in his direction, but the man only looked straight ahead.

"Why didn't you tell me about Jeff?"

Rusty waited for an answer. He was beginning to think Sam had not heard him. Finally Sam cleared his throat and spit.

"Well, first off, it's all history that I thought you didn't need to know about," he said, turning in Rusty's direction. "On second thought, maybe I was wrong and maybe you could have learned a lesson. Maybe you still can."

Rusty rubbed his hand against Sandy's mane while Sam told him about his seventeen-year-old son who, like Rusty, wanted to be a cowboy instead of going back to college. One bright, sunny, fall day Jeff was helping load steers along with Snake and some other hands when the bull board that spanned the opening to the railcar and loading chute slipped out of place.

"When Snake dove beneath that board, Jeff, like a fool, followed him. The board slipped and came down on Jeff and Snake. We tried to save him, but—"

"So it was an accident, like Henry told me," Rusty interrupted.

"I guess," Sam said, and turned toward the sounds of snorting cattle. "Looking back, if I'd insisted he stay back east, if Snake would have stopped him from running under that board, if... Well, woulda, shoulda, coulda ain't going to get these beefies counted and into the corral."

Sam made a clucking sound and Rusty said, "Sam, what happened with Henry? With his body, I mean?"

Their eyes met and Rusty felt a hot flash of fear that Sam was not going to tell him.

"Well son, the boys buried him out there near the widow's place. She said she wanted him near her garden."

"I feel like shit. I didn't get to say good-bye to him. I never get to say good-bye to people who die." Rusty turned away so the trail boss could not see his face.

Sam cleared his throat. "Lucy Shaw says you and Snake—"

"Call him Henry. His name was Henry."

"Right. And you're one of the few guys alive that he let call him by his given name since he came back from Argentina."

Sam looked out over the herd, then turned to him. "Lucy says you and Henry exchanged words before he died. What did you talk with him about? At the end, I mean."

Rusty followed Sandy's line of vision to a steer that was wandering off away from the herd.

"Oh, he said some strange things. And would you believe, he said I should go to school?"

"Yep, sounds like Henry. You have to understand, son, people like Henry have a lot of wagons they're either falling off of or climbing on to. What they say or do might not make sense today, but it will, someday. He was the best cowboy I've known."

Rusty looked over at Sam, surprised to see him smiling. He liked the way Sam's broad smile made the ends of his handlebar mustache curl upward.

"Sam, does it take a long time to grow a mustache like that?"

"Not if you get started early enough and don't plan on kissing the ladies for a few years while you're doin' it."

Rusty looked at the river of cattle flowing into the expanded corral. "Well, I like the cowboy life, Sam. A bit lonely out here at times, but peaceful."

"Yep. So what are you planning to do when we get 'em all shipped?"

Rusty looked at the man who'd been his teacher and talked with him like he wished his real Pa would do. "Ah, well, I guess I hadn't thought about it much."

Sam cleared his throat and looked out at the herd. "Another thing about being a cowboy these days is that you need another life so's to get through the winter months. Maybe you have a family to spend some time with. School'd be my suggestion, too."

Rusty was unsure if Sam was asking him about his family or telling him he no longer had a job.

"Well, I guess I could go back to Indiana for awhile, but it's a long way to go for just a few months. Or maybe head for the farm where my uncle lives in Woodson County. Maybe even back to the Slocums in Yates Center."

"Hmm. Long time since I been down to that part of Woodson County. Only passed through Yates oncest. Much of a place, now?"

"Not much."

"Pretty girls?"

"Not like here at the ranch."

Even though Sam was facing the open corral, Rusty could see the handlebars of his mustache twitch and knew the man was smiling. "Sam, I was wondering, what did Henry do in the winter months?"

"Not real sure. Stories swirled about him like twisters in springtime. If only half the stories are true he must have had an interesting life." Without looking back, Sam made a clucking sound to his horse and rode into the corral.

The tallgrass was changing from shades of dark green to purple to lustrous tones of gold and tan in the morning light. The shorter grass, the kind that nearly reached Rusty's boots when he was in the saddle—Henry called it switchgrass—changed colors all summer. Now it was darker tan than Sandy's butterscotch-colored coat. Even when it seemed there was no wind, switchgrass constantly swayed. This ever-changing ocean stretched as far across the prairie as he could see. He closed his eyes and tried to sort out the different aromas coming from the different kinds of grass like Henry said a real cowboy does to figure out where the strays might be feeding.

On the western horizon stood a windmill, one of the few on the ranch used to pump water into hollowed logs that served as watering troughs. Whenever the wind shifted in his direction, Rusty heard the clanking sound of its loose blades. The structure stood out there on the prairie like a flagpole marking the spot where some small victory in the battle with the land had been won.

"I've told you once, I've told you a thousand times, Wilhelmina: you are not leaving Chase County. Not even the state of Kansas."

"But Ma—"

"No buts about it, young lady. You have no idea what kind of trouble's out there."

"And you do?"

"Who's to take care of your father and me if you was to leave, anyway?"

Minnie watched her mother's red, cracked hands move up and down the backs of her arms as she stood at the sink, eyes drilling through streaks of grime on the window and settling on the barren, postage-stamp piece of dun-colored earth she called a garden. From Minnie's perspective, it appeared like her mother was being held in someone's embrace. She tried to imagine who would want to hug her mother. Pa must have, once.

Minnie knew what was coming when Rachel closed her eyes and blew at a wisp of hair that hung in front of her face. Soap bubbles from her hands created lacy cuffs on the sleeves of the cotton dress she'd sewn from bags that once brought chicken feed to the ranch.

"Daughter, over my dead body are you ever going to be as stupid as my brothers, or your father's brothers, and go to Colorado."

"But Ma—"

"Wilhelmina!"

"Okay, okay, okay."

Minnie stood and managed two steps before her mother's words stopped her.

"And put on some hat of your father's. It's cold out there. You'll catch your death."

"Okay Ma, okay," she said, as she removed her coat from the wood peg next to the door.

"And tell your father I'm not feeling so good tonight."

Minnie's eyes searched the lines of her mother's pale face for the truth. Fading sunlight coming through the window behind Rachel created a halo around her graying hair. Rachel rubbed the sides of her head. Minnie knew the signs that signaled a headache. Headaches and long naps seemed to come more often these days.

Minnie wanted to tell her mother to go tell Pa herself. A bit of conversation between the two of them might make evenings more pleasant. Instead, she said, "Ma, is there something I can get for your headache?"

"No. Just go help your father and give me some peace and quiet. And quit talking about Colorado."

Minnie jumped from the porch to the frozen ground rather than use the steps as she was told young ladies were supposed to do. *Quit thinking about Colorado—like quit breathing.* She pulled the button-less coat tighter. With shipping season near an end, her daily chores of preparing meals and picking up after men too dumb to pick up their own underplunders had lessened. Just a couple of hands hanging around, so cleaning the bunkhouse might be easier. These days she had more time for herself to read about places other than Kansas, and people other than cowboys.

Why would she want to leave such a glamorous job in such a glamorous place? Why would she want to leave her mother, who always acted more like a slave master than a mother? Why not marry one of these men who brought the stink and dirt of the corral into the house everyday? Heck, she could clean up after him and raise a brood of screaming little rats that looked just like him. She shuddered. Other girls her age were starting to do it. *No thanks.*

Minnie watched a flowing veil of snow temporarily mask the bunkhouse. She looked out toward the prairie and thought, in the months to come, any tallgrass left standing would comb snow out of the wind and create scenes of what she imagined the snowcapped mountains of Colorado must look like. In the right pocket of her apron, her hand found the Indian head penny she kept for moments like this. She thought about when her father had given her the penny on her fifth birthday and said, "Daughter, as long as you keep this you won't be penniless."

Instead of going to the barn to bother Pa, Minnie changed direction and walked toward the henhouse. What few eggs there might be should easily fit into her coat pocket and save her having to come out again later when she could be reading. Besides, gathering eggs would take her mind off Colorado. She lowered her head as she entered the confined space Pa had built for the few hens the family would need until next spring. The stench of chicken droppings made her eyes water. She pushed reluctant hens aside with one hand and grabbed eggs with the other. One of the chickens tried to escape and she used her right foot to pin the bird against the wall as she closed the door on her way out.

Walking back toward the house, Minnie rounded the corner of the bunkhouse and stopped. Standing in the doorway she saw that kid, Rusty, who seemed to be searching the prairie. *Well, maybe he's not all that much of a kid.* Even though she'd been cooking meals for him since he hired on, she'd rarely seen him since either Ma or Pa would take the meals to the bunkhouse. And during the few days he spent in the house, Ma told her to stay clear of his room because men had only one thing in mind when they saw young ladies.

He looked taller than she remembered. Yet there he stood with what Pa called that thousand-mile stare. All cowboys had it, few ever saw it in themselves. She could never tell if those cowboys were thinking about the future or something in the past they'd never talk about.

"Looks like the shipping season's over and done."

Rusty turned his head in the direction of the voice and released a breath. Minnie's eyes were the first things he noticed. One light blue like the winter ice on Merchant's Pond back home, the other the color of sand. He'd never seen a person with two different-colored eyes.

"Oh, sorry. Didn't mean to startle you," she said.

He tried to find a safe place on her face to settle his gaze. Her eyes kept shifting back and forth, challenging his. Flecks of straw hung in her hair and on her coat. They mixed with drops of water and sparkled like ornaments on a black Christmas tree.

He took a deep breath and said, "It's okay. I mean, I was just thinking, is all."

Minnie smiled, lifted her head, and turned as if searching for some barnyard noise. Rusty watched a shaft of light capture her hair, reflecting the color of the sun. Her face was wildly freckled—a summer face, the kind you want to remember when snow threatens.

She turned back and for the first time he realized her smile was crooked—a crescent moon leaning back, favoring the right side of her face. He couldn't help but smile back at her, as if they shared some long-forgotten joke, or intimate experience.

Movement distracted him and he looked down. Her right hand was extended toward him, palm angled upward, as if offering him something. Not the knife-like jab men projected when they shook hands. Rusty hesitated. Women didn't shake hands. Ever. He felt a bit lightheaded and thought he smelled chickens and lavender soap. Her image began to blur and he felt pressure in his chest.

Though hesitant to touch her, his right hand involuntarily reached out. His fingers, like iron filings drawn toward a magnet, slipped across her palm and were captured, cradled in its warmth.

Her grip was firm, like a man's but without calluses. The bone-crushing grip he'd come to expect of people on a ranch was replaced with softness. There was no shake, only soft pressure that seemed to carry a message: I'm here.

Minnie's hand fluttered to her side as Rusty's hand moved away and retreated to the safety of his pocket. Warmth abandoned his palm and moved up to where the tight collar of his new black shirt cut into his neck.

"Glad to see you're up and about, Rusty."

Her crescent-moon smile relaxed and her eyebrows rose slightly as her head tilted to the left.

"Oh, ah, thanks to you and your ma it looks like I'll live to tell the tale."

"Rusty, is it alright if I call you Russell?"

Too quickly Rusty leaned forward and said, "You can call me anything, 'cept late for dinner."

They both laughed. Rusty watched Minnie's cheeks darken as her eyes released his and looked toward the corral fence.

"Please, stop staring at me, Russell. I must look like ... well, I'm not at my best. I just came in from gathering eggs and that old banty rooster has more fight in him than some rodeo bulls I've seen. Comes at me every time I go out to gather the eggs. I don't know what we're going to do with him."

"Fry him, I'd say."

Again they laughed. As they did, Minnie reached out and rested her left hand on his forearm, then jerked it back.

"Oh Russell, it's so nice to have somebody around here who knows how to laugh."

Rusty's eyes searched her face, then the empty yard. He wanted to tell her something important, but couldn't think of a thing. For some reason he felt ashamed, or embarrassed. Neither said anything as they watched several old steers pull their own shadows across the now-empty corral.

"Ah, Minnie. Can I ask you something? About your eyes, I mean."

"Oh, sure, I guess so."

"Well, I never saw a person with two different eyes. Well, colored eyes, I mean. How did you get them?"

Minnie looked at the ground. When she looked up at him he realized she was blushing.

"Well, Russell, I didn't have a lot to do with it. My pa says, before I was born, God couldn't make up his mind as to which color he should use 'cause I was so pretty. So he gave me one of each."

"Oh," was all Rusty could manage.

Together they listened to the wind. Then Minnie, without looking at him, said, "Well, I should be getting inside with these eggs I have in my pocket before they hatch."

Rusty's breathing returned to normal. "Well, thanks again, for all you did for me. Fixing me up. I appreciate your pa keeping me around with the other hands to do some chores. I'm not sure how much help I am these days."

Minnie looked over toward the barn where they could see Granville grooming a horse.

"Well, I'm sure he thinks you'll get better care, at least better food, here than in town or wherever it is you'd have to go. And I know I appreciate having someone around that's closer to my age than that barn over there."

Rusty looked down at his boot tops, searching for something to ask her.

"Do you read much, Russell?" she asked.

"Well, ah, being a ranch hand and all doesn't give me much time for reading."

"I suppose not. You do a lot of reading in the off season then, when you're in school, I mean?"

At the mention of school, images of Miss Zerkle and Tom came to him. He thought about how he disliked going into that stuffy classroom with all the noisy little kids running around.

"Oh yeah, I like school and do plenty of reading there. I guess."

"Hmmm. Well, if you have any free time while you're healing, maybe we could read some books together. Now that shipping is over I have spare time, and I like to learn about places I've never been. And I've never been anyplace but here."

"Sure, we could do that," he said, looking out toward the sandstone blocks of the house hunched on the hill in front of him, then down at his feet.

"You know, Russell, anytime you want to come up to the house, I'm sure it would be okay with Pa."

A week later Minnie watched the doctor's car rock and sway as it navigated the ruts in the lane leaving the yard. She knew her father, standing at the window with his hands in his pockets, was watching too, and probably thinking the same thoughts.

"She's not getting any better, is she, Dad?"

He turned to look at her. "No, I'm afraid not. Doc Campbell says— well, have you and your ma made your peace?"

Minnie held his stare. As long as she could remember he'd been the tall, blue-eyed man, wearing blue denim works pants, mud-dappled boots, and blue denim shirt, sleeves rolled past his elbows regardless of the season. Although the shades of blue faded throughout the years, she could not remember a time when he wore anything else, nor smelled any different than the cattle he cared about. This morning, in the kitchen's blunt light, even the blue seemed to have drained from his eyes as she looked at him. She would not, however, turn away.

She rubbed her hands on the front of her apron before slipping them into its pockets, searching for her penny. "I suppose, as best we could, Dad. I couldn't tell her I knew that she's not my real ma. It's all a bit confusing, but now she seems to think I'd be better off with a life away from cattle and ranching. I'm not sure if she's talking about me or herself."

Granville smiled at her and pulled a chair away from the table. In a single move he spun the chair around and straddled it like a horse, his arms crossed and rested on the chair's back. He lowered his head until his chin was atop his permanently suntanned forearms. He looked at the barren tabletop and released his breath.

"Sounds like she's coming to her senses," he said. "Minnie, your ma's good as dead. Least that's what the doc says. Something he calls Bright's disease. I guess the end won't be pretty."

"Never is, is it, Dad?"

"Nope, unless you die in your sleep. Anyway, it's never easy on the ones still living. I agree with your ma, you don't have to hang around here and watch."

His eyes never left hers. In the silence of the kitchen she thought she could hear the ticking of his watch. She knew he was preparing to pull that watch from his pocket and make some excuse about having to check something, real or imagined, in the barn. It was the way he ended all conversations with Ma, her, or some cowboy.

Minnie was surprised when Granville did not move. She realized he was working on something in his mind. He had that damned thousand-mile stare in his eyes even though he seemed to be looking at the empty coffee cup a foot from his nose.

"You see, when one of your parents dies, no matter how old you might be, well, you have to assume some measure of the weight of the world. Part of the weight they carried, I suppose."

She could tell Granville was waiting for her to speak.

"Dad, I'm a bit confused."

"Welcome to growin' up, daughter."

Minnie dropped her eyes to examine the cracks in the linoleum floor. Her right hand wanted to move up and massage the back of her neck. The aroma of fresh-cut grass had filled the room since they closed the door to Rachel's bedroom. Her mind jumped around from what Miss Spencer at the library in Yates Center said last week about not keeping her talent under a bushel. Maybe she should become a writer. She also thought about Russell.

"Wait, I think I should stay and help you with Ma. That's my responsibility," Minnie said.

"No need, girl. God will give me all the help I need. God and Mrs. Fitzpatrick, that is, who promises to stop by every day."

Minnie could not look into his watery eyes. She walked over to the sink and rested her body against it as she'd watch Ma do a thousand times, to look out the window. The garden plot would need planting, and they'd have to get more chickens in the spring to feed the hands that would be arriving for the season. She wanted to take her shaking hands from her apron pockets and cover her ears.

"Dad, there's a thousand things around here that need doing. Ma might have been tough, but, well, she did a lot."

"More than I'll ever know, Minnie. But it's you we're talking about and you that have to get on with your life. Mine is here. I thought Sam's was here, too, but he says twenty-five years is enough and he's studying the idea of moving on. Your ma's life was here. It's what she chose. Now you have to choose."

Minnie continued to stare out the window. She reached up to rub the back of her neck. She could see the sun in the east, a yellow ball sliced into irregular pieces by branches of cottonwoods that had lost their leaves.

Granville broke the silence by clearing his throat and said, "Did I tell you I got a letter the other day from your uncle Roger? He says there's already a lot of snow in his pastures and if it wasn't so beautiful out there in Colorado, even with snow on the grass, he'd walk all the way back to Kansas just to get away from the cold weather."

"Did you ever see his ranch, Dad?"

"Nope. Never been. Would've liked to, but, well, this is my place, even if Mr. Raleigh owns it."

"I'd like to see Colorado. And I'd like to see England where Mr. Raleigh comes from and where the people talk funny."

Granville chuckled. "Then I think I should tell you that Roger says his cook up and quit on him, went back to Mexico. Next spring he'll need somebody handy in the art of feeding noisy, lazy cowboys who eat more than the cattle."

Minnie spun around. "Dad, are you saying what I think you're saying?"

"I'm also saying that I talked with Miss Zerkle at the school in Yates Center and she could use a smart gal to help with the students during the winter months. And she has a place to stay at her house if that smart young gal needed it. That's all I'm saying. In the spring I'll probably be saying something more."

The next day, before Minnie stepped onto the house's large front porch, she paused to look at the remaining swaying prairie grass. She always enjoyed the view in this direction through the grid of the screen and the frame of the door because it reminded her of a watercolor painting she once saw in a book of western scenes. A slight chill in the air had followed a couple days of warm temperatures and made her think about fall, then winter—and going back to school. She wiped her hands on the front of her apron. She clinched a book to her side with her left elbow as she looked west to where the sun played hide-and-seek with the outbuildings. House cleaning, including the small mess of the bunkhouse, a task she enjoyed least, loomed for tomorrow. The only good thing about Ma being so sick this year was that there were fewer commands to respond to. Cooking was the fun part of ranch life, something she could do anyplace—like Colorado—and be happy.

As she stepped onto the porch, the wind caught the screen door, pulling it from her grasp. The door banged against the side of the house and sent a crack like a pistol shot out toward the open prairie. Nearby, a thumping sound echoed the door's salvo, accompanied by a human voice. "What the—?"

Minnie stepped away from the door and leaned around the corner to see who was there. She jerked back when she found herself face-to-face with Rusty. She'd not seen him since they last spoke almost a week ago.

"Oh, sorry Russell. I didn't mean to frighten you."

A book on the floor caught her eye: *Trail of the Lonesome Pine*. He must have been reading and dropped it.

"Hi Minnie," he said as he stood. "You didn't scare me so much as wake me up."

"Oh, I'm sorry."

"It's okay. I was just taking a nap before I went to bed, I guess."

Both laughed. She noticed he wiped his palms on his trousers before he leaned down to retrieve the book and winced as he picked it up.

"Oh, it doesn't hurt that much when I remember not to use it," he said. "Doc told me yesterday the best things for quick healing were lots of rest and some of your fine meals."

Both were silent until Rusty cleared his throat and said, "I hope it's okay for me to be here, on the porch I mean. These chairs are better than what we have over in the bunkhouse, and the view is about as good as a guy could hope for."

"Of course it's okay. You have my permission to sit up here anytime you want. Of course, I'm not the boss around here, only one of the workers—like a cowboy without a horse."

Minnie smiled and looked at the porch floor. Rusty started to move the rocking chair he'd been sitting in. "Here, have a seat. I'll just pull that other one over."

"No such thing, Russell Starke. You're the injured party here. I'll get it. I'm not some helpless girl from the city, you know."

"I should say not," she heard him mumble as he settled back into the rocker.

Minnie dropped the book she carried onto the cushion, sending up a small puff of tan dust. She pushed the matching weathered gray rocking chair closer to Rusty.

"Planning to read?" he asked without turning toward her.

"Sure. This time of day is my own. I see you found something to read as well."

"Yeah. Can't say as I'm much on reading. Reminds me of school—a place I don't need reminding of."

Minnie hesitated and looked away from Rusty, down to the book in her lap. She rubbed her hands on its cover and traced its edge with her fingers. She sensed Rusty had turned and was staring at her. She felt her palms getting damp. Probably her neck was getting red, too.

"Why are looking at me that way, Russell?"

"Oh, sorry. I was just thinking, I have to admit, reading does make you think about other people and places."

Minnie folded her hands and locked her fingers atop the book. Without turning to him she said, "You ever think about going someplace else, Russell?"

"I came out here," he said, looking in the direction of the bunkhouse, not at her.

"Oh, of course, I know that. But what I mean is, well, someplace where you might start a different way of life?"

"I came here, didn't I?"

Minnie laughed and looked down at her folded hands. Her face felt warm.

"Okay Mister Smartypants. I guess I'm asking how it feels to just pack up and leave the thing or place you've known your whole life. I can't imagine jumping on a freight train and going off to Indiana to be a—What do they do in Indiana?"

"Well, Kendallville is a pretty exciting place," he said.

Minnie knew Rusty was trying hard not to smile.

"Oh is it? Tell me."

"Well, back there they build a lot of windmills, if they ain't smart enough to grow onions that is."

Minnie released a small laugh. She wanted to reach out and touch his arm but was held back by his eyes focused on her face.

All she could say was, "Well, I guess it's different for a boy, or man, I mean." She drew in a breath. "Russell, you once asked me about my different colored eyes. Can I ask you a kind of personal question about your family?"

Rusty looked away from her and she thought she'd made a mistake, moved too close, like when you try to approach a wild bird.

"Sure," he said.

She released a breath. "Well, I was wondering about your ma, not the stepma you ran away from. What was your real ma like?"

Minnie listened to him clear his throat several times and thought he was not going to answer. She tried to see what he was staring at on the porch floor. His eyebrows were pulled down and drawn together. Finally, he exhaled and quietly said, "I was just a kid when she died a couple years ago. I can't hardly remember what she looked like. She only told me not to do stuff if she thought I'd get hurt doing it. And she laughed a lot. She laughed a lot. Why you asking?"

"I've never told anyone this," she said. "And I don't know why I'm telling you, but my dad told me long ago that Rachel's not my real ma. He asked that I play along as if I was Rachel's real daughter."

Minnie could not look up from her hands.

"You mean she's really your stepma, but she thinks she's your real ma?"

"That's about the long and short of it. Pa says when I was born, God had to make a choice between me and my real ma, about who should live, and God chose me."

"Humph. How'd that make your pa feel about God?"

Minnie released a small breath and laugh. "He says he wasn't real happy at the time, but is pleased at the way things have turned out for him, if not for me. He says Rachel told him she'd learn to care for me like a real daughter. I guess it just never happened."

Rusty looked at the sun's amber light on Minnie's hair. He could see dampness at the corner of her brown eye and knew the warmth he felt beneath his shirt collar was not coming from the sun. He straightened, placed his shaking hands on the arms of the chair, and prepared to stand.

His body felt drained, so instead he leaned back, setting the chair into a rocking motion.

"Going someplace, cowboy?"

Rusty looked at her. His chest felt so tight he was sure his pounding heart was going to split him in two. She was smiling with that crooked smile that always made him want to laugh.

"Nobody's ever called me that."

"What? Cowboy? It's what you are, isn't it?"

"It's sure what I want to be. It's just that everybody thinks I should be something else."

He waited for her to say something. Instead, she softly cleared her throat and turned her face toward the sun. He had to lean forward to hear her words.

"Well, for what it's worth, Russell, you're a cowboy to me."

His mouth was suddenly dry. He felt moisture in the corners of his eyes. There was a slight shift of the wind and the scent of hay stacked in the barn flooded his head. He was sure his throat had swelled so tight that nothing would ever again make it to his stomach.

The word "thanks" reached his ears, and he was unsure if he had said it or if it had drifted in from someplace he'd not been in a long time.

He cleared his throat and said, "Well, I suppose I should go check on those two new horses your dad brought in yesterday."

"I suppose."

"They might need water or something."

"Or something."

He drew in a deep breath and said, "It was nice, well, I mean fun. Well, I'm not sure what I mean, talking with you like this, Min."

"Russell, there's no need for you to run off. We're friends. Why don't you just sit and tell me about the book you're reading?"

Rusty looked out over the prairie. He thought of Henry, the man who could easily cut steers from a herd or walk away from the Civil War, yet seemed to have no friends. Then he thought of blood running from the corner of Henry's mouth. The tallgrass did not move. Crickets had grown silent and the air felt heavy with the scent of cattle long gone to market.

"I suppose I could put off checking on those animals for awhile. Not too long, though."

"No, I wouldn't want to keep you from your chores by doing something like reading, or anything else you don't like to do."

Rusty turned his head to the right so she could not see his smile.

Three days later Rusty sat on the edge of his empty bunk, staring at the trail of mouse droppings beneath the cot across the aisle. When he moved, the bunk's web of metal springs squeaked and cut into the thin denim of his pants. He watched a mouse run along the windowsill, kicking up dust motes that floated through the shaft of sunlight that partitioned the empty room. The room, once filled with noise, now echoed with a silence that made his head hurt. It had been three weeks since the fire. The toughest thing about recovering from his injuries was that doc said he should keep his hands out of his pockets. He found the few hours of work that Granville asked him to do went by too quickly.

He felt ready to move on. Keeping busy doing light chores like sweeping out the bunk house and cleaning and hanging tack on the walls was not how he dreamed of cowboy life. Nor was having quiet conversations with Minnie, or times when she read stories to him about people and places he'd never heard of. Cowboys didn't do that. Henry probably never did that. He'd probably have found an excuse to be out riding—probably.

Rusty hefted the gray canvas bag, bulging with clothes. He rubbed his right hand over frayed edges of the shoulder strap that looked like the gray ends of winter grass. Letters that once proclaimed NEWS SUN had faded. He patted the raggedy bag that used to carry newspapers, and was still able to hold all his possessions as it had since he left Kend-allville. It worried him that he had more stuff than could fit behind a saddle. Extra things like a winter coat Granville had given him and a straight razor, once Henry's, that he slipped into the corner of the bag. The razor would be useful someday, if he lived long enough to grow a mustache and shave.

Footsteps on the gravel pierced the silence of his daydream. Before he heard her voice, he knew by the softness of the tread who it was.

"Russell?"

"Yeah? I mean, just a minute, please, Min."

With his good hand he struggled to roll the thin mattress into a tight bundle and wedge it between the end of the bunk and the wall. His eyes roamed the cavernous space of the bunk room. It felt so small when twenty cowboys were there.

"Russell?"

"Right. Sure. Be there in a minute. Packing is slow when you only have one good hand."

"I could help, you know. If you'd let me."

Her shadow fell across the bunk. She wore no hat and her hair, unafraid of being bullied by the wind, fell in front of her shoulders. He realized he'd never seen it pinned up on the back of her head like women in town.

Rusty could not see the dust on her coat sleeve that Minnie pretended to brush with her forefinger. She did not look at him.

"So, you really are going, Russell?"

"Gotta."

Her eyes met his. "You know, this cold spell isn't real. It'll warm up in a few days and Dad says there's still some work to be done in the barn, maybe even through the first of the year."

"Yeah, I know. But it's work for a guy with two good hands, Min."

"I like it when you call me 'Min,' Russell. It's short, more to the point."

"And I like the way you say, 'Russell.'" He felt his mouth getting dry. His heart was pounding higher in his chest.

Both looked toward the open door when the silence was broken by the sound of Doc Campbell's car coming up the track.

"I see my ride's here. Min, just let me say, ah, you've been as good to me as anyone ever has. Especially reading to me and all. I'm not one much for books."

"I noticed."

"I liked that first book, *Trail of the Lonesome Pine*, real well. I'd like to see Virginia some day."

She turned and looked out on the vacant prairie. "So would I, Russell, but we're Kansas ranchers, not travelers—not pioneers."

He released his breath and a strange, nervous sounding laugh came from somewhere in his throat. He kept his eyes locked on the toes of his dusty boots. He heard Minnie turn and start down the steps.

"Ah, Min, maybe, well, maybe I could come back in a week or so. When my hand gets feeling better and I figure out about some things in town."

She turned. "I'd like that, Russell. When you decide."

"Decide what?"

"About your life. You have to learn you can't depend on others to make decisions about your life—like some of us do."

Rusty leaned forward to hear the last of her words being swallowed by the wind.

After spending a week in town, Rusty hitched a ride back to the ranch with Doc Campbell. He knew Granville would find enough work to keep him busy. He tossed his bag into the empty bunkhouse and went outside to wait for Minnie. He leaned against the east side of the building out of the wind and tried to keep warm by twisting back and forth, both arms wrapped tightly across his chest.

He lifted his head and watched Minnie close the kitchen door and walk toward him, head down, hands clasped behind her back. She was wrapped in that same black, unbuttoned, cloth coat. She raised her head as she approached. He found it hard to believe he was looking at a woman who worked indoors all summer. His breath started coming in short gasps at the thought of sneaking inside her open coat to hide for the rest of his life. He tried to stand taller in hopes that his trousers would hide the shaking in his knees.

"So, what's it going to be, Russell?" Minnie said.

No talk about the weather or the apple butter he smelled cooking when he passed the kitchen. No mention of glad to see him again or how long he'd hang around this time. He unfurled his arms and dropped his hands to his sides. He twisted away from the bunkhouse wall he'd been holding up and let the wind push him toward Minnie.

He knew what the two glistening vertical lines on her cheeks meant. He started to push his right hand into his pants' pocket to touch his penny, hesitated, and instead slipped the shaking fingers into his coat pocket.

"I guess ... well, what do you think is best?"

"Doesn't matter. It's you we're talking about. What happened in town?"

"Nothing. I cleaned up around the station for Mr. Slocum, mostly. Town would be the best thing, I suppose, at least until spring. Then, well, I don't know."

"Sounds like you've really made up your mind this time."

Her words came at him fast and he wanted to crouch out of the way for fear of being stung.

"What about your brother?" Minnie asked.

He felt a twinge of pain in his hand as he reached to rub his dry throat, now so tight he could hardly breathe. "Oh, he's still in the army. I might stay in town to see if he gets home on leave before, well, before whatever's next."

The sound of an automobile engine starting distracted them and they looked toward the lane. They waved at Doc Campbell in the driver's seat, tapping his thumbs on the steering wheel.

"Seems like doc's visits are getting shorter. How's your ma doing?"

Minnie's head dropped and her voice grew soft. Rusty leaned toward her to hear all her words. "She's okay, I guess. Doesn't seem to change much, even after the doctor's visits. Spends most of her time in bed now, still giving me orders like she doesn't think I know what needs doing. I'm glad doc makes his visits, though, because, well, you know, so that you can come out with him if you want to."

"I, ah, me too, Min."

Minnie looked at him, then back over her shoulder at the kitchen window and doc's car. She turned slightly, using her body to block the view from the house and idling automobile. Quickly, she removed her glove and rested her bare left hand on his sleeve. Her forefinger slipped over his sleeve's cuff, touched the inside of his wrist, and ignited a flame.

"Can I offer you some advice, Russell?"

"Ah, I don't know, Min. You might suggest something like maybe I should take a trip to the moon or something. Then I'd have to figure out how to do it 'cause—"

"Hush! I just want to say, people offering you help are not trying to change you. And Russell, I'd plan to still be here in the spring if I thought you were coming back. I'd like to see other places, someday, so be sure to let me know if you're coming or going."

Minnie turned and walked toward the house. Rusty looked down at the place on his wrist where he could still feel her finger and promised himself to never, ever, wash that spot.

"Hey," he shouted. "I'm going to work here for the next week or so."

Minnie looked back over her shoulder as the wind lifted her coat collar and covered her smile.

He turned to stare into the bunkhouse and his bag lying on Henry's old bunk. *I'll hang around here at the ranch for another week, then decide what to do.* His hand felt well enough for some heavier chores, and since there were no other cowboys around, no one would mind if he used Henry's bunk.

By the end of the week the weather couldn't make up its mind either. It swung between summer and winter with a few hours of fall tossed in. Rusty sat atop the corral fence, his boot heels hooked onto the second rail for an anchor. He balanced his weight against the push and pull of the wind and wiped sweat from his hands on the few smooth places of the top log. Warm weather—Indian Summer, Pa called it—meant more time outside. Next to the barn he could see small patches of swaying tallgrass the steers somehow missed. Far away in the wind he heard the unmistakable song of a meadowlark, a bird he'd not known before Henry told him what it was.

The sound of a train whistle floated in the wind from beyond where the meadowlark sang. An unexpected growl from his stomach, triggered by the aroma of fried chicken, surprised him. He turned to look back at the ranch house and instead found himself staring at Minnie. He'd not heard her approach, yet there she was, not twenty feet away, looking up at him. The red-and-white-checkered tablecloth from the house's kitchen table guarded the contents of a basket hooked over her arm. She said nothing. Her crooked smile relaxed as she tilted her head. Her eyes remained on his face. Silence hung between them as precise as a picture on a wall.

"What is it, Russell? You had that thousand-mile stare about you."

"Nothing."

"Russell, what is it?"

Her eyes always delivered a challenge, even if her voice did not. How could he tell her he already missed her, missed this place, while she was still standing so close?

"Leaving the tallgrass just somehow seems like the wrong thing to be doing," he said, looking down at his feet. "On the other hand, you know, Henry's dead, Cliff's in the army, and, well, life got different all of a sudden."

"Hmm, let's see," she said, softly clearing her throat while looking down at the basket. "I've got fried chicken, biscuits, and the last lemonade of the season in this basket. What I don't have, and the thing I need most, is someone to share it with."

"That's hardly a problem," he said, as he released his grip on the fence railing and dropped to the ground with a thud that stopped the songs of the insects. Smiling at her, Rusty grabbed one corner of the tablecloth and in a sweeping motion snapped it out of the basket. He spread it close enough to the corral fence for them to use the cedar rails as a backrest.

"Min, this all looks good enough to eat!"

"Oh Russell, I do enjoy the company of such an observant man."

As Rusty reached for a piece of chicken he looked at her from beneath the brim of his hat. Her grin slipped from its usual position slightly right of center to a more normal location. She said nothing, just tilted her head to the left and looked at him. He felt his cheeks getting warm and knew he had missed something, something important.

"What? Is there something I was supposed to say, besides thank you, I mean? And that this might be the luckiest thing ever happened to that ornery chicken?"

He felt her eyes release their hold on him and he managed to take a breath. Still smiling, Minnie tipped her head down, rested her fork on the tablecloth, then looked up at him and said, "No, Russell, you say all the right things. You always do."

Sounds of insects returned and filled his head. He realized Minnie was not eating. He stopped and put the half-eaten piece of fried chicken back on his plate. He watched as she examined the prairie as if it was the first time she'd ever seen tallgrass. When their eyes met she stopped and looked at him with that same questioning stare that always made his palms damp.

Rusty felt goose flesh on his arms and coolness on the back of his neck. He gripped his plate tighter to stop his hands from shaking. She was looking directly at him, still smiling, still drilling him with those colorful eyes.

His heart pounded in his chest. He was afraid its sound would hide her words. His food-laden plate felt heavy.

Minnie cleared her throat to break the silence. "A bit ago, you started to say something about leaving the tallgrass—that it's the wrong thing for you to do. But, Russell, now I have something to tell you, I guess."

He swallowed hard.

"I've decided, well, it was Pa's suggestion, I suppose, to go back to school in Yates Center this winter."

Rusty wanted to swallow the chicken in his mouth, or at least take a drink of the lemonade, but none of his muscles would work. Minnie tortured him with her crooked smile, refusing to say anything. He tried to clear his throat but only coughed a bit.

"Well," she said. "Let me finish. It'll be a lot more fun, being back in school, if there's somebody in the school whom I know and could kind of show me around."

The lump of chicken in his mouth felt as large as a baseball when he swallowed. "I could do that, Min. I'd be glad to do that. I would, honest."

"That's wonderful, Russell. I was afraid you might be thinking about not going back to school."

"Not a chance, Min. The thought never entered my mind. I was going to tell you I planned to get some more education."

"Well then, I suppose we should make a plan, or at least eat this picnic before it gets cold."

Rusty watched Minnie bite into a chicken leg. When he thought of facing Miss Zerkle at school again he began to sweat.

The work of putting the ranch to bed for the winter was finished. Rusty knew the school bell in town was probably ringing and tomorrow, or the next day, he'd have to face Miss Zerkle. At least he'd be seeing Minnie in school. That should help. He looked at cottonwoods struggling for moisture along the river's edges; the color of their leaves matched the mud-clogged roads. In the distance he could see lamps aglow in some of the windows of the ranch house. The evening sky had turned to shades of orange. Darkness was closing in, fast. He wanted to watch sunsets from here every night. How could he tell Min something as stupid as that?

He dropped Sandy's reins and hoisted himself to the top rail of the corral. His boot heels hooked onto the second rail and he rubbed his hands along the roughness where horses must have been chewing. Sandy sidestepped away toward a patch of grass still green amidst all that had turned gold.

"Probably not even five and already getting dark," he said to two calves that had moved closer to investigate the lanky kid sitting on the fence. One calf nodded, the other pulled at grass beneath the bottom rail.

He looked north, past the big house toward the creek that ran through the distant pasture and examined its line of dancing cottonwoods. He could judge the power of the wind, now, by how it bent the trees—the excessive slant of the highest branches, all stretching their arms in the same direction. This evening they reached out like beggars trying to grasp the last of the pale golden sunlight.

All summer, riding fence or cleaning the bunkhouse, even those few nights he and Henry had spent riding herd, this had always been his favorite time of day. Work done, sun short of disappearing, bright colors of the land gone soft on the edges, he was free to watch time pass, cattle graze, calves chase each other. Time to work on some plan that he never seemed to finish. Free to think about—what? Now, what? He rubbed the back of his still-sore hand. Warmth from the diminished sun wrapped

around him, blanketing the fall chill. He thought about Minnie a lot and
that faint scent of lavender soap. Rusty's wall of thought was so thick the
rattling noises of Frank's truck rolling up behind him did not penetrate.

"Hey there!"

The sudden intrusion into his daydream catapulted Rusty, arms and
legs flailing, into the corral. He landed on his hands and knees, rolling on
the ground, trying to protect his injured hand. The two calves spooked,
kicking up dirt and cattle dung as they scrambled to get away from this
flying object.

Rusty gasped for breath. "Shit, Frank! You scared the shit outta me!"

He picked up his sweat-stained gray felt hat, now the color of corral
soil, and beat it against his leg.

Frank pounded on the side of the truck with his left hand. He
was laughing so hard Rusty could see tears in his eyes. Through fits of
coughing Frank sputtered, "Kid, you wouldn't believe the look on your
face, or how far you jumped."

Rusty reached down, picked up a chunk of dried cow dung the size
of a baseball, and hurled it in the general direction of the truck. It fell
short, as he knew it would.

Between laughs and gasps for breath, Frank said, "Let's get your butt
back to town. I hear there's some news about your brother."

"What?"

"Yeah. A little bird—well, she's not all that little—told me there's a
telegram just came in that might be of interest to you."

Rusty looked over at Sandy grazing near the corral.

"Don't worry about your horse. I called Granville and told him I was
coming out to fetch you. He'll take care of her. You'll just have to come
back out and get her later. Shouldn't be too much of a burden as I hear it."

"How'd you know I was out here, Frank?"

"Oh, I called the house and Min answered. She said she could see
you perched out here like a bird on the fence."

In town, Rusty bounded up the railway platform, taking the steps two at a time. He kept his head down so his hat would not become a victim of the wind. As he rounded the corner of the faded brown building, while trying to imagine what it was like to be the president of a railroad company, a dark shape loomed in front of him. He spun out of its way, slipped on a wet patch, and almost fell from the platform.

"Oh! Sorry Rebekah. Between the wind, sand, and everything, I can hardly keep my eyes open. Looks like the first snow storm of the season coming, doesn't it?" Rusty said.

"Good evening, Russell. Yes, eastern Kansas does have changeable weather, doesn't it?"

Rusty tried to turn away from her eyes. Movement inside the train station office saved him. Mr. Slocum, only inches away on the other side of the window glass, stared at him. The stationmaster was waving a piece of yellow paper, a telegram. Rebekah, however, blocked his way into the building and whatever news might be spelled out by the few dark lines on the paper.

Rusty looked around to see if anyone was within earshot. "Ah, you seem in a cheery mood this evening, Rebekah."

Both turned their faces away from the sharp edges of the wind. Rusty caught his breath, not wanting to look into Rebekah's eyes. He was never sure what to do or say when she stared at him like that. She would say nothing, only wait for him to ask something stupid or tell her something. God, he hated that.

"You're supposed to call me Edith, Russell. Yes, I am in a very good mood. And you might be interested in the why of it."

"Why?"

"Why I'm in a good mood or why you should be interested in my good mood?"

"Ah, I'm not real sure what you mean, Rebekah, err, Edith. I really don't have time for games this evening."

"Your brother, the corporal, my, ah, grown-up friend, is coming home on a five-day furlough, beginning Saturday! I just sent him a telegram to welcome him home."

Rebekah held a piece of yellow paper clinched in her small, gloved hand. The paper snapped and fluttered like a fish trapped in a net. She stepped around the silent Rusty, turned, and called back over her shoulder, "And you might wish to close your mouth before some of this sand blows in."

Rusty turned to look at Mr. Slocum inside the station. The older man stood with his head down, leaning on his desk with both fists.

In her rush to leave, Rebekah slipped on the same spot that had nearly pitched Rusty from the boardwalk. The package she held under her arm dropped into the mud. Rusty dropped on one knee to pick it up. As he handed her the errant box, she covered his hand with her own. Through her glove he felt the heat of her body.

"Better take it easy, Rebek—err, Edith, on these wet boards."

"Oh, you're so right, Russell."

She turned away. He could feel his heart pumping. Her words hung in the air between them. Two ties from her bonnet hung down her back and swayed counter to the movement of her hips. The railway station wall protected him from the wind as he forced himself to look back to watch Rebekah walk along Main Street.

His feet wouldn't move. He turned away from Rebekah's image and looked into the quiet darkness growing in the east, beyond the corner of the station building. A tapping sound on the window brought back his reason for coming to town. Mr. Slocum was holding a telegram against the inside of the glass. Rusty could see the man's smile above the yellow paper announcing Cliff's plans. He could also see that the telegram was addressed to Rebekah.

His mind rambled: Cliff was coming to visit for the first time in nearly six months. They'd have a great time, hunting and talking about cowboy life and army life. But why had Cliff sent the telegram to Rebekah and not him?

He stepped into the warmth of the station. The position of the building's bay window allowed him to continue looking along Railroad Street toward Main Street. Edwin Slocum followed the boy's gaze.

"Quite the attractive young lady, isn't she?"

"Yes sir, Mr. Slocum, she is that."

Rusty had six days to wait. Going to school during the day and cleaning up around the station in the evenings did not seem to make the time pass any quicker. He thought of how Minnie said time just flew by when she was reading. Maybe he'd give that a try. He enjoyed being back in the Slocums' house, talking with Mrs. Slocum about what life was like years ago on the prairie—how when real cowboys came into town on Saturday nights all the children would hide.

Finally Saturday morning arrived. As he swept the floor of the station for the third time, he glanced up at the Regulator clock, just as Mr. Slocum had instructed him not to do.

"Every time you look at a clock it makes the darn thing run slower," Mr. Slocum said. "Besides, keep at that sweeping and you're going to sweep the varnish off that floor, young man."

"Sorry, Mr. Slocum. I guess I'm a bit nervous."

"Won't make time move any faster, you know."

"I know, sir. Is that the correct time?"

Rusty looked up at the station's clock again to confirm that the train bringing Cliff nearly 400 miles from Ft. Sill was still late. Town residents watching for their army boys had been stopping by the station since the scheduled hour. Some spoke with him, congratulating him on helping to save the Shaw family in what seemed like the long-ago prairie fire. Nobody mentioned Henry. Rebekah came into the station, twice. Neither time did she acknowledge his existence, only asked Mr. Slocum when the train was due. Both times Rusty wanted to say she could wait with him, but when he needed it most, his tongue wouldn't work. All he saw was the blur of her green dress beneath her unbuttoned black cloth coat.

"Where's your brother going to stay while he's home?" Mr. Slocum asked.

"Oh, I forgot to ask if it was okay for him to bunk with me, in my room, since Alex is boarding in Cliff's old room now. I know Cliff liked sleeping in the barn on most warm nights, of which this ain't one."

"Not a problem, Rusty. You boys going hunting?"

"Yes sir. Frank, er, Mr. LaFevre and me cleaned some guns last night and I think we'll do some jack hunting if this wind lets up."

"Good idea. Nice bounty on those pests these days. Maybe you boys could pick up some extra cash. You'll need it for the girls, I suppose."

Rusty stood where he could watch through the bay window for the train coming from the east or Rebekah coming from the north along Railroad Street. He shifted his weight back and forth from foot to foot. Occasionally he rocked forward and back. In between shifting from side to side or front to back, he did a few deep knee bends.

"If you don't stand still, young man, you'll be the first person in the state of Kansas to wear out a pair of boots from the inside."

Rusty halted his movements and looked over at Mr. Slocum. "Can't help myself, sir. This is the biggest day of my life."

"Ha. Good thing you're still young then and got more to come."

Rusty stood on the wooden chair next to the telegraph key to peer through the clear upper part of the window. Above the heads of the people on the platform he could see a long line of black smoke coming from an engine's stack. He closed his eyes and thought about that first night when he left Kendallville, the red and yellow embers in his hair, the insects stinging his face, and the joy of running away from home.

Since working at the train station he'd become fascinated with the variety of train engines that passed through Yates Center. Where were they when he needed to get out here?

"Here she comes! Is that a Baldwin engine, sir?"

Mr. Slocum looked up from the telegram he was preparing and peered over the top of his eyeglasses at the large black shape creeping toward them.

"Yep, she sure is. You're getting good at knowing your engines, Rusty. There might be hope for you yet. Trains and telegraphs are the future, boy, not punching cows, especially those that punch back."

Rusty smiled. "Mr. Slocum, I appreciate you trying to teach me to be a railroad man, encouraging me to go to school and all, I really do. But I'm working on being a cowboy."

Outside, Rusty maneuvered a reluctant wooden box away from the wall and jumped on top to see over the gathering crowd. The towering Baldwin engine coughed and huffed, mixing clouds of ashes and steam with pea-size flakes of snow that were falling. The clanging of the engine's bell drowned the cheers of the crowd. Along the length of the passenger cars, doors began to swing open and porters helped deposit passengers and suitcases into the waiting crowd.

The wind and snow buffeted Rusty as he searched the crowd. Town and ranch families, loaded with baskets of food and warm coats for passengers arriving from warmer climates, swayed to the rhythms of the wind like an endless field of wheat.

"Kind of early for snow, don't you think, Russell?"

He turned to see where the soft words came from and met Minnie's eyes.

"Hi there, Min. I didn't see you there."

"Oh, I'm here, Russell. Wouldn't miss this opportunity to get out of cleaning up the classroom on Saturday to enjoy this fine weather." She tipped her head down to buffer an assault from a blast of snow. "Train's coming from the east, like the wind today. 'Wind from the east, not fit for man or beast,' is what my dad says."

Rusty looked down at the top of her bonnet and could see that her attention was on people exiting the cars. He was disappointed that the wind carried away the scent of new-mown hay or lavender he usually noticed when she was around. Her arms were crossed on her chest, protecting her ungloved hands. He wanted her to tip her head up and look at him so that he could see her colorful eyes. He knew he had to say something.

"Ah, Min. I was thinking."

"Yes?"

But he never finished. Just as she turned her face up to him, Cliff appeared in the doorway of the passenger car. His brother looked taller in his army uniform, somehow straighter. As Rusty started to raise his hand, he saw Rebekah pushing her way through the crowd. He could see her red hair alternately hiding her face then stretched out behind her like a flag. Her bonnet was lying on the platform, its long ties being trampled by well-wishers' feet.

"What's all the ruckus?" Minnie asked. "I can't see a thing from down here. Give me a lift up there with you."

Rusty could not take his eyes off Rebekah. "Ah, nothing really. Some folks just trying to get closer to the train and others aren't having it. That sort of stuff."

"Anybody I might know?" asked Minnie, no longer looking up.

He glanced down at the top of her head. People in the crowd nearby were looking up at him. He felt his palms become damp and his throat too dry to answer. He wanted to tell Minnie exactly what was happening, but didn't want to act like a radio announcer at a baseball game.

Rusty watched an older woman push toward the railcar, her path blocked by Rebekah. Birds' feathers crowning the woman's large hat flapped in the constant wind and threatened to give the hat flight. The woman managed to force her way closer to the base of the railcar's steps. It appeared the older woman was talking to the back of Rebekah's head. Suddenly Rebekah whirled, her face so close to the older woman's that the brim of the bird hat shielded them both from the weather. The crowd surged toward the train's steps, then ebbed away from the two women.

Rusty watched the older woman's arms begin to flail, mimicking the feathers on her hat. Rebekah's arms remained straight at her sides. He could see Rebekah's tiny, gloveless hands ball into fists as she thrust her jaw forward. Her lips stopped moving as she barred her teeth and lunged close to the older woman.

Above the argument, Rusty saw Cliff begin to cautiously descend the steps, his Stetson campaign hat in one hand to prevent it from blowing away, a small duffel in the other. Rebekah turned and tilted her head back as Cliff stepped forward. With the speed of a diving falcon Rebekah wrapped both arms around the unsuspecting soldier, pinning his arms to his sides as she pushed her lips tight against his.

The weight and thrust of Rebekah's body knocked Cliff backward against the brass handrail of the train car. Rusty watched his brother's eyebrows lift, his eyes rapidly shifting left and right.

All eyes on the platform focused on the handsome soldier and the red-haired girl in the green dress. Rusty jumped from the box. As he started to move, Minnie grabbed his coat sleeve.

"No," Minnie said.

"I gotta."

Rusty pushed into the crowd and Minnie grabbed the shoulder of the man standing next to her, boosting herself onto the crate. Someone else grabbed at Rusty's arm and said, "Looks like you better get in there and save your brother."

"Hussy!" The shout from the older woman in the feathered hat stopped Rusty and all other movement on the platform. He gulped for air as he pushed through the crowd. He broke through the last row of people facing Cliff, Rebekah, and the woman in the large hat with its lifeless birds trying to take flight.

Rusty swallowed and stepped between the two women. He faced his brother but was so close to Rebekah he could feel the warmth of her arm pressing against his. He sensed movement on his left. From the corner of his eye he saw a balled fist coming toward him. He turned, lowered his head to the right, and reached up to cover his face with his left hand.

His action partially deflected Rebekah's fist. It flashed past his ear and connected with the older woman's right eye. The lady's head snapped back, setting her fancy hat free to take wing. The stuffed birds came to life and floated onto the platform, joining the stew of sand and snow.

Before Rusty had a chance to say anything, Rebekah's other fist came around, predestined for the woman's nose. By leaning his weight against Rebekah's side, Rusty managed to knock her slightly off balance, causing her tiny hammer-like fist to land squarely on Cliff's jaw.

The meticulously uniformed soldier staggered backward, his butt hitting the steps of the passenger car first, then his elbows and the back of his head. He managed to hang onto his campaign hat as his duffel dropped between the two railcars.

Cliff's stunned expression matched those of others in the crowd. Rebekah's clinched fists returned to her sides as she wheeled in Rusty's direction. He could see little specks of spittle in the corners of her mouth.

"Now look what you made me do! Why don't you just leave me and your brother alone? Go back to Indiana where you belong. We don't need you here any more!"

"But I—"

Rebekah slammed her foot on whatever words Rusty might be thinking of saying. "Just shut up! As far as Cliff and the army's concerned, I'm his next of kin, now."

Rusty's mouth opened, releasing air and pain from his chest. He felt his face warming in the cold air. He turned away from Rebekah and searched for a path through the crowd. He could see Mr. Slocum standing next to Minnie, their backs against the station wall. The stationmaster's ever-present grin had disappeared. Minnie's right hand covered her mouth, and he thought of the first time he'd seen her like that, ages ago.

Rusty hesitated, turned back to his brother still seated on the step shaking his head, and tried to speak. Rebekah stood on guard duty at Cliff's side. She was looking down into the space between the railcars examining Cliff's wayward duffel. Rusty could see her body shaking in the cold.

"Cliff, I, well ..."

Cliff ignored Rusty's dilemma and stood, grinning at the crowd. He brushed the seat of his trousers, and to the delight of the audience said, "Maybe we should just give her a uniform and let her take a swipe at those Jerrys."

Rusty paid no attention to the crowd's laughter. He turned but his way seemed blocked by Rebekah's words: "Go back to Indiana" and "We don't need you." He felt light pressure against his right arm. It was Minnie standing between him and the milling crowd, her shoulder pressed against his. She stood close enough to hide the ungloved fingers of her left hand that encircled his right wrist. His heart stopped pounding and he felt his lungs fill with air. Her upturned face asked a question he did not understand. Tears appeared in the corners of her eyes and their dampness sparkled in the late afternoon sun.

"Russell, I think Cliff has enough company for right now. Let's us go for a walk."

He looked back at Cliff and Rebekah and followed their movement, arm in arm, as they made their way through the crowd along the platform. Minnie's voice had been soft, yet every word clear. He knew without looking that her lopsided smile was there. He leaned forward as far as he could without falling over and tilted his head enough to see past the hem of her black dress.

"Russell! What are you doing—"

"Min, I don't think those shoes you're wearing would last as far as I want to walk right now."

She looked at the ground, secreted her arm through his, and pulled him away from the crowd. "I was thinking only maybe as far as Hersh's Bakery, for the time being," she said.

As Rusty and Minnie turned to leave the station platform he searched through the people in the crowd to where Cliff had stopped and was staring in his direction. Cliff lifted his chin in acknowledgement. *Same way Pa has of saying hello.* He could see a smile forming on his brother's lips, but did not understand what was meant by Cliff's wink before his brother turned his attention back to Rebekah.

CHAPTER ELEVEN

Storms

The weather arrived in waves. Warm temperatures would raise the hopes of people, only to be shattered by days of bone-rattling cold. Dark winter days fell into a pattern as quiet as the snow covering the streets of Yates Center. For Rusty, school was now a time he looked forward to since Minnie was in the classroom most days. If she wasn't, he felt that getting through the day was like plodding through streets turned to mud. You just put your head down and moved on.

Afternoons at the station were the pleasant time. Mr. Slocum would happily disappear, leaving Rusty in charge of the nothing that usually happened. It wasn't long before Rusty and Minnie recognized the station-master's pattern. She would appear at the station less than two heartbeats after Mr. Slocum left.

"Why, good afternoon, Russell," was her usual greeting, as if she was surprised to see him at the desk. He'd look up from the magazine with pictures of new engines and try to act surprised that she'd stop by the station at the exact moment Mr. Slocum left.

One bright afternoon Minnie arrived with a large book in her arms. "Hey, great to see you, Min," Rusty said, standing so fast his thighs bumped against the edge of the desk, nearly tipping his coffee.

"I've got an American history book here, about the Civil War and Gettysburg, we might spend some time on," she said. "It's kind of like school work, but I think you'll enjoy it anyway. You told me Henry fought in the war."

He swallowed. "That's one of my favorite subjects these days since I'm trying to figure out what America's now doing in some European war. This train stuff is getting kind of boring."

"Right," she said. "Let's get started."

Thus would begin the two hours of the day he looked forward to most.

As Rusty stood on the Slocums' front porch, darkness spread before him to the west, while the gray line dividing ground and sky in the east widened. All around him light from stars shown like holes poked in a bucket. He pulled his coat tighter, jumped from the porch to the frozen ground, and thought about getting some coffee. It was Saturday. Miss Zerkle was sick so school was called off. Mr. Slocum would be going over to Regis for the day and had asked him to go in early to mind the station.

And what about Minnie? Would she stop by for coffee? Rusty thought about going back into the house for one of the books she had loaned him. Maybe he could read something to her the way she did for him. Maybe it was best to let her do the reading so he could just look at her.

He kicked at ice ruts in the road and thought of Cliff's parting words several months back: Keep your nose clean and don't take any wooden nickels. What did that mean? He had wanted to tell Cliff about Henry and working as a cowboy, but Cliff only wanted to talk about guns and marching and army things during the few times he wasn't visiting with Rebekah. Now Cliff was probably somewhere in France or Germany. Maybe fighting. *Maybe I should have Minnie get me a map of those countries.* He had received only one letter since Cliff left, and he'd memorized the words: "And Rusty, theres one more thing. I want you to keep an eye on Rebekah for me. Were real good friends and I dont want something bad to happen to her. Understand? I heard some talk around town about her. Maybe you did, too. But shes special to me. Maybe you dont understand that now, but you will, someday. I just dont want her forgetting me."

That strange tight feeling started in his throat as it did with any mention, even thought, of Rebekah. And now, if he saw Rebekah in the mercantile or crossing the street, she would smile at him, wink, and sometimes lick her lips. She didn't act like she wanted to be just friends. She always made him feel squishy inside when they talked. Once, in Hersh's Bakery while he was getting some doughnuts, she silently walked up behind him and blew warm air on the back of his neck. The embarrassment of pitching forward, the sound of his head thumping against the glass of the bakery case, still made his palms damp.

Rusty jammed his hands deep into his coat pockets as he turned onto Railroad Street and headed for the station. He could see the lights were on as Mr. Slocum prepared to leave. *Plenty of time to get coffee first. And since it's early, the doughnut selection should still be good.*

Rusty was trying to decide between the glazed or the cake doughnut when Frank's truck pulled into the space in front of the bakery and sat there with its headlights on. Rusty left the shop, making his usual promise to Mr. Hersh to return the mug by noon. The two doughnuts in the bag felt heavy. Just the thought of eating them made his mouth water.

He walked around to the passenger side of the truck and said, "What brings you here, stranger?"

Frank took off his hat and jammed it between the steering wheel and the windshield of the truck. "I have some disturbing news for you, kid."

"What's that?"

"Well, we just got a telegram that Cliff's been shot," Frank said as he turned toward Rusty.

"Huh? That can't be! He ain't dead, is he? What am I gonna—"

"Nope, no, he's okay, I guess. He's in a hospital someplace in France. Nobody seems to know what the hell is going on. Things about war are a bit confusing over there as much as they are here. Sounds like he caught a couple a Jerrys' machine gun bullets in the leg."

"What can we do?"

"Nothing, I guess, maybe other than pray. Come on, jump in. I'll run you down to the station."

"When did you find out, Frank? Why?"

As Frank pushed the truck into gear with one hand and crushed his hat back on with the other, he smiled and gave Rusty a sidelong glance. *Jesus H. Christ. Should I tell this whiny kid that I was hiding under the covers in her bedroom when old Mr. Slocum came knocking on the door early this morning?* "Well, I didn't get a telegram. It was Rebekah got the message and she told me."

"Rebekah got a telegram? She told you? But I'm his brother!"

Frank felt the whole truck shake when Rusty dropped into the passenger seat and stomped his foot against the truck's floor, spilling coffee on his trousers.

He started to speak, stopped, then started again. "Well, it sort of makes sense that she'd get the telegram. I mean, she's his, well, his girl I guess you'd say."

"Yeah."

He could see that when Rusty stretched his legs as far as they'd go inside the truck his tailbone rested against the front edge of the seat. Frank turned to look over his left shoulder at the lightening sky. Between the buildings he could see dun-colored prairie grass rising between patches of snow.

Mr. Slocum had left the station and a note for Rusty was pinned to the coat rack, along with a copy of the telegram the government had sent to Rebekah: Cliff was wounded and in a field hospital in France. A permanent address would follow.

Edwin Slocum sat in the bay window of the station staring at the empty rails that led into the distance. This was his workplace, his domain, his favorite spot on the planet. Best of all was his unobstructed view in all directions except to his back. To anyone who would listen, he said it was like living in a soap bubble. He looked at the silent telegraph key to his right, typewriter with paper in place to the left, and seven sharpened pencils lying next to a stack of clean yellow telegram forms in front of him.

Looking over the top of his reading glasses he had no trouble identifying the woman walking down Railroad Street toward the station. He knew the image of trouble when it headed his way. Framed by dim light escaping from storefronts, obscured by blowing snow, he recognized the simple outline of her head, never lowered, always in defiance of the incessant westerly winds. Rebekah Kern was one person in town everyone could identify, even at a distance. He knew there were stories about her, some new stories that included Rusty. *I wonder if the stories are true.* Were they stories like those every town had about some woman: a fixture like the heavy-thumbed butcher, the quiet burly man in the blacksmith shop, or the jolly railroad stationmaster? *Whatever the case, I think I'll make myself scarce.*

Without turning Edwin could examine Rusty's image reflected in the glass. The boy was busy practicing Morse code, tapping out dots and dashes with a pencil eraser on a pad of paper. A good apprentice, if only he could find a way to make him sit still.

The stationmaster unwound himself from his chair, stood, and cleared his throat twice. "Rusty, I'm going over to the café for some coffee. Think you can mind the station while I'm out?"

"Sure thing, Mr. Slocum. Nothing scheduled 'til morning, is there?"

"Right."

Edwin thought Rusty seemed in a better mood since he'd received a letter from his injured brother the day before. They joked that the letter almost beat the telegram that arrived less than a week ago and was supposed to be so much quicker. Rusty told him the letter must have been written weeks ago. The letter said Cliff was in a hospital in France and he promised to be home in time for spring planting, if he got lucky.

Without taking his eyes off the growing outline of the woman headed his way, Edwin removed his coat from the rack. He examined its patched sleeves and the places where two buttons had gone missing.

"And if any messages come in, should I tap out dot-dash-dot?" Rusty asked.

The stationmaster hesitated in his struggle against the overcoat and looked at the boy. "So, you've learned the response code for 'received' have you?"

"Yep, sure have."

"Well, that's great, young man. Only, you're not a certified operator so just stay away from that key."

Rusty smiled, then tapped dot-dash-dot on the writing pad with his pencil.

As the door closed, Rusty dug into his shirt pocket beneath the scratchy wool sweater Mrs. Slocum had given him. He opened the grime-stained envelope he'd received from Cliff. Holding the paper at its edges, he unfolded the letter, skipping over all the medical stuff about blood poisoning. He wanted to get to the part of the letter he hated most: Cliff and Rebekah would be getting married as soon as Cliff was back on his feet in Yates. She was to be treated like part of the family now.

A blast of cold air accompanied the whooshing sound of the station door as it opened. Rusty shivered but did not look up from the letter lying on top of the codebook. He was mildly surprised that Mr. Slocum was back so soon.

"Café closed?"

"Russell, I owe you an apology," Rebekah said. "I owe Cliff an apology, too, I suppose. Maybe I owe this whole damn town an apology."

He felt pressure build inside his head and his eyes refused to focus. His pencil hung in mid-stroke above the page. He tried to think of an escape route. Going through the still-opened door would be the only option.

Rebekah pressed a small green handkerchief to her face and pretended to wipe her nose, not her eyes. "Damn wind. Damn snow. Damn everything!"

"If it's a telegram you wish to send, Miss Kern, Mr. Slocum will be back in a few minutes."

"Oh, shut up! Don't be such a smart ass! You're supposed to call me Edith, remember?"

Air coming into the room through the open door felt as cold to him as Rebekah's stare. With several long strides he was at her side. Rebekah turned her face toward him, tilted her head back, and closed her eyes. Rusty thought he saw a smile beginning on her lips and felt her hand on his sleeve. He brushed past her to close the door, and stepped back.

"Better keep that winter weather outside where it belongs," he said in a voice more calm than he expected.

Rebekah spun toward him, her mouth hanging opened. She released a deep breath, but no words. Her eyes narrowed to small slits. He turned to follow her gaze through the window. Was she looking toward the lights of the café?

He could see her fingers curled into tiny fists. Her head tilted slightly to the left and through clinched teeth she said, "Russell, we've known each other a long time and—"

"Not long enough," he said, turning his head to avoid the scent of peppermint candy that always reminded him of his stepmother back home.

He felt his face getting warm in the cool air of the station. He continued to hold her stare even though his father's words filled his head, warning him against looking into the eyes of wild animals.

"Please. I'm saying please, Russell. Can't we just back up a bit? You know, make things different for us, easier for me?"

He looked at the tears welling in her eyes. *Why is it, if she has any interest in anyone outside of herself, she never gives any sign of it?* "What for? 'Cause I'm supposed to treat you like one of the family now? You're better off not being treated like one of our family. What's in it for a sixteen-year-old kid, anyway? Are you crazy?"

"I thought you were seventeen," Rebekah said.

"I lied, too."

Rebekah leaned toward him, fists still clinched, eyes growing wider. Rusty backed away, keeping his eyes fixed on hers.

Her teeth did not part. She hissed, "I don't lie. You're confused. You don't understand."

He licked at his lips, feeling the dryness in his mouth and the jagged front tooth. He broke off the staring contest and sought safety in the window. Mirrored in the window's glass he saw their images, two people arguing—not happy people. Beyond the reflections snow began again. He looked back. Her eyes were still locked onto his face. He bit into his lower lip, unable to find words in the desert of his mouth.

Rusty leaned back as he saw Rebekah's arm, swathed in shimmering green fabric, begin to rise. Her palm was open and he could see dark, tiny, moon-shaped imprints from her fingernails. She gently placed her hand on his sweater sleeve and lowered her eyes. "Russell, we can still be friends."

"I can't be friends with you, Rebekah. I think you want something more than to be friends. I'm only a kid, but I know that much. I just know, or feel—"

He turned toward the window, searching outside, hoping that Mr. Slocum would return to the station. All he could see was snow.

Rebekah tilted her head back and slightly to the right. Hesitantly, she turned her body toward him, moved in closer, reached out, and placed both hands behind his elbows. Rusty felt pressure on the backs of his arms as she forced his body toward hers. Her hands began to move up and down his sleeves.

He tried to ignore the short huffing sounds as his breathing marched in time with the pounding he felt in his chest. The warmth of her hands penetrated through the wool material of the sweater. His arms ached and he knew his knees were melting and soon he'd be little more than a puddle, like melted snow, on the station floor. He tried to blink away the stinging sensation in his eyes. His throat had swollen shut. He looked down at her. Her lips were moving but her voice sounded like it was outside the building.

"Russell, this is Edith in front of you, remember? I've always been your girl, just yours, you know that."

He felt a bit light-headed. He wanted to sit back on the edge of the desk and ignore her eyes, her hands, the flowery scent of her hair, and the clean aroma of soap on her skin. "Yes, I, ah, know. Edith must be wearing a different kind of perfume than Rebekah," he said.

"Huh? What? Russell, listen to me. I need you to be friends with Edith. Forget about Rebekah. Promise me, Russell?"

"Ah, I'm not sure I can do that."

A gust of wind rattled the windows. He found the strength to break the hold of her eyes and tried to imagine a favorable outcome if he decided to bolt for the door. The mix of swirling snow and sand in the street might sting his face; however, it would be preferable to the pain in his chest.

Rebekah dropped her hands from the backs of his arms, pulled the cloth belt of her coat tighter, and turned to leave. When her right hand reached the doorknob, she hesitated and looked back over her shoulder. With her left hand she reached out as if to slip her arm through his. Instead, she rubbed his forearm like she might pet a friendly dog.

He did not move. *No more words. No more questions.*

"Well Russell, are you coming or not?"

Beneath the weight of his sweater he could feel the hair on his arms respond. He rotated his head left and right to stop the prickly sensation in the back of his neck. Sweat trickled down his sides and he wanted to laugh. His tongue rasped against his chipped tooth and dry lips. He examined his shoes, released a long-held breath, and found the strength to look straight into her eyes.

"Well?" she asked again.

"Rebekah, I can't. First, I have to watch the station while Mr. Slocum is out. It's my responsibility. Maybe an important message will come in. Second—"

"There is no second! There's no 'first,' for that matter."

Her words hit him in the face and he closed his eyes. His heart pounded less. The churning inside his stomach stopped and tightness disappeared from his throat.

He took two deep breaths and opened his eyes as if awakening from a dream. Rebekah was still there, facing him, arms now folded across her chest, head tilted as if waiting for him to say something. Her eyebrows were knitted into a single line. The aroma of Mr. Slocum's sharpened pencils replaced Rebekah's scent.

The longer he waited, the more the color of Rebekah's cheeks deepened.

"You know, Russell, I'm not giving you another chance. It's now, tonight, or never." Her voice was quiet, her speech slow, words measured. "Your brother, if he comes home, will be home soon."

"And then you'll have to deal with him, whatever his condition," he interrupted.

"This is Edith talking to you. Rebekah will have to deal with Cliff. It's Edith who needs a good, whole man in her life. Don't you think so?"

"Well, it's not going to be me, Rebekah. I think maybe what you need is a cowboy to ride herd on you. That's what I think."

He watched her eyes narrow as she turned away from the door and back to him. The muscles on the side of her face pulsed.

"Just what does that mean?" she said. "You think I need somebody like that sick, useless, thankfully dead cowboy, Snake, don't you?"

"What?"

"You heard me. You're too young to understand. Snake was never man enough to be around real women so he chose to live alone. All he was good for was drinking and smoking and rounding up cattle. When it came to women, ha."

Rusty rested back against the desk. His heart pumped so hard it made his ears hurt. He wanted to scream and grab Rebekah by the neck and squeeze until her eyes popped out. He clung to the edge of the desk to stop his hands from shaking. In a voice more calm than he expected, Rusty said, "You're wrong, Rebekah. Henry was the best cowboy that ever rode. I was with him when he died."

"And you don't know what you're talking about, sonny boy. I gave old Snake, or Henry as you call him, plenty of chances to prove just how tough he really was. All he could do was touch the brim of his hat and say something like, 'Morning, ma'am' or 'No thanks, ma'am.' "

Rusty watched color fade from Rebekah's face. It turned white, like Ma's did that night she died. He pressed his lips together and knew at any moment his heart was going to explode and he'd die right there in the station.

"Well, good night then, Rebekah, ma'am," he said, and reached up to touch the brim of the hat he was not wearing.

Rebekah lifted her chin and narrowed her eyes. Rusty thought she might be planning to never leave the station. "What would your big brother think of you now? I'm his girl you know. You looked at me. You looked at my breasts. What will we talk about after Cliff and I are married and you stop by for dinner? Maybe you could bring that smelly ranch girl of yours, the one with the cow shit under her fingernails, to our fancy home for dinner. We could tell her, maybe even teach her, a thing or two."

Rusty shook his head and looked outside. He did not hear the station door open, nor Rebekah leave. He felt only the cold Kansas wind, laden with snow and sand.

CHAPTER TWELVE

Homecoming

As he waited for Mr. Slocum to come into the station, Rusty read the letter he'd received that day from Cliff, only a week after the first.

Dear little brother:

Just a short letter to tell you Im feeling better. Not much else to write about. I don't know if your getting my letters because I dont get one from anybody back there. Every day I hope to hear the Jerrys have turned tail back to Germany but it aint happened as yet. I hope your going to school like I told you. My leg is still in pretty bad shape but I think I might still be able to kick old Mr. Peakes turkey in the butt. Haha. This sawbones here wants to cut my leg off because of the red lines in it. I told him Id rather be dead than have one leg. He said thats what Im gonna be if he dont cut it off. Haha. Tell Frank and anybody who remembers me I should be home where you are by the time they start putting the cattle on the tallgrass. Cant wait to see that Kansas tallgrass. But you can keep those twisters. Haha.

Your brother,
Cliff

Rusty looked up from the letter to the stationmaster standing next to him, hands jiggling the coins in his pockets. The smell of bacon slipped from Mr. Slocum's jacket and made Rusty's stomach growl.

"Well Russell, that letter makes it sound like he's getting better."

"Oh, was I reading aloud?" He looked back at the creased paper. "Right. I can't hardly wait for him to come home. I'm thinking maybe we could start over. Him and me being cowboys, I mean."

When there was no response, he looked up at Mr. Slocum. The stationmaster was looking through the bay window toward Main Street. Rusty looked, too. All he could see was water-filled ruts of mud carved by automobiles and wagons, along with a dozen people, their arms hugging their chests, as if that could stop the spring rain from getting to their clothes.

"What's the date on that letter, Russell?"

Rusty looked at the stained envelope, then the top of the page. "Written more than a month ago. You'd think they'd use the telegraph, for goodness' sake."

Mr. Slocum said nothing. He took off his coat and began to straighten the books on his desk. Rusty glanced out the window in the direction of the bakery, then over toward the mercantile.

"Maybe I'll walk up to the cafe and get a bite to eat, sir."

Mr. Slocum looked up from his books, rubbed his eyes, and said, "Do what you think is best. I think I'd just go for the coffee. It's good this time of morning."

Rusty pulled on his coat and started for the door. "Thanks for the tip, Mr. Slocum. I can always depend on you for information on the quality of the coffee in Yates Center."

He waited for Mr. Slocum's rejoinder, humor he'd come to appreciate, but the stationmaster seemed more interested in his newspaper.

"Sir?"

"Oh, sorry Russell. Just thinking about this damned war."

Rusty shrugged as he left the station. He looked back over his shoulder to see Mr. Slocum still staring at the paper.

That same evening Edwin rubbed his eyes with his fists and through the self-inflicted haze, stared down at the words he'd just written. He tapped the eraser end of his pencil on the message as if trying to summon the spirit world and waited for an answer. He knew his duty: get information to the person designated as the recipient. But did he also have a duty to tell the person he thought would care most about this information? He stuck the eraser end of his pencil into his mouth and tested its resilience.

Edwin twisted in his chair and closed his eyes in anticipation of the wailing sound the chair would make. It always reminded him of cats engaged in copulation. As usual, he promised himself to apply grease to wherever it was that made this everyday action of turning around so annoying.

The clean sheet of yellow paper in his left hand offered no resistance as he slipped it between the typewriter's paper table and the roller. His forefingers poked at the keys while the pencil in his mouth swayed like a wind vane, pointing at the decoded words he'd written, and back to the neat lines of script appearing on the typed page.

Finished, Edwin unearthed the long scissors from his desk drawer. He carefully cut the lines of words into quarter-inch-wide strips. He closed his eyes as he leaned over the open jar of rubber cement and deeply inhaled that scent that always brought a smile as it filled his lungs. He brushed the sticky compound onto the backs of the paper strips and pressed the lines of bold black letters onto the smaller sheet of yellow paper emblazoned with the words "Western Union." Edwin squinted at the tiny signature beneath the larger letters and wondered who Newcomb Carlton, chairman of the board, might be. *What's the rich bastard doing today? Does Mr. Carlton know, or care, about the news one of his employees in far-off Kansas might be about to deliver? Does he know how many times his telegraph operators had to knock on some poor woman's door with a telegram that would inform her she was now a widow?*

Edwin pushed his hat on and stepped out of the station. He looked up into the darkening sky to watch bats scoop emptiness from the night, then turned in the direction he was not supposed to go.

Edwin reached the steps of his porch just as Rusty burst through the door, seemingly engaged in a battle with his coat. The hand holding his cap seemed wedged into the right sleeve, while in his left hand he held the remains of a biscuit.

"Ha! Just the young man I've been looking for," Edwin said. "Someone who can wrestle a bear while eating at the same time."

"Huh? Hey, Mr. Slocum. I was about to go down to the office to see if you needed some relief."

"No need, son. Closed for the night. I have a telegram here. Not for you, exactly, but certainly of interest to you."

Rusty jammed the remaining piece of biscuit into his mouth and reached for the piece of paper threatened by the wind.

"It looks like it's addressed to Rebekah Kern, sir," he said, his voice muffled by the biscuit.

"Don't you think I know that? Just read it and forget about where you saw it until she surprises you and the rest of the town with this news in the morning."

Edwin watched Rusty's eyes jump over the words as they went back and read through them a second time, more slowly.

"Wow! This says Cliff's coming home with some wounded soldiers. And he's well enough to travel here. This is great. When do you think he'll get here?"

"Well, best I can figure is that he must have arrived in New York about a week ago and the secretary of war or adjutant general or whoever's responsible for sending this telegram was too busy to let us know. Let me see what I can find out, soon as I deliver this to Miss Kern, that is."

Rusty watched Mr. Slocum walk toward Rebekah's house, turn the corner, and fade into the shadows before he could move back inside. He halted at the bottom of the stairs that led to his room, closed his eyes, and rested his forehead on his hand holding the banister. He felt a warm hand on his arm and looked up. His eyes met Mrs. Slocum's gray eyes, bits of fog drifting in the white dish of her face. She had her head tilted and looked up at him with the same expression he'd seen on dogs staring at the ceiling fans in the mercantile.

"Oh, good evening, Mrs. Slocum. Guess my mind was somewheres else."

"Understandable, Russell."

"Mr. Slocum says my brother's coming home soon."

"Won't that be nice," she said, and patted his arm as if she were rewarding an obedient puppy, "to have two of you in the house again. My boys never came home, you know."

Before he could respond, Mrs. Slocum walked through the drawing room and back into the kitchen. Rusty felt his heart pump faster and his breath come in small gulps as he climbed the stairs two at a time.

He sat on the bed and examined the frayed edge of the carpet where the oil lamp puddled his shadow beneath his feet. Downstairs he heard the front door snap like a distant rifle shot. The Slocums' soft voices filtered through the cracks in the floorboards, probably discussing the telegram. Would his brother have both legs? Rusty had never seen a cowboy with just one leg. Even being a carpenter with one leg would be hard. Should he run over to Miss Zerkle's house in the morning and tell Minnie that Cliff would be home soon?

He fell back on the bed, resting on the dirty and scarred canvas bag he preferred to a pillow. His eyes moved over the water stains on the ceiling and he wondered what life must have been like for Henry— before he became known as Snake. Were his stories of running away from Gettysburg true? Does it even matter if you're a deserter when you're trying to save your own life? *The patterns on the ceiling changed*

into herds of longhorn steers grazing their way to Kansas from Argentina.
He and Henry, who everyone except him called Snake, stopped at a house
for dinner and it was Ma standing next to a stove. She was laughing and
talking but he could not hear her words. He wanted to introduce Henry to
Ma but could not remember his friend's name. He heard Ma say, "Names
don't matter, Russell."

It was three days before Mr. Slocum passed on any more information about the troop transport train loaded with wounded soldiers. The train was working its way across country and Cliff should probably be on board.

Mr. Slocum said, "You have to remember, Russell, these government things don't always move as fast as we'd like. That train is an unscheduled one and has to make stops in a lot of out-of-the-way towns, dropping off soldiers and all. But we should know something the day before it gets here."

Two more days passed before notification about the train arrived. Keeping his hands in his pockets and balancing on one foot, Rusty used the rounded toe of his boot to scrape at clumps of dried mud clinging to the train station steps. When he tired of that, he walked into the station, glanced up at the clock, then over at Mr. Slocum asleep in his squeaky chair. Rusty shook his head. How did the man find comfort resting his head on a desk?

"Sir? Mr. Slocum? Time for some coffee, sir."

Mr. Slocum tipped upright and looked around the office as if he'd never seen the place. This time for a pillow he had used an inch-thick stack of blank yellow telegram pages. The paper left a crease down the right side of his face extending from his eye to his chin. It reminded Rusty of Shotsky's Creek that trickled between Kendallville and Orpham back home.

"Oh, Russell, glad you're here, lad. Glad to see you. Big day today, isn't it?"

The distorted view through the wavy glass of the bowed window softened the edges of the cottonwoods and created an undulating blue-green background for the tracks. He hid his shaking hands in his pants pockets and turned back to Mr. Slocum's smiling face.

"Sure is, sir. Somebody smart must have ordered this weather. Any word yet on that train, sir?"

"Sanders over in Nehosho Falls says the train cleared his station there just a bit ago. I bet if you laid your ear on the rail like those hobos do, you'd hear the train by now."

Rusty thought of Jupiter doing that so long ago. "Putting your head on the track is not always a good idea though, is it, sir?"

"Not if you're looking the wrong direction when the engine arrives, son," said Mr. Slocum, slapping his palm on the desk, laughing at his own joke.

Rusty turned his attention back to what was happening outside. In both directions windows framed a sky of such a hard shade of blue that a well-hit line drive might shatter the color. Closer to the station, below the blue line of the sky, Rusty watched a procession of people walking along Railroad Street. They carried baskets of food and blankets and seemed not to be in a hurry. Looking back to the east he saw a dark, crooked finger of smoke rising. It pointed its sharp nail to the south.

"She's coming, sir! And it looks like a lot of people coming over to meet it, too."

"Humph," said Mr. Slocum, looking up from his paper. "Probably coming to see something they hope they'll never see again. I'm afraid it's just the beginning, though."

Rusty watched the stationmaster snake his finger across the green-colored shade of his desk lamp to check the depth of the dung-colored dust.

"Yeah. Not a real happy celebration for some, son. But at least some of them, folks like you, will have their loved ones back, knowing they ain't buried in some muddy field in god-knows-where."

As Rusty started to answer, his breath caught in his throat. At the far end of the platform Minnie and Granville were standing next to a stack of crates. He used his tongue to wipe sweat off his upper lip as he moved toward the door.

"I see somebody out there I have to talk to, sir. Anything more you need me for?"

"Not now, young man. Let's get out there and be the first ones to welcome home your brother."

Rusty waited for Mr. Slocum to unbend himself from his chair. Just as he started, however, the telegraph key sprang to life and Mr. Slocum dropped back. The telegraph key's metallic clatter cut through the silence hanging between them.

"Oh, wouldn't you know. Run along. I'll be out to join you as soon as I take care of whatever this might be," Mr. Slocum said.

Edwin relaxed and prepared to translate the incoming message. Sweat started to form on the older man's palms as he decoded and wrote the opening line: WA226 48 Govt=Washington AP 10 111P

His eyes rose to the wall calendar and its painting of a locomotive plunging through a gigantic drift of snow in some place he'd never visit.

"These telegrams from the government are never good news these days," he said to the calendar. "And would you look at that date! This one is three days old, to boot."

He tapped his pencil on the lampshade and watched the irritated dust descend as he waited for the rest of the message to begin. The long and short spaces between the clicks seemed to be taking longer than usual. *New operator on the other end of the line.* As he deciphered the code, he felt his stomach began to churn and tighten. It was addressed to Rebekah Kern.

Rusty hesitated when he reached the middle of the crowd. He sorted through the growing mass of unsmiling faces, hoping to find Minnie and her father. Blasts of steam released from the engine's boiler behind him drowned music played by the Burdick Cowboy Band that had traveled over from Chase County for the day. His stomach rumbled as the aroma coming from cloth-covered baskets of baked goods reached him. Children stood quietly alongside their parents or grandparents while adults talked in hushed tones.

As he examined the crowd, he was met with occasional greetings from townspeople, along with farmers and ranchers dressed more for church than for work this day. The greetings consisted of little more than head nods. Robust voices more often used to stop a running steer were barely above a whisper. Some men reached up to touch the brim of their hats as he passed.

From behind, someone called his name and he turned to see Belle and George walking along the platform. Aunt Belle waved and started to yell something just as the train stopped moving.

All eyes but his focused on opening doors of the two passenger cars. Like distant rifle shots, he heard the crack as metal handles slammed against wood doorframes. Porters prepared to unload men barely able to walk. Rusty, still with his back to the train, continued to stare into the faces of the crowd looking for Minnie.

Her wheat-colored hair caught his attention. Its undulating movement and color easily separated her from her father, the only man in the crowd wearing canvas pants as if dressed for work. Minnie, however, was not looking east toward the incoming train. She seemed focused in the opposite direction at some disturbance.

Rusty searched in the same direction until he spotted Rebekah. Her bright green dress flashed, like a match struck in the darkness of gray and black suits and dresses as she pushed and shoved toward the edge of the platform.

When he turned back to look for Minnie, his eyes met Granville's solemn face. Minnie disappeared then reappeared closer to the building, standing next to Mr. Slocum. Men in the crowd, coats removed, sleeves of their white shirts rolled past their elbows, worked their way forward to help the wounded troops. There appeared to be more helpers than wounded soldiers. He could see Rebekah had made it to the front of the crowd and was being a hindrance.

Rusty moved toward the open door of the second passenger car, excusing himself as he pushed through the crowd. He could see pale faces at the top of the railcar steps searching the crowd until they found pale faces of loved ones below, bringing together tears and smiles.

Rebekah moved closer to him. Rusty did not want to speak with her. What could he say when nothing needed to be said? She looked up at him, released a huff of air through her nose, and turned her attention back to the railcar less than ten feet away.

In was soon over. The sound of shuffling feet faded until all Rusty could hear was the ticking of the engine's boiler cooling, a sound similar to Mr. Slocum's pocket watch laying forgotten on the desk. His feet would not move. He twisted his head toward the third car with its sliding door—a baggage car, not another passenger car.

Movement in the dark recesses of the passenger car caught Rusty's eye. A soldier on crutches appeared, working his way through the darkness. A campaign hat hid the man's face, but Rusty could see corporal's stripes on his left sleeve.

The soldier kept his head down and paused as if searching for something on the platform below. He leaned forward, pointing with his crutches and hesitating before stepping into the bright sunlight.

Rusty felt someone push against him and jam an elbow into his stomach. It was Rebekah. She drew herself to attention, raised her left arm, and offered a strange, two-fingered salute over her left eyebrow.

Rusty could see the soldier was unsteady on his feet, probably unfamiliar with how to walk with crutches. The soldier raised his head, blinked several times, and returned Rebekah's salute with a nod. It was not Cliff. Rusty stepped forward to offer assistance just as Rebekah spun toward him, blocking his way. Her face stopped inches from his. He could see her unblinking eyes were rimmed in red; spittle formed at the corners of her mouth. Her chest heaved and each time it rose, pressed lightly against him.

"Where is he? What have you done with my husband? I mean my fiancée?" she said.

Rusty's mouth opened but no words came out. He started to raise both hands in self-defense, stumbled backward, and bumped against a young woman cradling a child.

"Excuse me, ma'am, please," Rusty said.

He looked back at Rebekah—her hands were balled into fists, eyes wide like a steer's when it was being loaded into a cattle car. He moved around the woman holding the child.

"Please, I have to, ah, find someone," he said. His throat was dry and it hurt to breathe.

Rusty touched the brim of his hat, turned, and looked toward the end of the station platform. Over the top of the woman's head, near the corner of the station office, he saw Mr. Slocum talking with Minnie. Neither seemed to be paying attention to what was happening near the tracks.

Shouts came from a man standing next to the woman with the child, hastening Rusty's escape. "Make way! If you're not gonna help get outta the way!"

When he reached the station office he looked first at Minnie, her handkerchief covering her mouth and nose. Rusty could see tears had escaped the handkerchief and moved down the side of her face. He could see only her blue eye. She did not look at him as he approached. He turned to Mr. Slocum.

The stationmaster cleared his throat with such force it made Rusty wince. Mr. Slocum pulled at his nose with a red handkerchief. Rusty could see the man's tears disappearing into his beard.

Rusty looked back at Minnie. "Min? What is it? What's wrong? Is it your ma?"

Minnie looked down at the yellow telegram she held captive. She used her free hand to capture a tendril of hair that had escaped and tried to push it behind her ear.

Rusty stepped closer to her, unable to speak or breathe. His chest tightened and in the quiet world around him he heard only the drum beating in his chest.

Minnie said, "Oh Russell, I'm so sorry. So sorry."

Rusty turned to Mr. Slocum, who stood with his head down, running the right sleeve of his jacket back and forth across his nose. "Those damn people in Washington are so inefficient. So goddamned inefficient, Russell."

"What? Why?" Rusty said.

The stationmaster exhaled and nodded at the telegram Minnie held. "That was suppose to get here days ago, Russell. I'm so sorry."

Rusty reached out for the paper in Minnie's hand. He wanted to squeeze the telegram's words into a ball and throw them beyond the river. He wanted his world to stay as it was—or was going to be. He wanted to stop his hand as it reached out. His fingers felt the warmth of Minnie's beneath the paper as she managed to grasp his little finger with her own. He realized that trembling in her hand, not the wind, caused the paper to flutter like a frightened bird.

The name on the telegram was not his. Rebekah's name on the second line was the first thing to catch his eye as Minnie's finger relinquished its hold on him.

The message read:

THE SECRETARY OF WAR DESIRES ME TO EXPRESS HIS DEEP REGRET THAT YOUR FIANCEE CORPORAL CLIFTON A STARKE INFANTRY HAS BEEN REPORTED DEAD OF COMBAT WOUNDS ABOARD LIBERTY TRAIN 883 APR 11 TOWNSAND VIR PERIOD ADDITIONAL INFORMA-TION WILL BE SENT YOU WHEN RECEIPED= ULIO THE ADJUTANT GENERAL

Belle Hardy rocked back and forth trying to find comfort in dress shoes laced so tight she imagined herself as one of those little girls in China she'd read about. Her attention alternated among the last of the wounded soldiers hugging loved ones on the station platform, the thinning crowd of helpers, and an animated conversation she could see taking place at the corner of the station building.

Rebekah Kern's performance at the steps of the passenger car had been entertaining as well as upsetting. Belle saw Rusty standing with Mr. Slocum and Granville Gorham's daughter, and no one looked happy. Where was Cliff?

"George, something's wrong," she said, not taking her eyes off Rusty, who was leaning against the building holding a piece of yellow paper that could only be a telegram. "Cliff must have missed the train or something."

She turned to see George no longer watching the crowd disperse. He was focused on the baggage car. As she watched, Belle noticed one peculiar-shaped box that required six men to slide it along the floor, then lift from the doorway. The men carefully set the long box in the shade of the building.

"I think you're right, Belle. One of those crates down there looks an awful lot like a coffin," he said.

"George, you don't think they've sent a dead soldier home, do you?"

"No, I don't think they do that. It might be that one of the boys died once he got back here on American soil."

Belle hesitated before speaking, her eyes back on the conversation near the edge of the station house. "Oh, George, how terrible for his family. Maybe for ours."

Edwin looked down the length of the platform to where a large pine box was visible resting in the shade of the building. Two dark knots in the wood plank's side surface stared back at him. He had to say something to the Rusty. There must be some words of wisdom that would make fighting and dying seem like a smart thing to do. He felt a wave of relief when he heard his name called.

He turned to see Rebekah Kern approaching from the street. Both her hands grasped the front of her skirt and lifted it almost to her knees.

Her eyes appeared as mere slits and her lips were pressed together so hard they looked purple in the waning sunlight. Edwin shifted his attention to back to Rusty. The young boy's forearm was pushed against the station wall to provide a pillow for his forehead.

Edwin picked up the telegram Rusty had dropped, brushed away the sand, and shifted his eyes to Minnie, standing next to the boy. Her head was bowed. Her handkerchief covered her mouth and he could see her body shaking. The stationmaster released a deep sigh and walked toward Rebekah, hoping to deflect any encounter with Rusty she might have in mind.

"What is it, Miss Kern?"

"It is this: I demand you telegraph someone to find out where Clifton Starke is. He was supposed to be on that train, you know."

As he looked at Rebekah he could see her cheeks redden, her gloved hands balled into fists. He knew he should not look into her eyes. Their dark shade of green had a way of making him think of whatever it was he was ashamed of. Edwin looked down at the telegram and extended his hand toward Rebekah. "Well, Miss Kern, he is on that train. Or was."

CHAPTER THIRTEEN

Facing East

Rusty felt Sandy shift her weight. He took his eyes off the thin black line crawling between the blue of the sky and the green of the prairie. The colors seemed to separate as the train passed, then rejoined after its smoke was gone.

"What is it, girl?" he said, patting the horse's mane.

"Morning, cowboy."

"Hey Min. You're up early, as usual. Making breakfast for the new hands?" Rusty said as he turned to face Minnie for the first time since Cliff's funeral two weeks ago. He told himself the only reason for returning to the ranch was to take Sandy back to Uncle George's, then he'd move on.

He thought Minnie's crooked smile seemed more relaxed this morning. She looked different. It took a few seconds for him to realize she was not wearing an apron, her usual morning attire.

"You must have caught a ride up here with Doc Campbell," she said, and reached up to tuck a loose strand of hair behind her left ear before giving Sandy a pat on the neck. "I didn't know you were coming or I would have ... Well, it's good to see you, Russell. Have you been hiding?"

"Worse than that, Min. I've been thinking," he said and jumped down from the saddle.

She reached out and brushed her hand against his forearm. "I'm going to miss your little jokes—"

"What? Miss what? What—"

"I'm leaving, Russell," she said. Her smile was gone. Her eyes seemed to be dashing around his face looking for a place to land. "I'm not cooking this morning, or any morning, here. Dad's hired a new cook, a lady from town who knows how to deal with noisy cowboys since she raised a dozen kids." Minnie looked past him to where Henry's horse grazed at the far side of the field.

"Ah, I'm a bit confused," he said. "Leaving? You mean you're just going to take care of your ma, right?"

"No, Russell. I've made some decisions about, well, about me," she said.

Rusty felt his throat tighten, making it difficult to breathe. His eyes moved back and forth, trying to decide which of hers to focus on.

Minnie released a deep sigh. "Russell, I'm leaving the ranch. Dad and I discussed it. I want to see more of the world than just Kansas so I'm going out to Colorado to work for my uncle. He has a big cattle ranch out there and he needs a cook."

Rusty could not believe she was smiling. Each word made him want to back away. He swallowed and said, "What, well, what about after that?"

"Don't know. I'll figure that out then," she said and tipped her head back to let the wind play with her hair.

Rusty released the breath he'd been holding. He reached down and grasped her hand, trying not to smile as if this were some happy occasion. "I guess this is a day for good-byes then. I was trying to come up with a way to tell you I've about given up on the cowboy life," he said, and turned to look at Henry's mount in the pasture. "I think Sandy somehow knows. When I walked up to the fence she just snorted and walked away at first."

"Maybe she doesn't like good-byes, either. I know with Cliff gone it's tough—going to be tough—for you, but, well, you're the only one who can make decisions about yourself, Russell."

"Yeah, I think that's what all those books you've been reading to me have been trying to say." Rusty cleared his throat and looked down at the ground. She released his hand, reached up, and rested her palm against his chest.

"Okay cowboy. Maybe we'll meet again someplace."

"Yeah. Again. Someplace. Maybe," he said and slipped his hands into his pockets. He tipped his head back to check a passing cloud formation.

Rusty waited until he was sure she was gone and tears would no longer show on his face before he looked back toward the house where Doc Campbell's car waited. He looked at Sandy, who had her head over the top rail and was gazing into the pasture. He removed her saddle and bridle and watched as she walked back to Henry's mare. The two horses looked at him several times; however, he knew Sandy would not walk over again.

He waited in the doctor's car. When he heard the house door close he was afraid to turn to see if it might be Minnie coming back to say good-bye.

"Hey stranger," Granville said. "Minnie told me you were out here for one last look around, or maybe trying to steal a horse."

"Morning Granville. I don't know if it's a last look, but for now, well—"

"I understand. Don't worry about your mare. I'll set things right with George." Granville cleared his throat. "Well, I just want you to know that you're always welcome here. I don't know how much work they'll be, but there's always something to do around a ranch. Always something," he said, looking toward the barn. "Best I get at something, then. You take care," he said and reached in to shake hands.

Rusty grasped the man's hands and closed his eyes, preparing for the pain he knew was coming. He smiled and tried to match the ranch manager's grip with equal strength.

Granville turned and started to walk away, then stopped and looked back. "Can I give ya bit of advice, son?" he said.

Rusty hesitated, brushed some dust from the sleeve of his black shirt, and looked back through the car window.

"As long as it doesn't cost me anything. I'm a bit short on cash these days."

Granville leaned both hands on the window frame of the car door and looked down at his boot tops. Rusty could not see the boss's face and wondered what the man might be thinking.

"When I was about your age, and told my folks I was fixin' to leave the farm where I was working to go west and join the cattle drives, my Pa said, 'Better to be a pilgrim without a destination than cross the same miserable threshold every day of your life.' "

Rusty looked at the crown of Granville's hat and watched the man wipe his hands on the sides of his trousers before slipping them into his pockets.

He swallowed several times. "Granville, you know, when I came out here I was looking to learn how to be a cowboy. Now it hardly seems like it ever happened."

Granville backed away from the car and looked over toward the bunkhouse. "Well, I think you got a small taste of what it used to be, Russell, and a big taste of what it's like now."

Rusty watched the man who had given him his chance at being a cowboy turn and walk toward the barn, hands in his pockets, eyes focused on something a thousand miles away.

As they drove along the rutted road, Rusty looked at the tallgrass beginning to produce the carpet of green he knew would stretch on forever. When they reached the point where the road split, one branch heading for town, the other heading toward the north part of the county, Rusty asked the doc to stop and let him out.

"Thanks for the lift, doc. I'm going to walk up to the Hardy place and visit with my aunt and uncle for a bit."

Doc Campbell looked up the road. "Long way for a walk. Tell you what, I could use a bit of exercise myself. Why don't you take the car and I'll walk into town."

Rusty looked at the doctor then at the steering wheel. "Ah, I'm not so sure that's a good idea, Doc."

"Why, 'cause you've never driven a car?"

"Well, that would be a big part of it."

"Not much to it. Jump in here and I'll show you what you need to know. Better yet, you drive me in to town, then take the car out to the Hardys' place. I can get my exercise doing something else."

With fits and starts, Rusty had his first lesson in driving a motorcar. Later, as he drove into the Hardy ranch, causing the chickens to scatter around the yard, he noticed Belle standing at the door, arms across her chest. She moved toward him and he realized doc had not told him how to stop the engine from running.

"Tell me you haven't turned into an outlaw and stolen the doctor's car, Russell."

Rusty turned the key to the off position and jumped down from the seat. "No ma'am," he said, leaning against the front fender, arms across his chest. "Doc thinks I'm responsible enough to drive, so I thought I'd pay a visit."

Belle walked down the steps as George, attracted by the noise, came from the barn.

"George, look who's here to disturb our peace and quiet," Belle said and wrapped an arm around Rusty's shoulder. "If we had a telephone we could call the sheriff and have this guy arrested for car rustling."

"Maybe we should just shoot him and save the county the cost of a trial," said George as he wiped his hands on the front of his trousers. He extended his hand. "How ya doing, young man?"

"I'm okay, Uncle George. I just thought I'd come up here and, well, I'm not sure why I came up here," Rusty said, looking first at Belle, then George.

"It's called tying up loose ends, Rusty," said Belle.

"Feels more like quitting," he said, looking toward the dugout. "I thought being a cowboy would be more, well, last longer. I don't know. More work, maybe."

"Oh, you don't have to smell a barn full of cow manure to know what it's like to be a cowboy," George said.

"Well, I'll be," Belle said. "Russell, I think some of my teaching is finally taken hold of your uncle's brain. And since you're here, you might as well stay and have a bite to eat."

Over the meal the trio laughed about the days of living in the dugout with snakes and bugs. It ended with Rusty promising to write them a letter when he got back to Kendallville—if that's where he decided to go.

He stood next to the car looking down the long sweep of the patchwork quilt prairie to the west. Belle walked over to him. "Russell, let me give you a hug," she said and wrapped her arms around him before he could get his hands out of his pockets. He turned his head to the side when he realized she was going to kiss him.

When Belle released him he turned to George, who was walking toward the front of the automobile. "Climb up on in there, young man, and I'll give 'er a crank," George said without looking at him. "You leave a few of those bluegills in the lake back there in Kendallville—in case I ever go back for a visit."

"I'll save you a spot in the boat, Uncle George. And thanks for everything."

A week later, Rusty and Sam pushed Minnie's trunk along the stained wooden floor of the baggage car and into the care of a black porter. The trunk skidded and jostled on the rough planks, launching dust motes that danced in sunlight coming through the open door on the opposite side of the car. He felt a light brush of wind from the south tickle the back of his neck as the scent of the river replaced the smell of wood.

Sam looked up at the ancient black man who struggled with the trunk and said, "You be careful with that trunk. It's all she has in this world."

Rusty looked at the ragged sleeves of the porter's shirt, surprised at how much the old man reminded him of Jupiter. *I wonder where Jupiter is now.*

Sam turned to him and said, "Did you see the clothes on that man? You'd think the railroad would pay their people better so they could buy some decent clothes. He looks almost as bad as a hobo."

Rusty saw the black man's eyes shift in their direction, but he did not raise his head. When Sam turned and walked away from the open door, Rusty grabbed the edge of the doorframe and pulled himself up onto the floor as he'd done countless times with moving trains on his trip to Kansas.

"Let me give you a hand with that," he said, smiling at the porter.

"Thank you, sir. You seems to know how to get in and outta a side-door Pullman."

Rusty grinned at the man and released a quiet laugh. "First, the name's not sir, it's Rusty. Second, it's the only way to travel if you enjoy seeing the countryside at the least-possible cost. And third, I can tell by your clothes that you're, let's say, working your way west."

When the trunk was secure against the back wall of the baggage car, Rusty reached out to shake hands with the porter. "I know you'll take care of the trunk. Enjoy the trip west," he said.

The black man hesitated before extending his hand.

"Don't worry," Rusty said. "The white color won't come off on you."

Rusty walked around back of the baggage car and propped his feet against a rail tie as he leaned back on the hard edge of the car's floor. He heard the engineer release a blast of steam to relieve pressure in the boiler and knew that soon this car and everything connected to it would be moving. He turned so he could see Minnie preparing to board. She stood a hundred feet away, her back to him, talking with Granville.

Sam was tossing chunks of gravel at a signpost, displaying the bad form of a baseball pitcher. "Sam, my mind's made up. I'm not meant to be a cowboy," Rusty said.

Sam stopped and walked over to where Rusty was propped against the railcar.

"Well, you're already enough of a cowboy, Rusty. People have probably told you that so there's no need to chew that cabbage a second time, if you get my drift. Punching cows ain't for everybody."

Rusty watched Sam's mustache dance in the sun and brushed gravel from the top of a rail tie with the toe of his boot. "I suppose. Well, I did learn that being a cowboy is a lot more fun than what I first thought when I came out here."

"How's that, son?" Sam said, looking over at him.

"Well, I got beat up pretty good getting here, held a real cowboy's hand when he died, and now I'm watching the first girl I fancy walk away with hardly a word of good-bye. How much more fun can a guy ask for?"

"Ha, you got a point there, young man. Yeah, it's not only the cowboy's life that's different from what the books tell you. It's a different breed of cattle now. Different breed of men, too."

The jolt and uptake of couplers as each railcar urged the one behind it into life pushed Rusty to his feet. The sound of metal grabbing metal and the smell of ashes mixed with clouds of steam made him think of Indiana. He tried to push away thoughts of how Ma, and Cliff, and Henry, all left him without saying good-bye. *Well, Henry sort of said good-bye.* He felt a lump in his throat start again. His attention went back to Minnie on the steps, hatless, griping the brass railing. She turned toward him and he could see her crescent-moon smile slip out from behind the clouds as she disappeared into the darkness of the railcar.

Rusty sat on the side of the station's platform watching his boots swing in and out of his line of vision. He thought about a long-forgotten day on his trip to Kansas, passing through a nameless town, crossing over another nameless road. There was a kid about his own age standing next to the tracks, wearing a brown flat wool cap that matched the color of the road. A cigarette dangled from the corner of the kid's mouth. The sleeves of the boy's spotless white shirt were rolled to the elbows, one arm wrapped around a stack of books. As the train clanked past, he had locked eyes with the other boy. Just before he lost sight of him, he thought he'd seen the kid's free hand start to come up to wave, maybe even a smile start on the kid's lips.

The sound of the train's low whistle made him look up. All he could see was a distant image of the caboose. *The engine must be clearing the bridge over the river.* How had that sound, once so comforting, once so filled with adventure, turned so lonely? *Maybe I could just disappear. Just walk away into the heat and dust of the afternoon. There's no one who would really miss me, now.* The black smoke from the train's stack faded, leaving a smudge on the clean blue sky. He felt his heart begin to take on the rhythm of the engine: thunka-thunka, thunka-thunka, thunka-thunka.

Sam was sitting an arm's length away, looking the opposite direction at the empty train tracks that ran east from Yates Center. "Sam, Granville gave me a little money—a bonus, he called it. And Mr. Slocum gave me a round-trip ticket that will take me as far as Kendallville, or farther if I cash in the return part of the ticket and never come back."

"Are you fixin' to do that? Never come back?"

"Well, I have this idea that maybe I should know more about things than what I read in the barbershop magazines."

"Good idea. Maybe you can learn about the railroads—that's where the future is."

Rusty looked down the tracks to the west and smiled. "No sir. I've had enough of railroads in my life. I think I'll look for something safer, like those new aeroplanes I've been reading about."

CPSIA information can be obtained
at www.ICGtesting.com
Printed in the USA
FFOW04n2124071214
9235FF